IMMINENT HARM

A Cass Leary Legal Thriller

ROBIN JAMES

For all the latest on my new releases and exclusive content, sign up for my newsletter at:

http://www.robinjamesbooks.com/newsletter/

Chapter 1

"Honey, you don't wanna know."

Generally, when people say that it only makes me want to know more. But the look on Miranda Sulier's face took the wind out of me before I could hit her with the witty comeback I had in mind.

The woman had just celebrated her fiftieth anniversary of working as a legal secretary. She'd been at it longer than they even had a word for it. Paralegals, legal assistants, law clerks, filing clerks, those were all the fancy names for things Miranda did every single day of her working life. I wouldn't be surprised if the woman could walk into a courtroom today and eviscerate even the most seasoned trial lawyers. Today though, she gave me a cold stare as she shut her laptop before I could see what was on it.

"How bad?" I asked for the seventh time.

She gave me a grim smile and sat back in her leather office chair.

"You've got a month. A solid month."

"For everything?" I asked. "Utilities. Rent." I paused. "Payroll?"

"Yeah," she answered.

"Miranda," I said. "I mean the complete payroll. Not just Tori's. Yours too."

"I'm fine," she said.

"Do not give me that," I said. "And a month is not so bad. I can do a lot in a month. It's an eternity."

The front door blew open, and a four-foot-eleven tornado blasted in. My law partner, Jeanie Mills, hoisted her briefcase on Miranda's desk.

Miranda carefully picked it up and set it beside her. Later, she would sort through Jeanie's indecipherable (to me anyway) chicken scratch on sticky notes and make sense of it all. Jeanie had a habit of scrawling said chicken scratch on the fly when she was at the courthouse. Miranda assembled it all into an organized calendar for Jeanie, who refused to use anything more technologically advanced than a flip phone.

"Everything go okay?" I asked, though it was clear from the line in Jeanie's forehead that it hadn't.

"Peachy," she said. "The Wilhelm divorce settled. Finally got the bastard to agree to spousal support. Lump sum. Would have enjoyed raking him over the coals every month for the next twenty-odd years, but Kathy's a hell of a lot more reasonable a woman than I am."

"Good," Miranda said. "We need the billing. Did you also get him to agree to Kathy's attorney fee?"

Jeanie's face cracked into a sly smile. "An installment plan, but yeah."

"Good," Miranda said. She eyed me once more. "That'll make it six weeks."

"Eons," I said. "No worries."

I stuck a hand in the air and wiggled my fingers in a wave as I turned and headed up the stairs to my office.

It was all a lie. I was worried.

Ever since I had represented my deadbeat father in a murder trial earlier in the year, my community standing had taken a hit. My old man had a knack for burning every bridge he crossed and screwing over every friend he ever made. The fallout from his disastrous Delphi homecoming was worse than I anticipated this time. It was a reminder to everyone in town that I was one of *those* Learys. Plus, there was the little matter of the bribe I gave him to send him packing for good this time. While the gesture had done my family a world of good, it had all but depleted my cash flow.

I swear I wouldn't have done it if I'd known my billings would dry up too.

I heaved the battered leather bag I used for a briefcase onto one of my client chairs then plopped down behind my desk.

My desk. The thing was spotless, not so much as a paper-clip out of place. A harbinger of doom far more ominous than anything Miranda pulled up in her ledger.

I'd been through worse. A lot worse. I had started this practice just two years ago with almost nothing but gas in my car and that beat-up leather bag. Now, I had the best staff any lawyer could ask for and both feet firmly planted in the county legal community. Things would get better.

They sure as heck couldn't get much worse.

A soft knock on my door pulled me out of my head, or perhaps a more southern part of my anatomy.

Jeanie poked her face through the crack.

"Got a sec?" she asked. With her, it was always a rhetorical question. I waved her in. "What's up?" I asked.

Jeanie moved my bag and sat in the chair opposite me. She pulled a folded business card out of the pocket of her navy-blue blazer and slid it across my desk.

"He wants to talk to you," she said.

I picked up the card and scrunched my nose as I read it. "Judge Tucker?" I asked.

Jeanie nodded. "He wouldn't tell me what it was about. That's his personal cell phone written on the back."

"So why didn't he just call me? "I asked.

Jeanie shook her head. "I suppose you can ask him. I'm just the messenger."

Judge Kent Tucker was Woodbridge County's newest District Court judge. He had narrowly won an election not long before I came back to town. I didn't have any active cases in his court now as I primarily practiced one floor up in Circuit Court.

"Why do I get the feeling this can't be good?" I asked.

"Come on," Jeanie said, smiling. "Things will turn around. They always do. Plus, you've been through a heck of a lot worse than a little professional dry spell."

I loved her. There was no judgment in Jeanie's tone. Of course, I'd earned it from her if there were. She begged me not to get involved in my dad's latest legal turmoil. Still, she never said I told you so and I knew she was always in my corner. Even if it was to give me a good swift kick in the rear end on occasion when I needed it.

"Give him a call," Jeanie said. "Who knows, maybe he wants to ask you out."

If I had been drinking coffee, I would have spit it out. "That's the last thing I need."

"I mean, he's cute," she said. I rolled my eyes, but she was already getting up to leave. She closed the door behind her while I fingered Judge Tucker's bent business card.

Raising a brow, I slid my phone across the desk and punched in the number.

JUDGE TUCKER DIDN'T WANT to meet in my office or his. Instead, he picked a diner attached to a truck stop off M-50. He was waiting for me in a booth with his back to the door as I approached.

"Judge?" I said. Tucker turned. He was handsome, with a thick head of light-brown hair, deeply tanned skin, and bright-green eyes. He rose to meet me and extended his hand.

"Cass," he said. "Thanks for meeting me. I know how odd this must all seem."

I took the opposite bench and folded my hands on the table. I ordered an iced tea and a toasted bagel when the waitress came.

At forty-two, Kent Tucker was one of the youngest judges on the local bench. His election had been a bit of a coup as he had only lived in the county for about five years before that. He'd made a small fortune as an asbestos lawyer, from what I was told. A lot of people thought he bought his way to the bench, but I'd so far found him a fair and thoughtful jurist. It also helped he didn't have deep family connections in town like most of the good ol' boy network around Delphi.

"Well, I'm curious," I said. "You didn't say much on the phone."

Tucker sipped his own iced tea and gave the waitress a polite smile as she set down my bagel. The judge was working on a club sandwich. When the waitress left, I quietly scraped off about an inch of cream cheese from each half of my bagel before taking a bite.

"I need your help," he said.

I dabbed the corner of my mouth with a napkin. "I figured that much out already. What's going on?"

He tapped the blank screen of his phone before answering. "It's my sister. I'm worried about her."

Being an out-of-towner, I knew little about Kent Tucker's

family. Hell, most of Delphi would have considered him an out-of-towner even if he had lived here twenty years. He hadn't.

"I've tried to look out for her," he said. "But she's had a rough go. Not that a lot of it she didn't bring on herself. We weren't close growing up. Ten years apart. I had an older sister, Cindy. We were kind of inseparable. She passed away when I was eight. My parents kind of had Annie to, I don't know, replace Cindy. We lost her in a car accident. My mom was driving."

"I'm sorry," I said. "That must have been a pretty awful time for your family."

He shrugged. "I was just a kid. It wasn't Annie's fault, but it was hard not to resent her for even existing at that time."

"I can imagine," I said.

"I wasn't always there for her," he said. "My parents' marriage fell apart. I think Annie grew up blaming herself for a lot of it. Kinda hard for a kid not to think she wasn't enough for them to hold it all together, you know?"

I took a sip of my tea. I'd never spoken to Judge Tucker except in open court or a polite hello in the hallways. If anything, I always found him stoic. As far as I knew, he didn't really socialize with anyone outside the courthouse. Being a judge could be a lonely life in that way. It could cause problems if he went on golf outings or lunched with lawyers who appeared before him. Which was why I was doubly stunned as to why I was sitting here. And why he just unloaded most of his life story on me, a near stranger to him.

"What's going on, Judge?" I asked.

He let out a breath. Judge Tucker kept his eyes down. "Like I said, Annie's had a complicated life. I should have been there for her more than I was. By the time I was mature enough to figure that out, it was too late. She doesn't always trust me."

"She's in trouble," I surmised. "What is it? Money or a man?"

Judge Tucker finally looked up.

"Ah," I said. "A man. Is she married to him?"

He tightened his lips. "Brian," he answered. "Brian Liski."

"How bad is it?" I asked.

"I've seen some bruises," he said.

"Do they have kids?" I asked.

He shook his head. "Thankfully, no."

"Has she reached out to you?" I asked.

"Not overtly. But as distant as we've been over the years, I do know my sister. She moved here to Delphi when I did. She'd just gotten out from under a different bad relationship. She has a knack for those. We're getting closer now. Until she married Brian, I was the only family she had."

I smiled. "I've got a kid sister like that too."

His face fell. He knew about my sister Vangie's troubles. Everyone did.

"Yeah," he said. "That's one of the reasons I thought of you."

"What is it you want me to do?" I asked.

"Cass," he said. "Annie, my sister. She's a little in awe of you. She followed some of your more notable trials in the last couple of years. On more than one occasion, she's asked me if I knew you personally."

"I'm flattered," I said.

"I'm hoping you can talk some sense into her. I think if she knew someone like you would be willing to go to bat for her, she could work up the nerve to deal with Brian once and for all."

"Wait," I said. "Do you mean to tell me she hasn't asked for my help?"

"No," he said. "But like I said, I know her. She covers when I'm the one asking. She doesn't want to disappoint me, and she hates that she's had to ask for my help before. I've told her that's silly, but she's stubborn."

I couldn't help but smile. Oh yes, his Annie sounded a lot like members of my own family. "Judge," I said. "I sympathize with how tough this has to be for you. Believe me, I've been in your shoes. But if Annie doesn't ..."

"Cass," he said, his tone growing grave. "I think she's running out of time."

A chill went up my spine. I didn't know Kent Tucker well at all, but I recognized the fear in his eyes, and it triggered something inside of me.

"Just talk to her," he said. "It's all in her head, but I think she feels like she's all on her own. I'm afraid it's going to make her take chances she shouldn't. And I don't want to be sitting here someday hating myself for not trying everything I can think of."

"Talk to her," I said.

"She's financially dependent on this guy," the judge said. He turned his phone around and showed me a picture of his sister. She was pretty. Dark haired with a wide smile and deep dimples. In the picture, a man I presumed was Brian, her husband, had his arms wrapped around her. He was kissing her cheek. With everything Tucker said, the image gave me the creeps.

"Financially dependent, huh?" I said.

"Yes. I mean, she tries. She went to college for a while. Never graduated. She was going to be a dental hygienist. Then an X-ray tech. For a while she had an Etsy store and sold homemade greeting cards and invitations. She's a pretty

8

good artist. She does calligraphy and things like that. When she married Brian, she started going to cosmetology school. She just started at a hair salon. But I know my sister, that won't last long either. I've been the one paying for all of that until now. Now, she thinks Brian's her savior. Between the pair of them, I don't think they have a pot to … er … you know what … in."

I sat back and shook my head. "So, you want me to pursue a case with a client who more than likely doesn't want my help and who can't afford to pay me even if she agrees to talk to me?"

Judge Tucker charmed me with a sheepish smile. "I'd say that's about the size of it. And I'll owe you."

My face fell. Then his did. "No," he said. "Not like that. I'm not talking about something unethical. I just mean if I'm in a position to put in a good word or throw some business your way …"

The truth was it wouldn't at all hurt me to get back in the good graces of at least one member of the Woodbridge County judiciary. Plus, Kent Tucker was no fool. He knew I was a sucker for lost causes. Annie Liski fit the bill, for sure.

"Sounds like this is right up my alley," I sighed.

Kent Tucker's face softened with relief. "She works at a salon called Bella Donna. You could, I don't know, maybe make an appointment with her?"

"Great," I smiled. I ran a hand through my hair, wondering how much he expected me to sacrifice to the cause. Sliding out of the booth. I left a ten on the table. "I'll see what I can do. But no promises."

Judge Kent Tucker's hopeful expression kind of melted me. Oh yes. I was a sucker for lost causes, for sure.

Chapter 2

Two days later, Annie Liski had a cancellation, and I
found myself in the waiting room of the Bella Donna Salon.

"She'll be just a second," a young, friendly receptionist
told me. I pegged her at about seventeen with shimmering
green hair and a tiny waist. Her name was Reese.

Reese set me up at one of the hairstylists' stations and
offered me something to drink. I was about to decline but
Reese was so polite I asked for bottled water.

As she went to get it, I got a better look at Annie's station.
She kept everything neat, tidy, and in its place. A sticker of
her name spelled out in ornate calligraphy framed the top of
her mirror. From what Judge Tucker said, I guessed she made
that herself. In one corner at the bottom of the mirror, I
noticed a picture of Annie in a simple, champagne-colored
wedding dress holding a bouquet of red roses. Brian Liski had
his arms wrapped around her waist. He was tall, lanky, with
big hands laced together. They made an attractive couple,
enough so that the picture was good enough to come with the
frame itself. But Annie was the stunner. Brian was plain-

looking and had an expression on his face that made you think maybe he couldn't believe his luck.

"So sorry I'm late," a soft voice gushed behind me. Annie Liski rushed in, sliding her massive purse off her shoulder. She tucked it into a cubby beside her station and gave me a huge smile.

"I'm in no rush," I said. "I'm just glad you could fit me in on such short notice. Your receptionist said your next appointment wasn't until next month."

No sooner had I gotten the words out before Annie's phone went off the first time. She glanced at it and swiped the screen.

"One second," she said. "I'm so sorry. My husband doesn't like me driving on the highway, so I always promise to check in."

She did with a quick "thumbs up" emoji and slipped her phone in the back pocket of her black jeans.

It didn't have to mean anything. Brian could just be a concerned husband and nothing more. But it was the first of many alarms to go off for me that day.

"You have amazing hair," she said, coming toward me. She slid her fingers through what I considered to be an unruly mess right now. My natural color was sort of a dull blonde, fading to almost brown in the winter. Up until a few years ago, I'd bleached it platinum. The ends of that had taken almost two years to grow out and now I just had light ends.

"Thanks," I said.

"What are we doing today?"

I realized I hadn't thought that far. I came here to introduce myself to Annie and let her know I was available to help if she needed it. That was the extent of my promise to Judge Tucker.

"I love the ombre look on you," Annie said. "Or we can work on blending some of this."

Never mind Kent Tucker's concerns, I'd asked around. Annie Liski was new at this, but rumor was she had a knack for color.

"You know," I said. "What do you think?"

"Your skin is flawless," she said. "And fair. I'd love to see more of a butter blonde on you. Do you want to try?"

I tilted my head and looked in the mirror. Annie was looking at me with an artist's eye. She pulled different strands away from my face and held them up to the light.

She really was quite pretty. She wore a Joan Jett and the Blackhearts tee shirt with the sleeves rolled up. She had tight jeans and heels that seemed impractical for the job she did, but Annie moved in them as if they were part of her. Her own hair was dark. From a distance, it looked black. But up close, I could see it was more of a deep brown.

"I'm willing to give it a go," I said.

"Great," Annie replied. "Just give me a minute to mix up your color, Cassie."

"Just Cass," I said.

Annie paused. Her smile changed a bit as if she had to remind herself to keep it in place. Then she turned and went to whatever magical back room Bella Donna had where she whipped up my color.

About ten minutes later, she came back. Annie had turned silent and serious as she began the meticulous process of foiling my hair.

Now that I had a captive audience, I found myself not having the first clue about how to broach the subject of Brian Liski. It turned out, I didn't have to. Once Annie had me settled, she took a step back.

"So, Cass Leary," she said. "You know I've heard of you." Not missing a beat, she slid an infrared halo dryer over my head. It seemed a lot more civilized than the noisy, giant hood dryers I was used to. It also allowed us to talk.

"Should I be scared?" I asked.

Annie smiled. "I'm kind of in awe of you," she said. "I followed the Coach D murder trial."

"Ah," I said. It was my most famous. I defended a young girl who'd been accused of killing Delphi High's legendary basketball coach. That one had garnered national attention. It had also taken me almost two years to live it down to certain people in Delphi who idolized the man no matter what awful things he'd done.

"Well," I said. "I'm only glad I was able to help bring justice to everyone hurt. That's all I could have asked for."

Annie nodded. She checked on one of my foil wraps then folded it back up.

"So why are you really here?" she asked.

Annie leaned back, perching herself on the edge of her workstation.

I could have pointed to my porcupine-like foils. I could have told her that I had heard she was great with color. But as Annie Liski stared at me with her serious, green eyes, I decided to just cut the crap.

"Your brother is a little worried about you," I said.

Annie's entire demeanor changed. Gone was the confident woman who'd wrapped my hair with nimble, experienced hands. She looked over her shoulder and her color went a little gray.

"He worries too much. And he's not so great at minding his own business," she said. She checked another foil then tilted the dryer toward the front of my head.

"He's just trying to be a good big brother. I've got a little sister and brother too. It's part of the job description."

"He's never liked Brian," Annie said.

"Maybe not," I said. "And I can't say that I know Judge Tucker very well. But I've so far found him to be level-headed. Does he have a reason to be worried?"

Annie blinked rapidly. "Brian's got a temper," she said. "He's passionate. He and Kent are just total opposites. I'm getting tired of being in the middle all the time."

"I understand," I said. "And look, this is awkward for me too." Annie leaned in. Satisfied at whatever she saw under the foil, she led me to the nearest sink.

It felt like heaven as she pulled off the foils and let the warm water penetrate to my scalp. Her hands were quick and strong as she washed my hair then wrapped a heated towel around my head. When she did, I saw an old bruise around her wrist. She'd tried to cover it with a pair of bangle bracelets, but it certainly looked like someone had gripped her there way too hard.

Annie quickly shoved her bracelets back in place and I followed her back to her station.

"I'm fine," she said. "I told you. Kent just worries too much. Brian's not perfect."

"Is he hurting you, Annie?" I asked.

"You're not my lawyer," she said. "This isn't your office."

I realized she may have a different purpose in claiming that. I met her eyes. "Annie, I can consider this a legal consultation. Whatever you tell me, I'll keep it confidential."

She pulled the towel off my head and rubbed some product between her hands. She laced it through my hair.

"I do love him," she said, her voice breaking.

"I know."

"I'm not ready for this," she said.

"I know that too," I said. "But you know who I am. Do you have what you need? I can get you …"

"No," she said. "I know all this. Kent's left me a bunch of brochures. Stuff on personal protection orders. I can't do that. I can't drag Brian through court."

"Are you looking for a way out, Annie?" I said. She turned on the blow dryer. In less than five minutes, she had my hair styled in a soft wave. I could never get it to do that. Whatever magic product she used had made the texture of my hair totally different too. I would never be able to replicate it on my own even if she gave me everything she used.

She turned my chair so I could see myself in the mirror.

"Wow," I said. She'd turned my ordinary dark blonde into a sunny, golden color. I liked it. Actually, I loved it.

"I don't know," she said; her eyes were bloodshot. "But I do appreciate you reaching out. I said I know who you are."

Her words tugged at me. I took a chance and put a light hand on her arm.

"Good," I said. "Then you know the kinds of women I've helped before. Your brother's a good guy."

She wiped her face and took a breath. She was about to cry right there in the middle of the salon. That wasn't my objective at all.

"I know," she said.

I put a business card face down on her counter. "My cell phone's on it," I said. "If you ever just want to talk."

"Six weeks," she said, not touching the card.

"Huh?"

"Your color," she said. "I think you can probably go six weeks. Four would be better."

"I'll make an appointment before I leave."

Annie nodded. She turned her back to me. Her phone

rang again. This time, when she pulled it out of her pocket, I saw "Bri" pull up on her caller ID. He'd called her twice in an hour. It could mean nothing, only I knew it didn't.

Annie Liski had given as much as she was going to. She needed help. That was clear. But she also needed time. I thanked her then went to the reception desk to pay my bill and leave her a generous tip.

Reese was there waiting for me with that big smile. She set up my next appointment. Annie disappeared, heading to the back room to mix up her next client's color.

Reese handed me back my change. She gripped my hand when I tried to take it.

"She's scared," Reese whispered.

"What?"

"Annie," she said. "You're here about Brian, right?"

My heart flipped. Lord, had this girl been eavesdropping the whole time?

Everything I'd said to Annie was true. I couldn't answer Reese's question. But she didn't let go of my hand.

"You're Cass Leary," she whispered.

I nodded.

"Yeah. I'm not surprised Judge Tucker sent you here to talk to her. I'm glad."

Finally, Reese let go of me. She held up a finger though. I waited. Reese pulled out her phone and opened her pictures. When she turned the screen toward me, my stomach twisted in knots.

She showed me a picture of Annie taken from the side. She was leaning down to pick something up beside her work-station. The image was a little grainy as if it had been zoomed in from a distance, likely as far away as Reese's reception desk. But from this angle, Annie's hair fell to the side. Her neck was mottled with bruises, the kind you get when someone tries to strangle you.

"Last month," Reese whispered. "She doesn't know I have this. Will it help?"

I wanted to tell her yes. But the truth was, until and unless Annie let me, there was very little else I could do.

Chapter 3

No ONE's ever heard of Finn Lake and that's the way I like it. Though technically still part of the famous Irish Hills chain of lakes in southeastern Michigan, Finn isn't big and flashy like Devil's, Wampler's, or Vineyard Lake.

It's quiet here. Tucked away, it takes a little doing to get here off US-12 and usually only we locals ever do. At just shy of four hundred acres and an average depth of five feet (though it dips down to thirty-five feet in some spots) we have the perks of an all-sports lake and great fishing with none of the chaos of a "party lake."

Yes. I'm fine with it that nobody knows we're here.

I pulled up my new gravel driveway. It was still weird not seeing the little faded yellow house my great-grandfather built and my grandad left to me. Last year, it had burned to the ground. This year, I'd built something new.

I took a moment as I stepped out of the car and slid my sunglasses down. I still couldn't believe the place was real. I had purchased the empty lot next door and wrestled with the township to join it with my existing plot. Now, I had a three thousand square foot, two-story dream house nestled among tall pines set back on the only peninsula on the lake.

Behind me, the moving truck pulled up, right on time.

"Hey, Ed." I waved to the driver. He'd gone to school with my younger brother Matty. He and *his* four brothers had started a moving company ten years ago.

"Wow," Ed said as he popped down from the driver's seat. "I mean, really ... wow."

"Thanks," I said.

The house wasn't just my dream. Decades ago, my great-grandfather drew out plans for something just like this with a wide, wraparound porch and giant bay windows giving stunning views of the lake from almost everywhere in the house.

There were now two structures on the land. The main house with four bedrooms, and a two-story garage big enough to house the pontoon, my brother's fishing boat, my car, and every other water toy I kept accumulating. Finally, I'd built a small apartment above that garage ready to accommodate any Leary who needed the respite. Well, not any Leary. The hell with my father anymore.

I walked to the back of the truck and gave Ed directions on where everything went. Then I got the heck out of the way.

I took a moment to walk out to the water. My brother Joe had laid intricate paving stones all the way down. My brand-new aluminum dock had been another of Joe's ideas. No more heaving three-hundred-pound planks of wood around twice a year.

Moving into early June and the water was calm for now. Finn Lake just didn't get a lot of boat traffic. Even on the fourth of July, we'd maybe get twenty boats over the whole lake.

It was quiet. Calm. My happy place. I breathed in the

fresh lake air then turned as I heard another vehicle pull up beside Ed's truck.

Joe and Matty were here. I waved to my brothers as they hopped down from the cab of Matty's pick-up. Matty looked good and my heart lifted.

He spent the first part of the year in a ninety-day stint at rehab to get his drinking under control. For the past two months, he'd been in a sober living house in Hillsdale. He was still deciding where his next step would take him.

I rushed up the hill to greet him. "Hey, you," I said to Matty.

He'd put on some weight. His hair was a little too long, but his eyes were clear, and he smelled good.

"Hey, yourself," he said. His eyes flickered and I knew he was trying to figure out what else to say. Nothing. The answer was nothing. It was enough that he was simply here today and in one piece.

"I still can't get over it," my older brother Joe said. Taller than Matty, he looked the most like our father with a thick head of wavy brown hair and wide jaw.

"Come on," I said. "While Ed's crew is busy on the main floor, let me show you the guest house."

Matty and Joe exchanged a look. I ignored it. I took Matty by the hand and we rounded the house. There was a small path from the porch of the main house leading to the outside stairwell of the outbuilding. We walked up one by one.

I handed Matty a key. He paused, then opened the door.

It was a studio apartment. One large room with a kitchenette and living space. I had them install a queen-size Murphy bed in the wall. Like the main house, the guest house had the best view of the lake from a floor-to ceiling window. And here on the second floor, you could see clear to the opposite shore. I put Grandpa Leary's telescope right by the window.

"Cass," Matty said. He twirled the key in his hand.

"You don't have to decide right now," I said. "I just wanted you to know this was an option."

He walked to the window and looked out at the lake. "I know. It's just ... you've done so much for me."

"We don't have to talk about this now," Joe said sharply.

"No," I said. "We don't."

We heard some rumbling and swearing down below. Matty put the key on the window ledge and headed downstairs. I started to follow but Joe put a hand on my arm to stop me. He waited until Matty was all the way down the stairs and into the main house before turning me.

"You have to let him be," Joe said.

"What?"

"Matty's doing great, but he's fragile. His counselor is pretty adamant that he's got to break some of his old patterns if he's got any hope of making things stick this time."

I crossed my arms. "Old patterns? Me? I'm a bad habit?"

Joe pressed his thumb and forefinger to the bridge of his nose. I got the feeling he and our little brother had rehearsed the conversation Joe and I were about to have. I took a breath and tried not to get defensive.

I failed.

"He needs to be checked on, Joe," I said.

"Cass, he loves you. I love you. But if Matty can't figure out how to stand on his own two feet or fall off them, then we're gonna be right back here with him sooner rather than later. You can't mother him out of this disease."

"I just want to know he's okay," I said.

"He is," Joe said. "Or he will be. He's good, Cass."

Something occurred to me. With it, I felt the heat of anger fill my lungs. "You've been visiting him," I said. "How often?"

Joe sighed. "His counselor asked me to come to a few of their sessions over the last few weeks."

"You," I said.

"Now don't get upset," he said.

I stepped away from the window. "Is he blaming me for this?"

"No," Joe said. "God, no."

"But his counselor thinks I'm enabling him," I said.

"We all are or have been," Joe answered. "Every time we bail Matty out. It's helping more than hurting."

"So what," I said. The thing was, I knew all of this. Heck, I'd said it myself at least a dozen times over the last year. And yet, it was so hard to step back.

"You're amazing at what you do," Joe said. "Cass, we all know it. We know we'd be lost without you. I'd be lost without you. Now it's time for us to maybe help you."

"Help me?"

From the corner of the window, I watched Ed, his brothers, and Matty carry in my king-sized mattress. Sure, maybe it was way bigger than one person needed, but I'd always wanted one. Also, the dogs had taken to sleeping with me lately. I fully realized it meant I was starting to become one of *those* people.

"There's something I've been meaning to talk to you about," he said. "When Dad left. Cass, did you give him money?"

Our father was another sore spot among us. Joe pretty much wanted the man to drop off the face of the earth. Matty and our younger sister Vangie still wanted a relationship. Me? I was fine with him being on the planet, I just wanted him out of Delphi.

"What if I did?" I asked.

Joe's nostrils flared. "Dammit, Cass. You know he'll just come back for more."

"No," I said. "He won't. Not this time." I believed it.

"How much?" Joe asked.

I didn't want to tell him. He'd kill me. But it was worth every penny to get the toxic old man far away from all of us.

When I wouldn't answer, Joe started to pace. "Never mind," he said. "I already know. He told Matty."

Great. "So, it's okay if Dad talks to Matty but not if I do."

"Dad called him," Joe said. "Matty ended up hanging up on him and blocking his number. But not before Dad ratted you out. Cass, that was your life savings."

"No," I said, spreading my hands. "You're standing in my life savings. And it's all been worth it. Besides, I'm fine."

It was a wee bit of a lie. I *would* be fine. Soon.

"Look," Joe said. "For once, why don't you let someone else help *you*?"

"Someone?"

"Me," Joe said. "Okay. Me. Are you able to make payroll?"

"Stop," I said.

"Cass."

"Joe."

"Unbelievable," he said. "That man's a cancer. You know he is. And you left yourself over a financial barrel for what?"

"For peace," I said, louder than I meant. "Your peace. Mine. And God help him, Matty's. He's gone. Dad's not coming back. Ever. Not to Delphi."

Joe dropped his head. "I know."

His words stunned me more than if he'd shouted back at me. Had my brother just agreed with me?

"Okay," I said. "Good. So, we don't need to talk about it again."

"Let me help you for a change," Joe said. "I'm in a position in which I can. For once. People of this town seem to be holding your paternity against you but that hasn't been the case for me."

"I'm fine," I said. "Business will pick up. I've already got some things in the works."

"That's not what I've been hearing. And I hear a lot. I know you had a bunch of clients dump you after Dad's trial. And it's insane. For whatever reason, my clients have stuck by me. And I just got hired for a big job in Ann Arbor. If you need a boost, I can give you one. So, let me."

"Thanks," I said, meaning it. "But I really am fine."

"Consider it a loan," he said. "With interest."

"Joe." I went to him. I touched my brother's face. "If it gets to that point, I'll let you know. I promise."

"Okay," he capitulated. I loved him. I truly did. For so much of my life, it had been Joey and me against the world.

I had more to say, but another loud crash drew my eye. A fourth vehicle slammed to a stop in the driveway. My eyes widened as my sister Vangie got out. My niece Jessa spilled out of the car with my two dogs, Marbury and Madison, in tow. The pair of them bounded down the hill and dove into the lake. Jessa already had a suit and her life jacket on as she tore off after them, squealing with laughter.

"Looks like you're going to have a full house," Joe said, sliding an arm around me.

My heart swelled. That was all I ever wanted with this place. It was all Grandpa Leary ever wanted either. I felt a little of his ghost among us that day and it made me smile.

Ed, his brothers, and my brothers had the house unpacked by sundown. By then, Matty fired up the grill.

It was a good day. One of the best I could remember for the longest time.

Chapter 4

TUESDAYS at four had quickly become my favorite time of the week. I sat in the same corner booth at Sweet Delights pastry and coffee shop sipping a vanilla latte while the proprietor, Terrence Romaine, served me a Kruller fresh out of the oven.

"I'm going to need a bigger booth if this keeps up," I said to him. Terrence smiled. He was about to say something when the chime jingled at the front door. Terrence gave me a knowing wink then quietly excused himself as my standing date walked in.

Detective Eric Wray had an old-school charm. Like most of us, he knew everyone in town by name. Unlike most of us, he made a point of saying hello to everyone even when a fair number of them distrusted the cops and found creative ways to insult him.

I got that same little flare of heat I always did when his eyes found mine. He spared a quick nod for Terrence, then slid into the booth opposite me.

"How's business?" I asked.

"Booming, like always," Eric said. In his case, that was never a good thing. He didn't ask me how mine was. He already knew. Of all the people who had warned me not to entangle myself with my father's legal trouble, Eric had led the charge. To his credit though, he never once said I told you so.

He gave me a cockeyed grin then made a circular gesture, framing my head. "Your hair," he said. "It's different."

I smiled. I'd spent the weekend with both of my brothers. So far, Eric had been the only guy in my life to notice.

"I like it," he added. Lord. I exhaled. Lately, being around Eric made me feel like a high school girl.

"Thanks," I said. "I tried out a new stylist."

"I'm sorry I couldn't stop by to help Saturday," he said. "How about I make up for it this evening?"

I took a sip of my latte. Eric's eyes shone. I waved my hand. "It's fine. I already told you that. How'd your sting go?"

Along with his duties as a violent crimes detective, Eric also served on a statewide vice task force. Occasionally, he'd disappear for days as they worked on drug or prostitution stings.

He cleared his throat. "How'd you know that's where I was?"

I smiled and sipped my coffee once more. Eric grimaced. "There really aren't any secrets in this town, are there?"

Laughing, I set my cup down. "Not really."

"It went fine," he said. "You'll probably read about it in the news in a day or so. And that's all I can say."

"Of course," I said.

"What about tonight?" he asked. It was an innocent offer, I knew. Eric and I were in a sort of weird place right now. We enjoyed each other tremendously. He knew all my secrets and I knew his. But we'd been taking things very slow.

"I could maybe use some help hanging some pictures," I

said honestly. "Joe and Matty are good at the heavy lifting. Not so good with the finer details. I need a stud finder."

Eric wiggled his eyebrows; I rolled my eyes. "Happy to be of service. I've just got a few things to finish up at the office. How about I grab some hamburgers from Mickey's and head over around seven?"

"I'd like that," I said. Just then, my phone buzzed on the table beside me. It was Miranda.

"Sorry," I said. "I need to take this."

I turned slightly away from Eric. "Cass," Miranda said, a little breathless. "Sorry. I know you were planning on leaving for the day, but I think you need to head on back."

"What's going on?" My pulse started to pick up speed. I didn't like Miranda's tone.

"Um, there's a young lady here. She has your business card. She said her name is Annie and that you'd know what it's about. Cass … she looks rough."

Eric caught my eye. I held up a finger.

"Got it," I said. "Just have her wait in my office. I'm over at Sweet Delights. I'll be there in five minutes."

I hung up the phone. "I'm so sorry. I …"

Eric held up a hand. "Don't sweat it. Do you think you'll be late?"

I took a twenty out of my purse. Eric gave me a stern look. I wanted to protest that it was my turn to pay. He was having none of it. I decided to pick my battles and slid the bill back in my purse.

"Anything you need help with?" he asked.

Sometimes, I swear the man could read my mind.

"Maybe," I said. "I'll let you know. On the help and whether I'll be late."

"Understood," he said, and I knew he did. He reached

across the table and touched my arm. Just that little gesture sent electricity zinging through me.

Yes. Someday soon, Eric Wray and I were going to have to figure out exactly what this was. I said a polite goodbye to Terrence and waved to his wife Alicia in the back. Then, I adjusted my purse strap higher on my shoulder as I made my way out the door. Terrence's chime clanged loudly behind me.

ANNIE LISKI DIDN'T JUST LOOK rough. She looked defeated. She sat in one of my office chairs with her dark brown hair covering the side of her face. She wouldn't look up at me at first.

"Annie," I said. I sat in the chair beside her rather than the one behind my desk. I wanted to reach out to her but resisted the urge. The last thing she needed was someone invading her personal space without permission.

"What happened?"

In some ways, it was a dumb question on my part. This was not the woman I met the other day at Bella Donna. She seemed more broken, scared. She'd withdrawn into herself.

She kept her head down, that hank of dark hair concealing the left side of her face. The room went deadly silent except for the rhythmic tick of my wall clock.

Finally, slowly, Annie lifted her head and tucked the hair behind her ear. I stayed still as stone, forcing myself not to gasp as I saw what she'd been hiding.

Annie's ear was crusted with blood. She had an ugly, purple bruise across her cheekbone. Her thick lashes were caked with more crust and tears. Her bottom lip was split.

I folded my hands in my lap. "Tell me," I said.

"It was my fault ..."

"No," I cut her off. "It wasn't."

"He's so tired when he comes home from work. Twelve-hour days. Sixteen-hour days. He works for his uncle in Taylor. It's such a long commute. He wants to move out there but I'm the one who hasn't wanted to. I'm just starting to build up my client list here. I like it in Delphi."

"Annie," I said, keeping my tone neutral, my voice soft. "This is not your fault."

She looked at me. "It isn't what Kent thinks."

"Did Brian do this to you?" I asked.

"Twice," she said. "We've been married for almost four years. There were just two other times. It's when he drinks."

It usually was. I had to make myself unclench my fists. Annie needed a safe space to tell as much of her story as she was comfortable with. My job was to listen, not judge.

"I love him," she said, her voice breaking. "It's not easy."

"No," I said. "It isn't. It's the hardest thing there is."

"You've helped a lot of women like me?" she asked.

"I do what I can," I said.

"I don't want to leave him," she said. "I want him to get help. You have to understand. Most of the time he's so good to me. I don't have to work. I do it because I enjoy it. Brian has nurtured that. He's paid for all my start-up costs. Whatever I need. He wants me to succeed. It's just, sometimes the pressure gets to him. I know when it's about to happen most of the time. I leave him alone. He handles it. And everything's fine. It's just, last night I was tired too."

"It's okay," I said. I wanted to tell her that it would be okay. But I couldn't presume to know Annie Liski's pain. I could only be here for what she asked.

It took her a moment. A breath. A pause. And then, she asked.

"What would be the first step?" she said.

"The most important thing is to make sure you're safe," I said. "Can you stay with someone? Your brother perhaps? A friend. Or I could work on getting you into a safe house. There are shelters around here that work exclusively with women like ..."

"No," she said. "I don't want to go to Kent's."

"Your brother loves you," I said. "He's trying to do what he thinks is best for you."

"I'm okay," she said. "Really. I mean, legally, what's the next step?"

"Divorce, if you want it," I said. "But also, a personal protection order. I'm serious. Keeping you safe is the only thing that matters, Annie."

"How does a personal protection order work?" she asked.

"It's an order from the court mandating that Brian stays away from you. It would cover even phone harassment. If he threatens you again or gets within spitting distance of you, he can be arrested. But you need to understand that it's just a piece of paper. It's still critically important we have you out of that house and somewhere he can't hurt you."

"What if"—she looked up at me—"when he finds out ..."

"We'd request what's called an ex parte order," I said. "It means we'd ask the judge to enter the order without first notifying Brian. He'd be served with it after the fact. It would buy you time to get out of there. And Annie, I don't want you alone with him again. No matter what. If there's something you need from the house, you have your brother or preferably a deputy sheriff go with you. Not one of your girlfriends. That would be my recommendation."

She drew in a sharp breath. "It's so much. It's all just too much."

"It is," I said. "But it's manageable, Annie. I promise."

She nodded but it seemed more from nerves than agreement. I was worried about her. Deeply.

"A PPO," she said. "That's what Kent said too."

"Does he know about this latest incident?" I asked.

"No!" Her eyes got big. "No. And Cass, I need you to promise me that you won't tell him."

"I can't," I said. "Not without your express permission."

"Even though he's the one who came to you first?"

"Not even then," I said. "If you want to be, you're my client, not Judge Tucker."

"Okay," she said, her shoulders dropping with relief. "Okay. I mean, I know he'll find out eventually. As soon as we file, even. But I'm just not ready to deal with him today."

"I understand."

Her color brightened. Now that Annie had the makings of a plan, it seemed to empower her. I felt the weight of her trust and it pulled at my heart.

"When?" she asked.

"Today," I said. "I'll work on preparing your paperwork this evening. I'll need an affidavit from you. You'll need to put it all in writing, Annie. Everything you're afraid of. What's happened. Have you made a police report yet?"

"Do I have to do that?" she asked.

"I recommend it."

"No!" she started to rise from her seat. "No police. This was a mistake. I need to get out of here."

"Okay," I relented, though hated it. "Okay. Just your story. We can request the PPO on your statement. Though, I'd like to take some photographs."

She sat back down. "I thought you would."

"Okay," I said. "Then, I'll take the order to the courthouse myself first thing in the morning. We'll have the best chance of a judge granting it without a hearing that way."

33

With the prospect of the police off the table for now, Annie calmed right down. Though I didn't like capitulating on that, it was better than having her bolt.

"Just sit tight," I said. "I'll get you a pad of paper and a pen."

She wiped a tear from her swollen eye. "Thank you," she said, her voice hoarse. At that point, she reached for me.

I took a chance. I moved toward her. Annie collapsed against me. I hugged her. She was Kent Tucker's little sister and she reminded me so much of my own.

When she calmed down a bit, I went to get that pad of paper. I shot a quick text to Eric Wray.

"I'm so sorry," I typed. "It's probably going to be a long night at the office. Raincheck?"

Three dots blinked back at me for a moment. Then he sent back a heart and three words that made me smile.

"I can't wait."

Chapter 5

WE GOT LUCKY. I had Annie meet me at the courthouse as I filed her petition and affidavit for the personal protection order. We drew Judge Moira Pierce and I had a hunch she might have questions.

She did.

Bailiff Ted Moran poked his head out of her chambers. "She wants you to go on the record in five," he said.

Annie stiffened beside me. I gave Ted a quick smile and gestured that we'd be right there.

"I can't," Annie said, starting to hyperventilate. She dressed smartly in a pair of black dress pants and a yellow blouse. She brushed her hair straight, covering half her face as she had at my office. Her bruising looked even worse today as the blood settled. She tried to cover it with heavy makeup, but the mottled purple showed through.

"You can," I said. "All you have to do is tell the truth. I'll ask you some questions in front of the judge. That's all. Brian's not here."

"What's going to happen?" she asked.

"We're here to try and get your protection order entered

without a full hearing and notice to Brian beforehand. To do that, you need to convince the judge that you're in imminent risk of harm and that Brian having a heads-up about all of this will put you in more danger."

She fidgeted on the bench beside me. "Right," she said.

"You ready?" Ted poked his head out again.

"Yes," I said. I put a light hand on Annie's back. She rose with me and we walked into the courtroom together.

Judge Moira Pierce was an attractive woman with chestnut-brown hair cut into a smart bob. She only recently started letting the gray show through. She ran an efficient courtroom and with any luck, this would all be a formality. Then came the hard part. Getting Annie to actually abide by the terms of the PPO if we got it.

Judge Pierce rifled through the documents I filed earlier. She peered over her reading glasses. Her expression was kind, but serious.

"Mrs. Liski?" she asked.

"Yes, Your Honor," Annie spoke up.

"I trust your lawyer has explained how we're going to proceed."

"She has, Your Honor."

"Good. Counselor, you may go ahead and put your proofs into the record."

Judge Pierce's clerk swore Annie in. She sat at the counsel table beside me for this one rather than taking the witness stand. I think it put her a little more at ease.

"Thank you," I said. "Mrs. Liski, let's have you state your full name for the record."

The court reporter sat with her fingers poised to type.

"Anne Marie Liski. Um ... my maiden name is Tucker. Do you need that?"

"That's fine," I said. "Annie, can you tell the judge why you're here today?"

"I need ... that is ... I'm afraid my husband is going to hurt me again. He ... I'm asking for a restraining order. So I can get help from the police if he comes near me again."

"Annie," I said. "Why are you asking for this order at this time? What happened this week?"

Annie cleared her throat. "My husband, Brian Liski. Um ... he's also ... his given name is Branislav. Do you need that? He doesn't use it though. He hates it. Um. He has a bad temper. He ... the night before last, we got in an argument. I mean, I nagged. I was angry that he didn't call to tell me he was going to be late coming home. And he just ... he lost his temper. He got physical. He ... backhanded me. Across the face."

Annie tucked her hair behind her ear, revealing the ugly welt on the side of her face.

"Annie," I said. "You've just shown the judge an injury on your face. Because the court reporter is typing everything down, can you describe how you were hurt?"

"I have a black eye," she said. "And a split lip. My ear is cut."

"How did all that happen?" I asked.

"Brian ... the ear when he backhanded me. I fell backward. I tried to get away, but he was pretty much over the edge then. He grabbed me by the arm. I tried to pull away from him but that made him even more angry. He threw me against the wall in the living room. I lost my footing and landed hard on the ground. I think that's when my lip was split. He hit me again when I tried to get up. That's when ... that's how I got this."

She gestured toward her eye.

"Annie," I said. "Was that the first time your husband was ever physically violent toward you?"

"No," she almost whispered it. "No. It was the third time. I mean, he's thrown things at me and threatened me. But two other times he's struck me like this. Once last year he twisted my arm so hard I dislocated my wrist. And once ... um ... he put his hands around my neck and I ... I passed out."

"Has Brian threatened you?" I asked, my heart pounding.

"Yes," she said; her voice had gone flat. "He did that the other night. I told him I was going to leave, that I couldn't take it anymore and that I wanted him to get help. He told me if I tried to leave him or got the police involved, he'd make things so much worse for me."

"Worse how?" I asked.

"He said what he did that night would be the least of it." At that point, her voice finally broke.

"Mrs. Liski," the judge interjected, "Does your husband have any guns in the house?"

Annie nodded. I nudged her. "Yes," she said. "He has a ... I don't even know what kind it is. A nine-millimeter something? He taught me how to shoot it. He's taken me to a gun range a few times. He keeps it locked in a safe in our closet. Judge, please help me. I didn't want it to come to this. I've tried to work things out. But I'm scared. I'm terrified. Brian hasn't been himself lately. I don't want him to be arrested. I think if he gets the right kind of help it might be okay. I just ... I can't be around it anymore. And if he knew I was here today, I just ... I'm scared of what he'd do. It would escalate."

"Can you tell me how?" the judge asked.

"Your Honor," she said. "I'm in fear for my life. My husband has a volatile temper. He has warned me if I ever try to leave him, or if I go to court, it would be the last thing I'd ever do."

Judge Pierce's voice interrupted. "Mrs. Liski, are you telling the Court that the respondent, Brian Liski, has expressly threatened to harm you if you file for divorce?"

"Yes, ma'am," she said. "Not harm. Brian said he'd kill me. He said he'd wring my neck again."

Judge Pierce wrote something down and pursed her lips. I knew Moira. She didn't show it outwardly. She was a good judge. Inside, I think she was seething on Annie's behalf.

"Have you sought medical attention for your injuries?" she asked.

"No, Your Honor," Annie answered.

"I wish you would," Judge Pierce said. "It has no bearing on my ruling today, but I want to make sure you're taking care of yourself."

"I understand," Annie said.

"Have you filed a police report? I don't see that in the exhibits attached to your petition."

"I haven't," Annie answered. "Cass, my lawyer ... she advised me to. I'm not looking to have Brian arrested right now. I mean, if he comes near me again. If he just stays away ... I just ..."

She couldn't finish her sentence. She broke down beside me and cried.

"Well," Judge Pierce said. "I'm going to trust that your attorney will advise you on your next course of action. For the moment, I'm going to grant your petition for an ex parte personal protection order. Ms. Leary, you'll coordinate with the sheriffs for service on the respondent, Mr. Liski?"

"Of course, Your Honor. Thank you," I said.

"So ordered," she said. She signed my proposed order with a bit of a flourish then handed the paperwork to her clerk.

Judge Pierce had a full morning docket and would be

eager to get through it. I put a gentle hand on Annie's arm, and we left the courtroom together.

"What did she mean about the sheriffs?" Annie asked.

"I have to make arrangements for Brian to get copies of this order," I said. "Don't worry. I'll handle all of that. You keep a copy and do what I said. Stay far away from Brian. If he comes near you, call the police and tell them you have this order. If he tries to call or text, you let me know. It's like I told you before. This is an important step, but it's a piece of paper. Don't put yourself in a position where you might be alone with Brian. No matter what he says or promises. Do you understand?"

She nodded and wiped her eyes. "I get it. I do. And Kent's been telling me all this too."

As she said it, Kent Tucker himself turned down the hallway and made his way toward us. Of course, he had ears in the courthouse and already knew Judge Pierce's ruling.

His face was ashen as he made eye contact with me. I gave him a curt nod to let him know things were in motion on my end. He mouthed a thank you.

Annie crumpled against her brother as he put an arm around her. He whispered to her and she melted.

"I'll be in touch," I said, not wanting to intrude on them. Annie thanked me. Kent produced a tissue from his pocket and wiped his sister's eyes.

I had a few other filings to do this morning and made my way to the elevator. The thing was ancient and slow. By the time the doors began to shut, a hand shot out and stopped them.

Kent Tucker gave me a smile and stepped in with me. He waited until the doors shut before turning to me. I noted a glisten in his eyes. He'd been crying too.

"Thank you," he said. "I don't know what you did to

finally get through to her, but thank you. I knew she'd listen to you."

"I appreciate your faith in me," I said. "A lot of this is going to be up to Annie now. Do you think she'll cave?"

Judge Tucker shrugged. "God, I hope not. Brian's a loser, Cass. A leech. But the more I tried to tell her that, the more she seemed drawn to him. This though ... I can barely look at her."

I had the impulse to tell him everything would be all right. I knew better. Things might get harder for Annie before they got better.

"Is she staying with you?" I asked.

"No," he said. "She won't. She's got a friend, one of the other women she works with. It won't last forever. I was going to ask you about getting her into a safe house. I think it would be better if Brian didn't know where to find her."

"I agree. She was reluctant when I broached the subject. I'll try again and I'll make some calls. Maybe if it's all arranged and all she has to do is show up ..."

"That's exactly what I was thinking," Tucker said. "Cass ... I ... I owe you."

I smiled. "I'm doing my job."

"No. I don't mean ... Well, you know what I mean."

"I do," I said. "And you're welcome."

Judge Kent Tucker looked like he was deciding whether he should hug me. The relief in his eyes was palpable. I understood it. I knew what it was to worry about a sibling who just couldn't stay out of their own way. I think he got that. I think it's one of the main reasons he came to me for help.

He settled on squeezing my arm. The elevator doors opened, and Judge Tucker cleared his throat and turned all business again.

"Counselor," he said, then made a gentlemanly gesture, ushering me out of the elevator before him.

He straightened his tie and headed the opposite way down the hall. I adjusted the weight of my bag and turned toward the main hallway.

Detective Eric Wray stood slack-jawed in front of the clerk's office door. He tracked Judge Tucker's retreat with cool eyes and then focused them on me.

The two deputy sheriffs he stood near made hasty good-byes, picking up on the shift in Eric's mood as I walked up. I gave them a quick wave then met Eric's eyes.

"Stop it," I said.

To his credit, Eric looked chagrined. He found that sly smile of his and leveled it at me. I looked left and right, making sure no curious eyes could see us, then went up on my tiptoes to give Eric a quick peck on the cheek.

"Why do I get the feeling you're up to something I'm not going to like? Again," he said.

I answered him in the same way I'd just answered Judge Kent Tucker.

"I'm just doing my job," I said.

Eric let out a chuckle. "That's what you always say, Leary. Come on. I'll buy you lunch."

I almost turned him down. It would serve him right for the alpha male crap he'd almost pulled. But it wasn't really my style and I was getting damned hungry.

Chapter 6

I MADE a stop at the sheriff's department before heading back to the office. The sooner Brian Liski was served, the better. Word would get out quick that he was Judge Tucker's brother-in-law. I didn't know if Brian himself had been much on their radar before now, but Delphi took care of its own.

Deputy Jed Simons handled a fair number of the PPOs I secured for clients. A former marine, Jed had done two tours in Iraq. He'd also been an all-state linebacker for Delphi High School fifteen years ago. He was big, burly, and scary as hell, if you just went on looks.

"Hey, Jed," I said.

"Whatcha got for me?" he asked. I caught him just leaving to start his shift and met him in the parking lot. Jed stood outside his patrol car looking like he could pretty much lift it one-handed if it came down to it.

I gave him a copy of the signed order. He took a quick look at it. "Liski, why do I know that name?"

"They run a pawn shop up in Taylor," I said. "But that's the extent of my knowledge. You know this is Kent Tucker's sister he's married to."

Jed squinted. He ran a beefy paw across his jaw. He still wore a military buzz cut and the sun glinted off the spiky tips.

"Do you know if anyone's been out to that house before?" I asked.

"I'll ask around," he said. "I don't think so. I'd have heard about it by now. Whatever was going on, I don't think Tucker asked for anyone to keep an eye out. I woulda heard."

"That's what I figured. Well, he's for sure asking now."

Jed nodded. "Is she out of the house?"

"She is," I said. "Staying with a friend. She's hoping he'll just go back to Taylor and stay with family."

"If he's smart, he will," Jed agreed. "This dirtbag won't find a lot of sympathy from any of us once this gets out. What else do you know about the family?"

"Not much," I said. "Just what I told you. Depending on how this goes and how much pushback he gives on the divorce, I'm sure I'll have to find out a whole lot more."

Jed nodded. "Yeah. I'm kinda thinking maybe he's got a brother? Cousins, maybe? I told you, the name's ringing some bells. It could be nothing, but this pawn shop you mentioned, any chance there's some, uh, extra stuff going on?"

I adjusted the strap of my messenger bag on my shoulder to redistribute its weight. "I wouldn't rule it out. I just want to get my ducks in a row with the order. That's priority one."

"Gotcha," Jed said. "I'll make sure it happens. I'll get the word out locally too. You got a picture of this dickhead?"

I'd taken a screenshot off Annie's Facebook page. I turned my phone so Jed could see it, then texted it to him. He waited for it to pop up on his phone. "That'll do," he said.

"Thanks," I said. "You should know. Annie, the wife, she says Liski's got a gun he keeps in a safe in their bedroom."

"Yeah," he said. "Not surprised. I appreciate the heads-up.

He might have to be served in Taylor. I know somebody good for that."

"Thanks. Though I think he's home now."

Jed checked his watch. "He's home right now?"

"I think so."

Jed bunched his shoulder and spoke into the radio he had strapped there. He turned sideways and rattled off a series of numbers to his dispatcher. "Who's working the north end?" he asked. After some static, the dispatcher responded with a name. "Thanks," Jed responded, then he shot me a wink and clicked off.

"Thanks, Jed," I said.

"No problem. You gonna be in your office later this afternoon?"

"I should be," I said.

"I'll swing by with the proof of service as soon as we get your guy."

"Thank you," I said, touching his elbow. "I owe you one."

"Yeah, yeah," he answered. "That's what they all say."

"Just be careful. This jerk made hamburger out of Annie Liski's face two nights ago."

Jed scowled. "Well then, I hope he doesn't give us any trouble."

He was being sarcastic. I'm not going to lie and say I wouldn't like Brian Liski getting a taste of his own medicine, but I didn't want Jed or anyone else putting themselves in unnecessary danger or in a bad position.

"Just watch your back, Simons," I said. He gave me a crisp salute as I turned and headed for my car.

Chapter 7

It was after three by the time I made it back to the office. The parking lot was empty save for Jeanie and Miranda's cars. That was a bad sign. I had no appointments scheduled for the rest of the day either. The truth was, other than Annie, who I'd taken pro bono, I had no new business lined up. If things stayed this way, I was going to have to start taking court appointments again.

I found Miranda and Jeanie huddled in Jeanie's first-floor office. Jeanie sat with her feet up on her desk.

"How'd it go?" she asked. Miranda turned and gave me a wave.

"PPO's being served as we speak. Divorce papers are filed. Brian Liski is about to have an awfully bad day."

"Serves him right," Jeanie said. "That poor kid. How's she holding up?"

"She's scared," I said. "She's also embarrassed."

"She has no reason to be," Miranda said. "She hasn't done anything wrong."

"I've told her," I said. "The trouble is, she's still in love with the guy."

47

Jeanie let out a heavy sigh. "You think she'll take him back?"

"I don't know," I said, and I honestly didn't. "I think the fact that she's gone forward with all of this is a good sign. I'm working on getting her some help as well. I'd like her to start talking to someone with experience. She seems open to the idea. The hardest part is going to be keeping Kent Tucker from doing too much for her."

"Hmm," Jeanie said. "An overprotective sibling?"

"Stop," I said, narrowing my eyes at her. Her face split into a wide smile.

"Hey, it's my job to jerk your chain," she said. "It keeps you humble."

"And what's my job?" I asked, then instantly regretted it.

"Oh, we just keep you around to look pretty," Jeanie said.

I matched her smirk. "Well, I'm glad to provide your daily entertainment."

"We're just gettin' warmed up," Jeanie said.

"Hey," I said, changing the subject. "Where's Tori?" Tori was my law clerk, and a fantastic one at that. I'd kind of stolen her from the U.S. Attorney's office last year.

Jeanie and Miranda passed a look. I didn't like it.

"She was going to talk to you," Miranda said. "See how you felt about her coming in two to three days a week for a little while."

My heart fell a little. "It's a dry spell, you guys. That's all. We don't need to start laying anyone off."

"Pipe down," Jeanie said. "Don't get your shorts all in a twist. Tori's taking the bar exam in six weeks. It was my idea to lighten her load. I was going to talk to you about it."

I felt like a first-class jerk. I should have discussed that with Tori myself weeks ago. With everything that had been going on lately, it flat out slipped my mind.

"Of course," I said. "Six weeks?" Sure enough, the Michigan bar exam had been given at the end of July since the beginning of time. It gave me flashbacks myself.

"Miranda, text Tori and tell her she doesn't have to come in until after the exam. I don't know what I was thinking. She'll still get paid, of course. We paid her exam fees and for her bar review course, didn't we?"

Miranda smiled. "Taken care of, boss."

"Thank you," I said.

"Have you gotten around to actually offering that girl a job when she passes?" Jeanie asked.

"I haven't … I mean … I assumed … Lord. She could make a lot more at a bigger firm. She knows that, right?"

"She knows," Jeanie said. "But for whatever reason, she finds you charming and easy to work for."

I shook my head. I was going to get nowhere with these two yahoos. "Get back to work," I said. "At least *look* busy, will ya?"

Jeanie hurled a few lighthearted and choice swear words at me as I headed up the stairs.

As much as I missed hearing Tori clacking away on her laptop in the office next to me, it was nice to have a little bit of peace and quiet. It gave me a chance to get organized. I ran through my active cases and billings. Miranda had been right the other day. I had about six weeks left of positive cash flow before things started getting dire. As much as I hated it, I was going to have to do some schmoozing in town and put myself back on the court appointment list. I didn't even want to think about how I was going to float an extra lawyer's salary when Tori passed the bar.

About an hour later, I got a text from Jed Simons. It read simply, "We got your guy. I'll bring the proof of service over in the morning."

"Thanks," I texted back. "You're the best."

"Can confirm," Jed answered, making me smile.

I punched in Annie's number to tell her the news.

"Hi, Cass," she answered.

"Annie, I just wanted you to know, Brian's been served. Both the PPO and the divorce papers. The order is enforceable now. If you see him, if he tries to contact you, you call the cops then you call me. Okay? And you are not to contact him under any circumstances."

"Thank you," she said. I could hear the relief in her voice.

"You're at your friend Maggie's?" I asked.

"Yes," she said. "On Spielman Road. Brian doesn't know where she lives."

"Okay, good," I said. "Is there any chance he's had access to your phone that you didn't know about?"

"I don't think so," she said. "Why?"

"Probably nothing," I said. "But it wouldn't be the worst idea for you to get a new one."

I didn't tell her my bigger fear just yet. I wouldn't have put it past a guy like Brian to put a tracking app on her phone.

"Yes," she said. "Actually, Kent suggested that too. I'll take care of it and text you with my new number."

"Good," I said. "Annie, I know this is hard, but you're doing great. It's going to take some time, but things are going to get better. I promise."

She paused. I could hear her breathing. Her voice sounded so tiny and far away when she finally answered. "Thanks," she said. "For everything."

"Just doing my job," I said.

We hung up. I closed my laptop and decided to call it a day. It was just past five. Jeanie and Miranda had already cleared out.

I turned off the lights and headed downstairs. It was the

first time I'd be home before about eight o'clock all week. The dogs probably wouldn't know what to do with me.

I made it as far as my car door when a shadow fell over me. I hadn't heard another car pull up. I hadn't even heard his footsteps. But when I turned, I was face to face with Brian Liski.

He wasn't a big man. Maybe five-six or -seven. He wasn't broad or particularly muscle-bound like Jed Simons. But Brian Liski had a cold, hard look in his eye as he waved a fist at me. In it, he held the crumpled-up PPO and divorce complaint.

"Mr. Liski," I said. My phone was in the bottom of my giant bag. I held my keys in my hand. "It's not appropriate for you to be here right now."

"Her brother put you up to this?" he asked.

"I'm going to need you to leave."

He sneered. He waved his fist again and his knuckles were scabbed over. I realized with cold horror he'd likely scraped them on Annie's face the other night.

There was an alley off the parking lot. I couldn't see Liski's car anywhere. More than likely, he'd been hiding in the shadow of the big blue dumpster behind my building. God. He'd been waiting for me to come out.

I could scream if I had to. We were smack in the middle of downtown Delphi. Someone would hear me, for sure.

"Annie and I can handle this all on our own," he said. "We don't need her brother's help. Or yours."

"Really?" I said. "Have you seen Annie's face lately?"

"It's not what you think," he said.

"Spare me."

"I'm contesting this," he said.

"You do that in court, Mr. Liski. I suggest you get your own lawyer and have him or her contact me."

He lunged forward. I flinched and stumbled back against my car.

"This is bullshit," he hissed. "You have no idea what you've done."

"Is that a threat?" I asked, growing bolder. He curled his lips back and pointed at me.

"No," he said. "I don't make threats. But I do protect what's mine. Remember that."

He got too close. Sweat trickled down my back. I took a breath, planning to scream but never got the chance.

A second shadow descended out of nowhere. He must have come from the other direction, behind my car. At well over six feet, Eric Wray towered over Brian Liski. He grabbed him with both hands; lifting him up by the shoulders he threw him against the side of the building.

I dropped my bag.

"You come near her again ... you so much as lift a finger at her or any other woman, you'll never see the light of day again. You got me?"

Eric's tone was dark. His eyes glazed over in what I can only describe as bloodlust. Liski's breath came quick. Eric had knocked the wind out of him.

"Eric," I said. I had no doubt in my mind what Eric was capable of. "Eric, don't. He's not worth it."

Eric jabbed his index finger into Liski's chest. "Get the hell out of here," he said.

We'd drawn a bit of a crowd on the other side of the street. Two civilians, two deputy sheriffs who worked the metal detector at the courthouse. They knew Eric was also a cop. They stayed at the ready but held back.

Liski straightened his shirt and threw the crumpled court documents on the ground at my feet. The act nearly sent Eric back over the brink. I put a steadying hand on his arm.

"Don't," I whispered.

He turned to me. His lips became a bloodless line. "I'll kill him," he said, "if he ever comes near you again."

"I know," I whispered. Eric jerked his chin at the deputy sheriffs. They nodded back and moved off down the street.

Chapter 8

THE NEXT DAY, I made a phone call to someone I hadn't talked to in a very long time. Special Agent Lee Cannon. Cannon had made a name for himself working organized crime. He'd once tried to throw me a lifeline when I was working for the Thorne Law Group in Chicago. That line had ended up being attached to a cement block, though that hadn't been Cannon's fault and I didn't hold it against him. Lee had tried and failed to bring down the Thorne family for their more nefarious dealings. Things I'd spent a decade trying to stay away from until I no longer could.

It felt like a lifetime ago now. At the same time, I knew it was often only a phone call away.

"Why do I get the feeling I'm not going to like where this conversation is headed?" Lee asked.

"Good to hear your voice too!" I said. In a way, it was. Lee was a good guy at heart. I'd known him to be a straight shooter. Though he tended to view things in black and white. It made him good at his job.

"Relax," I said. "This one should be easy. I just kind of wanted to pick your brain on something."

"Okay," he said, drawing the word out.

"Is there anything you can tell me about a Liski family in the Detroit area?" I asked. I'd printed out screenshots from the family pawn shop's web page. There wasn't much to it, but I had some of the family names in front of me.

"They run a pawn shop in Taylor. It's called the L & M," I continued. "Peter Liski is listed as the owner, but I know he runs it with several of his sons and nephews."

Cannon paused. "Why do you ask?"

I decided there was really no reason to be anything but straight with Cannon. "One of the nephews," I said. "A Brian Liski. Given name, Branislav. He's married to a client of mine. She's trying to remedy that."

I could hear a keyboard clacking on Cannon's end. "What are you asking me?"

"You know what I'm asking," I said. "I'm just trying to gauge how big a hornet's nest I might be stirring up with this. This Brian, he's hurt this girl. Badly."

"Does he have a record?" Lee asked.

"No," I said. "A few speeding tickets. That's all. His family though."

"Liski," Cannon repeated. "Yeah, the uncle. A Ukrainian national."

"That's probably right."

I didn't like the sound of Cannon's breathing on the other end of the phone. I could pretty much guess at the exasperated expression he wore with it.

"I'm going to suggest you tread lightly," Cannon said. "I can't say as I've had personal dealings with this family, but that pawn shop is on the Bureau's radar. That one and a few others."

"I figured as much," I said. "Laundering?"

Cannon laughed. "You know I can't get into specifics. But

you're not new at this, Cass."

There was an edge to his voice, almost an accusation. It was in me to take offense, but I knew I deserved at least some of it. Still, though Cannon liked things black and white, I lived most of my life in shades of gray.

"Can you at least tell me who they're connected to?" I asked. There were mob connections, and there were wannabes. If Liski's family fell into the latter category, it would make my life a whole lot simpler.

"Does it matter?" he asked.

"And you wouldn't tell me much anyway," I said, then reconsidered. He'd actually told me quite a bit. "Right. Tread lightly."

"This girl," Cannon said. "Your client. The wife. Does she want to talk to me?"

"I'm not sure she knows anything worth saying. Honestly, at this point I'm just trying to figure out how dangerous these people might be. Can you at least tell me whether they're part of an active investigation?"

"You know I can't," he said. "And right now, that's not even something I know. I'd have to check in with the Detroit field office."

"Would you?"

"Cass," he said. "Even if they are a target of an investigation, you know I can't divulge that. What I *can* do is try to warn you if you're stepping into something you shouldn't. Let me make some calls. In the meantime, why don't you just assume you are. We'll both sleep better that way."

"I do appreciate the concern," I said.

"You appreciate it," he said. "But you never heed it."

He grew silent for a moment. Then, "Cass," he said. "You are staying out of trouble, aren't you?"

There was more I wanted to ask him. My last association

with the Thorne Law Group had been, like all things, complicated. I had reason to believe my ex-fiancé and client, Killian
Thorne, was about to go head to head with his brother, my ex-
boss, Liam Thorne. I'd spent more than a year trying not to
care, thinking no news was good news. If anything had
happened to Killian, I would have heard about it.

"I'm trying," I said. "What about you?"

"I'm doing my job," he answered. "And I prefer it when
my job and your job aren't in opposition. Are they this time?"

"No," I said. "Promise. I've just got a client I care about
and I'm trying to keep her from getting hurt any more than
she already has. And I'm *really* hoping this jerk she's married
to is of the garden variety."

"I get it," Cannon said. "Has he tried leaning on you?"

I debated whether to tell him about the parking lot incident. Lee Cannon and I weren't exactly friends. He was
someone I trusted, though. And someone I knew tried to do
the right things in the world. People like that were rare. It was
bad enough Eric was now mixed up with Brian Liski.

"Nothing I can't handle," I said.

Lee laughed. "If you really thought that, you wouldn't
have called me in the first place, Cass."

He had a point. I let my lack of response serve as confir-
mation for now.

"Listen," he said. "I'll put a feeler or two out. If I hear
anything that I can share, I'll let you know. Just be careful."

"Always," I said. "You too."

"Always," he answered. He drew in a sharp breath and for
a moment, I thought he had something else to say. When he
didn't, I knew better than to press him further. We said our
goodbyes and I found myself wondering what to hope for.
That Agent Cannon would call back with dirt on the Liskis
or not.

Chapter 9

I brought reinforcements for my meeting with Annie Liski. Jeanie Mills was hands down the best family law attorney I knew. As much as Annie trusted me, this needed to be a team effort.

Delphi being Delphi, Jeanie had already heard about my incident with Brian Liski earlier in the week.

"You okay, kid?" she asked. "I'm not going to give you too much crap for making me hear gossip from the courthouse staff rather than you. But seriously, are you okay?"

"I am," I said. "But I want to impress on Annie even more how important it is she enforces that personal protection order to the letter."

"You file a police report?" she asked.

"He didn't actually commit a crime," I said. "But I wrote everything down while it was fresh in my mind."

"Eric needs to keep it under control," Jeanie said. "I heard he threw the guy against a wall in front of four witnesses."

"He deserved it," I muttered, but knew what she meant.

"Well," Miranda said, appearing in the doorway. "Liski's already tried to file an assault charge against Detective Wray," she said. "I got a call from my friend at the sheriff's office. And Nancy Oleson called from the circuit court clerk's office. He's filed a petition for his own PPO against Wray. Judge Castor caught it. He wouldn't grant it without a hearing. It's scheduled for next week."

"Great," I said. "I'm not surprised." I decided not to tell her about my phone call with my FBI contact so far. I'd wait to hear if Cannon found anything he could share.

"The charges against Wray won't stick," Jeanie said.

"No," I said. "But it'll make just enough trouble for Eric."

"Yes. Honey, it's not the first time Eric's landed in hot water trying to defend you. He did the right thing. Don't get me wrong. But I could see the DPD command or IA suspending him just to make a point."

"I know," I said. That was my concern as well.

The front door opened behind Miranda, and Annie Liski walked in.

"Go right on in," Miranda told her with a smile. "Can I get you anything? Coffee? Bottled water? We have some pop in the fridge."

"Thank you," Annie said. "I'm okay."

She didn't look it. Annie looked downright ill. Her hair was uncharacteristically disheveled. She clutched her purse against her chest as if she needed it for a shield.

"Annie?" I asked. "Is something wrong?"

She tucked a hair behind her ear. The swelling on her face had gone down to almost nothing. The make-up she used to cover the bruising was doing its trick now. And yet, she looked even more wounded somehow.

I knew what it likely was. This was real now. Brian had been served with the papers. The hard part was just beginning.

I gave Jeanie a look. She saw the same thing in Annie, and

it was one of the main reasons I wanted her here. Annie needed to know that as hard as this was, we were on her side and we knew what we were doing.

"Sit down," I said.

Annie took the seat beside me. Jeanie stayed behind her desk.

"Brian texted me," she said.

"Did you text him back?" I asked.

Annie's silence was a yes, I knew.

"Tell us what happened," I said.

'I'm doing well at the salon," she said. "But I just rent the space. I've been working on a plan to buy Donna out. Donna Harris. She's the owner. Now ... I mean, that's out the window. I didn't have the capital to do it myself. I'd asked Brian to help me. Donna called me today and said she's not going to renew my lease."

"What?" Jeanie and I said it together.

"I think Brian, or his family, talked to her. I don't know. But she's kicking me out at the end of the month. It's not just me, she says. She's going to do a remodel. I don't know. It came completely out of the blue. And she sounded, odd on the phone. Like she couldn't hang up fast enough. She sounded scared."

"I don't like it," Jeanie said.

"Let me check into it," I said. "See if there's something going on with Donna we don't know about."

"He's trying to cut your legs out from under you," Jeanie said, pulling no punches. "We're not going to let him, Annie. This is nothing but a tactic."

"He's under so much stress," Annie said, choking past her words. "His family doesn't always have his best interests at heart."

"Annie," Jeanie started, her voice going hard.

"No. I know," Annie said. "I'm not making excuses. I'm not ... forgiving him. I wanted him to leave the business. Brian's never worked for anyone but his family. His cousins have big houses, fancy cars. Brian works there longer than they do. He stays later. They flit in and out and take all the credit. I wanted it to just be us, you know? The hell with the Liskis. Brian was always good with his hands. You should see some of the things he's built. He could be a carpenter."

Good with his hands. I swallowed past what I wanted to say. He'd used those same hands to hurt her.

"I never wanted to seem like I was pitting Brian against his family. They've never liked me. I mean, I don't speak Ukrainian. I don't even know where my ancestors came from. I mean ... they came from Ann Arbor, you know? To the Liskis, that's a character flaw."

Annie sat quietly for a moment. Then she nodded. But I didn't like the look in her eyes. I started to feel like she'd made a decision without me.

"Annie," I said. "We'll get you through this."

"Honey," Jeanie said. "There's something else we haven't talked about. Is there any chance ... has he been unfaithful?"

Annie reared back. "Why do you ask?"

"We always ask," Jeanie said.

"I didn't think you had to prove that to get a divorce," Annie said.

"You don't," I answered. "But if Brian's been cheating on you, it's the kind of thing a judge can take into consideration when deciding on spousal support ... um ... alimony."

Annie shook her head. "No. I don't know. I don't think so. I thought so for a little while. There was this woman who called our landline. Once, a few weeks ago, she called me on my cell. She wouldn't leave her name. She just said she wanted to talk to me and a couple of times she asked for Brian.

But she sounded like the rest of them. Like Brian's family. It was a while ago."

"Do you still have her number?" I asked.

"No," Annie said. "I'll check my phone later. I don't even care anymore, to be honest. But the bank accounts," she said. "He said he owns all the money."

"We talked about that," I said. "I've already secured a temporary restraining order and served it on the banks. Brian can't withdraw the money. We're going to protect you as best as we can. How are you set for cash right now?"

"All the bills are in Brian's name," she said. "My friend Maggie, who I'm staying with? She isn't charging me rent right now. But if Donna kicks me out of the salon, I won't have any income, Cass."

"We'll file a motion to get you some temporary support from Brian," I said. "I'll file it today."

"Are you sure Brian doesn't know where Maggie lives?" Jeanie asked. "Honey, I know it's tough, but I don't think it's safe for you to be where he can potentially find you. It wouldn't be hard for him to have her followed home from the salon. He may have hired a private investigator. If he's playing dirty, we have to assume nothing is off the table. I don't like that you haven't changed your phone. That needs to happen. Today."

Annie's eyes widened.

"He came here last night," I said. Though I'd debated telling Annie that part, she needed to know. "Jeanie's right. Brian's volatile. Especially when we serve him with the support request, it could get worse."

"I don't have anywhere else to go. Kent has offered but ..."

"Brian knows where Kent lives too," I said. "Annie, there's a safe house just outside of Delphi. It's only ten miles from here. It's a beautiful place. It won't be forever. Hopefully, just a few days."

"A battered women's shelter?" she asked.

"Yes," I said. "It's private. Confidential. You can get support there."

"I can't afford that," she said.

"There's no cost to you," I said. "It's run by a private foundation under a state grant. They only take a handful of people at a time at most. I've already spoken to the director there. Her name is Renee. You can go today. I've taken the liberty of arranging it. I know it's sudden, but that's to your advantage. Will you go?"

She sniffled. Jeanie handed her a tissue. "It's not great at Maggie's. I mean, she's great. But she has a husband and kids. They're all sweet and supportive, but I don't know."

"You have options," I said. "Resources. You're not alone, Annie. I promise."

"Thank you," she said. "I really mean that. I just ... I sit here, and I don't know how I got here. How it all got so ... big. You know?"

"Honey," Jeanie said. "I've been at this a long time. You did everything right. And even if you hadn't, this isn't your fault. Listen to Cass. She's scrawny but she's tough. We'll help you get through this. I can't tell you how long it's going to take you to feel like you've made it to the other side. But you will make it to the other side if you trust us. You hear me?"

For all her gruff bluster, Jeanie Mills was just a big old softie. I knew how much she wanted to wrap her arms around Annie. In a sense, she already had.

I also knew the most important thing I could do besides helping ensure Annie's safety was help her take back her power. A homework assignment was in order.

"So," I said. "The more information I have about Brian's

finances, the better. I do not want you going back to that house by yourself. Does he use an accountant?"

"He does," she said. "Um, it's a cousin of his though. I'll get you his number."

"It's a start," I said. "I can subpoena all of his records but that'll take time."

Annie nodded. I didn't like that he used family. My hunch was Brian would try to hide assets. However, there was more than one way to skin this particular cat, so I told Annie to let me worry about it.

We finished up a few more loose ends with her, then I gave Annie a pink business card with the safe house number and address written on it.

"Okay," she said. Her whole posture changed. She looked as though she had just set down something heavy. "I'll go this evening. I'll get my things from Maggie's, and I'll go."

"They're expecting you," Jeanie told her. "You just show up and tell them who you are. No one else but us will know you're there."

"That's important," I said. "Don't tell Maggie. Don't tell any of your other friends. At least, not right now. Confidentiality is a two-way street."

"I understand," she said. "And thanks. I really don't know what I'd do if you weren't in my corner."

"Well we are," I said.

Annie rose. I stood with her and started walking her toward the front door. With her hand on the doorknob, she froze. Smiling, she turned to me and pulled me into a hug that startled me.

I hugged her back.

She was sad, but I could feel her strength. As Annie Liski headed toward her car, I knew in my heart she'd get through this.

Chapter 10

As soon as Annie left, Jeanie made a call to the safe house to finalize her arrangements. Annie was going to call and let us know as soon as she was settled. I admired her bravery. Though our situations weren't the same, I knew what it was like to uproot your entire life in an afternoon. I'd done the same thing two years ago when I left Chicago and my high-powered law firm life behind. I'd hit the highway with little more than a few boxes of my belongings in the back seat and tried not to look back.

The difference was, I was running back to family in Delphi. Mine was a homecoming. Annie Liski was heading into the unknown. But she couldn't be in a better place than the shelter we picked out. She would be safe and surrounded by new resources and people who had expertise in helping women like her.

I finished up my few remaining projects for the day and left the building. This time, Eric was waiting for me. He parked alongside my Jeep. I knew better than to argue with him. I gave him a quick wave and he followed me home.

It was warm still, over eighty degrees, the perfect evening

for a pontoon ride. I had some leftover lasagna from the night before. I heated it in the microwave, poured myself a glass of wine and grabbed a beer for Eric while he started the boat and tossed off the mooring lines.

Marbury and Madison tore down the hill and jumped on board. They slathered Eric with doggie kisses. He gently pushed them down and took the food and drinks from me. The pontoon had a small table in the center. He set everything there while the dogs hopped up on the benches on either side of the boat. Once we got going, they'd be on duck watch. There was even a muskrat sliding around out there somewhere. My niece Jemma named him Olaf. Because, why not?

I put our drinks in the cup holders and pushed off from the dock while Eric steered. We went out to the middle of the lake by the sand bar and dropped anchor. We had an hour or so until sunset. The dogs busied themselves watching for fish off the back of the boat. Olaf and the swans were hiding somewhere else.

Eric picked a classic rock station and cracked open his beer. This was just about as good as it got as far as I was concerned. "How's Annie?" he finally asked.

"Coping," I said. Eric sat in the captain's chair. I sat opposite him with my feet stretched out.

"How much of a headache are you going to have to deal with regarding Liski's charges?" I asked.

Eric picked at the label on his beer bottle. "Guy's a scumbag. I'm not worried."

"Really? I think maybe I want you to be a little. Just ... promise me you'll behave yourself and not let your temper get the best of you. I can handle Liski. With any luck, I'll have him slinking back to Taylor and his family with his tail between his legs."

Marbury started barking and ran to the front of the boat. A flock of geese had just landed.

"Hey," Eric said. "I think that's an insult to animals with tails."

Madison nuzzled his leg as if she agreed.

"That's my girl," Eric said. He scratched her behind the ear which sent Madison straight to her back twitching her legs.

"Fine," I said. "Take his side."

"Aw," Eric said. He came over to me and started rubbing behind my ear. "Don't get jealous. There's plenty of me to go around."

He made me laugh. Eric sat in the small space I made for him. His fingers threaded through my hair.

His eyes flashed as the sunlight caught them. He ran a thumb across my cheekbone. Heat flared in my core. It got hard to breathe when he got this close. Hard to think. He made me not want to.

Eric leaned forward and caught my lips with his. He tasted good. Sometimes, I just wanted to lose myself in him. Someday, I hoped I would, even for a little while.

"Just be careful," he said. "Liski's dangerous. I have a bad feeling about that guy."

"So do I," I said. "I, uh ... I put some feelers out about him. And about his family."

Eric bristled. I was poking the edges of a sore spot between Eric and me.

"Cass," he said. "I think you better tell me who you've been feeling out."

Part of me felt indignant. I wasn't used to answering to Eric, or anyone else, for that matter. Even though I'd been back in Delphi for two years, I often still thought of myself as flying solo.

ROBIN JAMES

"I have a hunch that Liski's family might be ... um ... connected," I said. "That pawn shop he works at. The one his family owns. I don't know for sure, but it's got the earmarks of one that might be a front for something else."

I didn't have to tell Eric my full line of thought. He'd been a police detective for a very long time. "You know anything concrete?" he asked, staring out at the water.

"No," I said. I knew him well enough to know he had a different question on his mind. He wanted to know if the feelers I'd put out reached all the way back to Killian Thorne and my old associations. I decided to put his mind at ease. I reached for his knee.

"I talked to a contact of mine at the FBI," I said.

Eric smiled. "They won't tell you anything," he said. "Hell, they wouldn't tell *me* anything if I called."

"I get that," I said. "But I figured it was worth a call."

"You could have called me," he said.

"I have. I do. But on this one? I need you to steer clear. Liski's not worth your badge. He's got you riled up. He'll use that. Let's not give him any more power or help than he already has. Okay?"

Eric's gaze cut right through me. "If you think I'm going to sit back and let that scumbag come near you?" He leaned far forward. When provoked, Eric Wray was a formidable adversary. And I knew just how far he would go to protect the people he cared about. It took my breath away. The sky turned pink behind Eric.

"I know," I said. "But I really do think once he realizes he's not going to win ... when he knows Annie won't back down ... he will."

"I hope you're right."

"I meant what I said though," I said. "Liski knows how to

push your buttons, I think. He's not worth you risking your career."

"You let me worry about my badge. And I don't give a damn about any of that when it comes to someone trying to hurt you, Cass. I hope you know that."

"I do," I said. "And I appreciate it."

I had more I wanted to say. I started to, then my phone buzzed. I'd almost forgotten that I brought it out here. I would have let it go to voicemail, but Jeanie's name popped up. She didn't usually call me after hours unless it was something important.

Eric sat back as I answered.

I never even had a chance to say hello before Jeanie started talking. "Cass," she said. "Is Eric with you?"

"He is," I answered.

"Good," she said. "I'm sorry to ruin your evening. I just got a call from Renee Windham. You know, the safe house we sent Annie to."

My heart turned to stone. I sat up and dropped my feet to the floor.

"What is it, Jeanie?"

"Honey, she never showed."

"What?"

"Annie," she said. "She called ahead like we told her to and said she was on her way. That was over four hours ago. But she never showed up. No one's seen her. No one's heard from her. It could be nothing. Only ..."

"Got it," I said. I made a circular gesture to Eric. He went to the back of the boat and started pulling up the anchor.

"We'll be right there," I said.

Chapter 11

"IT'S NOT RIGHT," Jeanie said.

I found her pacing at the back door of the office. She was smoking a cigarette, something I hadn't seen her do in years. She had a cancer scare a little over two years ago. This was bad.

"What do you know?" I said. Eric stood behind me, a solid presence while Jeanie was falling apart. That, more than anything, had my heart racing.

"She was supposed to show up at the safe house by five thirty. A social worker was waiting for her. She never arrived."

It was almost ten now.

I stared Jeanie down. She rolled her eyes then extinguished her cigarette.

"I tried her cell a few times," I said. "It goes straight to voicemail."

"Not even that now," Jeanie said. "I just tried a minute ago and got a message that her mailbox is full."

Eric pulled out his own cell phone. I keyed into the back door and got Jeanie to come inside. She was sweating. A tiny pulse in her neck jumped.

"It's wrong, Cass," she said. "I feel it. I've been down this road before."

I knew what she meant. Jeanie had been handling family law and domestic violence cases for over forty years. She'd seen it all. And her instincts were never wrong.

A ball of heat formed in my chest. "It's early," she said. "She probably just got cold feet."

Eric stepped inside, his expression grim. Jeanie's demeanor spooked him for the same reason it did me. "Jeanie," he said. "I've got a crew out looking for her."

"She's not with her friend, Maggie," Jeanie said. "Maggie hasn't heard from her since she left for work this morning. They've got a Ring doorbell. It shows Annie getting in her car that was parked in front of their house at ten thirty. She was probably on her way here. We had an appointment at eleven. She went back there right after like she told us. But she was gone again by noon. Where's she been for the last ten hours?"

"I've sent another car to check in on Liski," Eric said.

"He's supposed to be at the pawn shop up in Taylor," I said.

"That'll be easy enough to check out if he's not at their house. I have a few contacts in Wayne County."

"They won't do anything," Jeanie said, her voice rising with panic. "I know how this goes, Wray. Annie's over eighteen. She's not technically missing for forty-eight hours."

Eric's expression turned grim. "She's a woman who just served a PPO on her asshat of a husband. Same guy who then showed up and threatened Cass right in front of me. This isn't a normal situation. We're all on the same page here. I'll do everything I can. Plus, I'd be the one to catch this case anyway if ..."

"Don't," I said. "Don't even say it yet. Jeanie, maybe Annie didn't want to go to the safe house, after all. Maybe ..."

"Maybe nothing," she said. "Even if she chickened out of going, she wouldn't just ghost all of us."

I winced at Jeanie's choice of words.

"You talked to Tucker?" Eric asked. "See if she reached out to him?"

"I texted him earlier," I said. "He hasn't answered yet. I didn't tell him what I was worried about. I didn't want to ... Christ. I can't tell even *him* Annie was heading to the safe house. She's my client. He isn't. The only reason I told you was ..."

"Right," he said. "Let me give it a shot. We're beyond confidentiality now."

Gone was Eric's reassurances that this might just be Annie driving around clearing her head. He went into full police detective mode. Eric went back outside to make a series of calls.

"If anything happens to that girl," Jeanie said, on the verge of tears.

I wanted to tell her that it wouldn't. I wanted to reassure her that I would fix everything. Only I knew this one might be too big for even me.

"Jeanie," I said. "Have you called the hospital?"

She squeezed her eyes shut. "Not yet."

"I'll do it," I answered. "Right now, as much as we need to find Annie, we need to know where Brian is."

Eric came back inside. "I gotta go in," he said. "I want to coordinate with my guy up in Taylor. The pawn shop closed at seven. There's a crew heading over there to see if anyone's still there. So far, Annie and Brian's house is quiet. No cars in the driveway or the garage that they can see."

"Eric ..." I said.

"You gotta let me do my job," he said. "You sure you're the last two who saw or talked to Annie today?"

"As far as we know," I said. "But I have no idea what she did after she left Maggie's. She was supposed to go get a new cell phone. Maybe she did. Maybe that's why we can't get a hold of her."

It wasn't though. I knew it in my gut. Annie would have called one of us or my office. Someone.

"Jeanie, I need the number of this social worker at the safe house," Eric said. "Hell, I need everything. Give me this Maggie's number. Start writing down every one of her friends or coworkers and where I can reach them."

I ran up to my office and pulled Annie's physical file off my desk. The list of contacts Eric wanted was a pretty short one. I hoped they would all cooperate with him. God. I hoped it wasn't already too late.

I wrote down the numbers on a steno pad and tore off a sheet for Eric. He thanked me.

"Okay," he said. "I need the two of you to sit tight."

"Eric ... I ..."

"I mean it," he said, his voice rising. "Brian Liski is dangerous. I know you know that. I don't need you poking this particular bear anymore right now. I don't want to have to worry about your safety along with Annie's. This guy has weapons. He knows who you are. In fact, don't go back home. Go to Jeanie's. You okay with that?"

"Of course," she said.

"Good," he said. "And you stay there until you hear from me. I don't want you out of pocket until I know exactly where Brian Liski is. We clear?"

I gritted my teeth. I wanted to be with him. I wanted to make calls. I wanted to just *do* something.

"He's not a serial killer, Eric. This is about Annie, not me."

"You don't know what he is right now," Eric said. "If he

did something to Annie ... Just ... for once, for the love of God, will you just do what I say and not fight me on it?"

I put my hands up in surrender. "Okay. But will you please check in with me?"

"Yes," he said. "Also, I'll have to. If we don't ..." He frowned and looked at Jeanie. "I might need to take a formal statement from the both of you."

"We understand," she answered.

"If you think of anything else that could be helpful in finding Annie, let me know. I'll be reachable on my cell."

"So will I," I said.

"Don't go to your house," he said. "I mean it."

"I get it, Eric, honest. I don't need to. I keep a change of clothes and other essentials here at the office. I'll just throw it into a bag."

"I'll wait," he said. He stood with his arms crossed.

I got my things and came straight back downstairs. By the time I did, a Delphi P.D. patrol car had pulled into the parking lot. My knees went weak.

"That's me," Eric said. "I just want to make sure you get to Jeanie's safely."

"You really think that's necessary?" Jeanie asked.

"Look," he said. "We don't know what's really going on with Annie. It's entirely possible she *did* just decide to drive around or whatever. It's also possible that we're not the only ones looking for her. If that's true, it makes sense that Brian would try to corner you or Cass once he realizes she's really and truly making a break from him for good. So, yeah. I think it's best if you lay low at your house for a bit. And I want to make sure that asshole isn't lying in wait ready to follow."

"Thank you," I said. "I'll wait to hear from you. But I'm going to need to call my brothers."

"Do," he said. "I suspect they'll know within the hour that

there was a black and white parked outside your office. I don't need them charging over here or at your place making unnecessary noise."

"Got it," I said. "Good thinking. Just ... promise me you'll let me know the second you hear anything."

"I will. Consider that a two-way street. If Annie calls, I'm your next call."

"Of course," I promised. Jeanie had already started out the front door. She held it open. I locked eyes with Eric. He froze for an instant, then leaned down and kissed me.

"Be safe," he said.

"Back at ya, Detective," I answered. Then I followed Jeanie out the door.

Chapter 12

I slid into the passenger seat of Jeanie's RAV4. I almost wanted to take the keys from her. The woman drove like a bat out of hell. Even with Delphi P.D.'s finest tailing her, she drove fifteen over the speed limit. We arrived at her condo in under ten minutes.

Jeanie had recently moved into the Shady Woods subdivision. I thought it was the most unfortunate of names the developer could have chosen. Jeanie thought it was hilarious and a selling point. It was a retirement community populated by, as Jeanie described it, a bunch of nosey, old, white farts. She'd served on the Homeowner's Association and managed to ruffle the feathers of pretty much every fart in the place.

But it was a safe, quiet neighborhood and she didn't have to worry about her yard in the summer or her driveway in the winter. Plus, there was an on-site handyman, though Jeanie mostly pestered my brothers to handle what she needed, which they did without complaint.

"Second door on the left in the back," she said. "Bed's already made up."

"Thanks," I said. I was surprised when I walked inside.

Jeanie had the house professionally decorated in soft pinks and blues. It looked ... well ... respectable. Quaint, almost. I couldn't help but smile.

After I set my things in the guest room, I joined Jeanie in the kitchen where she'd already cracked two beers.

It was nearly midnight. She downed her beer quickly. I only sipped mine.

My phone started to blow up. Just as Eric figured, my brothers already knew about the police car outside my office this late at night. I couldn't tell them much as I still wanted to protect Annie's privacy.

I called Matty first and had a brief conversation. He was still in Hillsdale and yet the events at my office had reached him. I hoped that for once, the small-town gossip mill would work to Annie Liski's favor. Someone had to know something.

"Cass," my brother Joe said when I called him next. "Just tell me what I need to know."

"That everything's fine," I said. "Just ... a little drama with a client. Please don't make a big deal out of it."

"Don't you think that ship has sailed?" he asked.

"Do me a favor," I said. "Stay away from the lake house the rest of this weekend. Tell Emma the same thing. Things just got a little hairy with the abusive ex of a woman I'm trying to help out. It's temporary. It's being taken care of."

"Christ," he said. "Is Eric involved? Is this the same abusive ex who showed up at your office? Cass, this isn't just a little hairy. You're lying."

"I'm fine," I said, appreciating the concern but also really wishing I were an only child sometimes. Briefly. "Please, please, please don't make this into a bigger thing than it needs to be. I've got enough to worry about. Just, stay home. Tell Emma to stay home. Can I trust you to take care of Vangie? I don't want her over at the house for the next couple of days either."

"Yeah," he said, sighing. "As long as you promise to answer your phone."

"I have been. I did!"

"This time."

"I will," I promised. The last thing I wanted was my family worrying about me as much as I worried about Annie. No sooner had I thought it before a second call started to come through. Judge Tucker. I said a quick goodbye to my brother and said hello to Annie's.

"What's going on?!" he asked, breathless.

I realized there was little I could tell him that wouldn't break confidentiality. "Who have you talked to?"

"I've been trying to get a hold of my sister," he said. "She isn't answering. Then I hear you've got cops outside your office. Were you going to tell me Liski came after you?"

I covered my face with my hand. There really was nothing that happened in this town that didn't become news. If Eric hadn't talked to Tucker yet, he soon would be.

"When was the last time you talked to Annie?" I asked.

"Cass, what's that got to do with anything?"

My eyes caught Jeanie's. She turned her palm up, gesturing toward my phone. I knew what she was trying to convey. I might as well tell Judge Tucker what I knew. He was going to find out soon enough anyway when Eric got to him.

"Judge," I said. "We're having a little trouble locating Annie right now. It's not time to worry yet. I need you to sit tight."

"Did he do this? Did he hurt her? I'll kill him. I'll ..."

"Stop," I said. "Just stop right there. Detective Wray is helping, okay? I expect he's going to call you soon. If you want, I can give you his cell phone number." I knew that's exactly what Eric would want. I had to trust him to handle the investigation without any help from me.

Still fuming, Judge Tucker at least calmed down enough to take Eric's number. We said our goodbyes and I shot Eric a quick text to warn him Judge Tucker was going to reach out. His answer was brief.

"Thanks. Was on my way to talk to him next anyhow. No news yet. Sit tight."

I was starting to get a headache. Jeanie poured me another drink.

"This isn't going to end well," she said. "Cass, I know it. Brian called her, is my guess. She said too much. He convinced her to meet him one last time."

"Don't," I said. "There's no point to it. We're doing everything we can. Let's just ... I don't know."

"Talk about something else?" she said, smirking. "Fine. So, tell me what's going on with you and Wray."

"Oh," I smiled. "That."

"You sleeping with him yet?"

I nearly spit out my beer.

"That a yes?" she laughed.

"It's a none of your business," I said, but knew that would get me nowhere. "But no. We're taking it slow."

Jeanie shook her head. "Like hell you are. He's head over heels. You know that, right?"

"He's married," I reminded her.

"He's married so his would-have-been-ex-wife still has access to his health insurance. Cass, that marriage was over years ago. It was just rotten luck that Wendy had that accident. She's gone. She's never waking up. Rumor I heard was Maple Valley is looking to move her out of that facility. They need the bed. She's pretty much just receiving palliative care."

"Rumor?" I asked. "Lord. Hasn't anyone heard of HIPAA in this town?" I joked it off, but it concerned me. Eric had never said a word about Wendy's condition deteriorating. On the other hand, it was a subject we barely broached but one that formed an invisible barrier I hadn't been yet willing to cross.

"Well," Jeanie said. "I'm glad. Not about Wendy. But about you and Eric. You both deserve some happiness. And you deserve a guy who thinks you're the cat's ass. Which you are and he does."

I smiled. "Thanks. And thanks for this. For putting up with me tonight."

Jeanie waved me off. "It gives me one less thing to worry about."

The heaviness in the air settled again. Jeanie dropped her head.

"She's gotta be okay," she whispered. "That poor kid has just gotta be okay."

I bit my lip to keep from assuring her that she would be. I didn't know. And with each passing minute, I knew the chances of Annie Liski's happy ending faded.

Chapter 13

JEANIE AND EVERYONE in my office tried to stay busy the next morning. But our concern for Annie seemed to cling to the air we breathed. My calls and texts to Eric went unanswered. Though it frustrated me, I knew what he'd say anyway. When he could tell me something, he would. By eleven o'clock, I didn't know whether I was hoping to hear from him or not anymore.

I managed to finish half of a summary disposition brief on one of my remaining workplace harassment claims when Miranda's soft knock on the door pulled me out of it.

I heard loud footsteps and a shout from downstairs. "Sorry," Miranda said. "Judge ..."

She didn't get the sentence out before Kent Tucker appeared behind her, red-faced and with his normally perfect hair disheveled.

I rose from my seat. "Judge," I said. He cast an apologetic look at Miranda then brushed past her.

Kent Tucker was a stoic man. Professionally, at least. He handled the transition from private practitioner to judge with more grace than most, withdrawing from the local bar social circles. He remained aloof when I saw him in court halls. But now, the man was quite simply falling apart.

He held one fist with the other hand, rubbing it with worry. He paced in front of my desk, declining my offer of a chair.

"I knew it," he whispered. "She wouldn't listen."

"No news at all?" I asked.

He shook his head. "It's been over twenty-four hours since anyone's seen or heard from her. She hasn't answered my texts. Not her friend Maggie's either. Not yours?"

"No," I said.

"You're not just saying that?" His voice broke. "I mean ... she's your client. I'm not asking ..."

"No," I said. "This is different. I wouldn't withhold information like that from you."

"She doesn't do this," he whispered. "She checks in. She's on her phone constantly. There's just been nothing. Nothing. And she knows exactly what we'd all be worried about, Cass. Annie would *not* just ignore all these calls and texts."

"I know," I said. I wished to God I could say something encouraging. Think of some alternate scenario where the mystery of Annie Liski's whereabouts wouldn't end in the worst-case scenario. There just wasn't one.

"Why didn't you tell me Brian came after you?" he asked, turning to me. Though we'd talked about it briefly last night, he was right. The news about Liski's harassment hadn't come from me. Tucker's eyes were glassy and bloodshot. I doubted the judge had slept at all last night. Neither had I.

"Well," I said. "For one thing, it kind of just happened. For another, it wasn't something you needed to add to your plate."

"He filed for a PPO against Detective Wray," he said. "That's how I know."

"Courthouse rumor mill," I said. "I hadn't even had a chance to really tell Annie about it yet."

"I was going to tell her," he said. "I warned her a thousand times not to meet with Brian once she moved out. I told her the statistics."

"Do you know for sure she did?" I asked.

"I mean ... what did she say to you the last time you spoke?" he asked.

Tucker didn't seem entirely present. I started to wonder if maybe he'd been drinking. I didn't smell anything on him. Come to think of it, I didn't think I'd ever seen him take a drink. Certainly not at any of the local bar association holiday parties or functions.

"Everything's okay," he said. "That's what she always said. Brian's not who you think he is. He loves me. Don't worry about me."

Then, Tucker turned. He took two powerful strides. His anger overcoming him, he smashed both of his fists into my wall. The force of it seemed to shake the whole building. His hands went through the plaster.

He doubled over and pulled his fists into his stomach. I came around the desk.

"Shit," he muttered. Never mind drinking, I'd never, ever heard the man swear.

"You're bleeding," I said. "Let me see."

He let me guide him to a chair. I knelt in front of him and pulled his hands toward me. They were a mangled mess, the right one worse than the left. The skin on his knuckles was torn and blood trickled down his wrist.

"Stay put," I said. "Let me get something to wrap that with."

"I'm sorry," he sobbed.

I smiled. "You've met my brothers, right? This isn't

exactly the first time someone's punched a hole through one of my walls."

"I'll pay for it," he said.

I waved my hand in dismissal. "Again ... two hot-headed Irish brothers. The Learys should buy stock in spackle."

I played it off, but I was worried. I just hoped Eric got a hold of Brian Liski before Kent Tucker did.

I ran down to the office kitchen and grabbed our first aid kit and a clean dish towel.

"What was that?" Miranda asked. Naturally, she'd heard the commotion.

"Angry brother versus wall," I explained.

Miranda barely batted an eye. She simply reached around me for the cupboard and pulled out a plastic bag. She then filled it with a handful of ice from the freezer.

"Thanks," I said.

"No word yet?" she asked.

"No," I answered. I took the supplies and went back to the judge. He stayed quiet and mostly obedient as I gently cleaned the plaster out of his mangled right hand, sprayed some Bactine on it, then the left one, then wrapped them both with gauze.

"Ice," I said, handing him the bag. "Lots of it. That'll look worse tomorrow."

Defeated, he nodded. "I need to get back to work."

I rose. "You can't. Judge, you're not going to do anyone any good taking the bench today. Least of all yourself. Clear your docket. Go home. Try and get some rest. I promise, if I hear anything, I'll call you. If you hear something before I do, then you call me."

He looked up at me. "Thank you," he said. "I should have made Annie come talk to you sooner. Maybe if I had ..."

"We don't know anything yet," I said, though it sounded hollow even to me.

"Right," he said. Then he quietly rose from the chair. I walked him downstairs.

"I mean it," I said. "You're in no condition to be at work today. And nobody expects you to. Go home. Is there other family you can be with?"

He shook his head. "Our parents passed a long time ago. Right now, that seems like a blessing. It's just ... it's just me."

I half expected Miranda to come flying around the corner to offer to take him home. She had a knack for collecting strays. Though a judge would be a first. But she hung back. I saw her turn away from us and dab her eyes with a tissue.

"Thanks, Cass," he said. "I wish ... I hope you'll get the chance to know Annie even better after all of this. She's not ... she's more than a victim, you know?"

"I do," I said. We stood in awkward silence for a moment, then Judge Kent Tucker walked out of my building a quiet, broken man.

Chapter 14

A FEW HOURS LATER, just as I was about to leave for the day, Eric showed up. He came up the stairs so quietly, I hadn't even heard him. I startled at first, then relief flooded through me as he gave me that patented, sideways smile.

"Please tell me you have good news."

His smile faltered. "We haven't found her yet."

"Have you found Liski?" I asked.

He worked a muscle in his jaw.

"Right," I said. "Ongoing investigation."

"Something like that," he said.

"Well," I said. "Let me ask it another way. Did you come here to escort me home? And can I expect a police presence near the house tonight?"

He considered me. "No," he answered.

"He's in custody," I said, my heart tripping.

"That's what I came over here to tell you."

"I can go home?" I asked.

He nodded. "You can go home. You've still got your security system hooked up?"

"Of course," I said. "Nobody gets in or out without the

thing beeping or recording it, or both. I'm like Fort Knox up on that hill, thanks to you and my brothers."

"It's not like you haven't given us all cause to worry, Cass."

I felt bad. My tone came out harsher than I wanted. My lack of sleep wore on me. I may not have punched any walls, but I wasn't handling any of this much better than Kent Tucker.

"I don't want to lose her, Eric," I said. "Have you … can you tell me what Liski said?"

"I'm heading over to the station now," Eric said. "They just picked him up."

"Have you arrested him?" I asked. Eric stayed silent. Right. Ongoing investigation and all of that.

"You're going to interrogate him," I said. It was a statement not a question. I had a terrible thought. I'm not proud of it, but I envisioned Eric hurting Brian Liski the way he'd hurt Annie and it gave me pleasure. Eric must have sensed something shift behind my eyes. He had a warm smile for me that worked to calm me, just a little.

Eric stepped further into my office and saw the hole in the wall.

"Matty or Joe been by?" he asked, pointing to it. I couldn't help but chuckle.

"Actually, no," I said. "That one's courtesy of another pissed off brother. Annie's. Judge Tucker was here earlier this morning. He's hanging on by a thread."

Eric nodded. "I can imagine. You all right?"

I was about to say yes. I would say I was fine. But something broke inside of me as I thought of all the bleak possibilities Annie Liski likely faced. Before I knew what was happening, a sob escaped my throat and Eric was there.

He pulled me against him. "You have to find her," I whispered.

"We're doing everything we can," he said.

"Her cell phone. You've pinged it?"

It was Eric's turn to chuckle. "I know how to do my job, Cass."

"I should have done mine better," I said. "I should have stayed with Annie. Driven her to that safe house myself."

"She's a grown woman," Eric said. It was a small thing, but he still spoke of her in the present tense. It gave me hope.

"We both saw the evil in that man's eyes," I said. "Why the hell didn't I ..."

"Stop," he said. "If Brian Liski is responsible for something happening to her ... then *Brian* is responsible. And we don't know that yet."

He didn't say it was going to be okay. I think I might have lost it completely if he had.

"This hurts," I whispered.

"I know," he said.

I grabbed my messenger bag while Eric turned off the lights. It was Friday. We'd made plans earlier in the week to have dinner together. That was out of the question now. He didn't have to tell me he might be dealing with Liski late into the night.

"I can still send a car to follow you home," he said. "If you feel ..."

"I feel fine," I said. "I want them out there, not babysitting me. They need to be looking for Annie. Or, God forbid, being ready if someone else like her needs help tonight."

Eric nodded. We walked to the parking lot together. He'd pulled his car beside mine. His was still running.

"I'll check in tomorrow. You know I can't talk about an active investigation, even to you. But ..."

"I know," I said. "And thanks." I went on my tiptoes to give him a peck on the cheek.

He hugged me then waited for me to slide behind the wheel of my car. There was something in his eyes. A haunted look. As much as Annie's fate hurt me, I knew this one might leave a mark on him as well.

I waved goodbye and said a small prayer for Annie. This would mark night number two with no word.

I didn't know it then, but there would be two more nights like it. Then, on the morning of the fifth day since her disappearance, the world came crashing down.

Chapter 15

"SOMETHING'S GOING ON OUT THERE," Joe said.

On the fifth morning after Annie Liski's disappearance, he sat on the back of the pontoon.

It was the first near ninety-degree day we'd had. The water was calm, not a cloud in the sky. My brother had gotten an early start and caught a pile of bluegills. They were still in the live well of his fishing boat.

I joined him on the pontoon bearing two cups of steaming hot coffee. Earlier, I'd called Miranda and told her to take the day off. None of us were handling Annie's disappearance very well or getting much of anything done. For the longest time, I'd wonder what might have happened if I'd just gone into work that day.

"What are you talking about?" I asked, blowing over the top of my mug.

"Over by the boat launch," he said. "There's something going on out there."

I shielded my eyes from the sun. In the distance, I could see three boats anchored close together.

Before I could make any other observations, Joe hopped

off the boat and stepped in the shallow water. He had the WaveRunner beached and pulled it out.

"Joe," I said.

"Just stay put," he said. "I'll be right back." He tore off, spraying a jet of water behind him.

"Where's he off to like a bat out of hell?" My sister Vangie stood at the end of the dock. She and my niece Jessa were eating a late breakfast inside. Vangie didn't need to go into work until later in the afternoon. Her blonde hair lifted as the breeze picked up.

"I don't know," I said. "Joe's spidey sense went off."

I waited and sipped my coffee. Vangie watched from the end of the dock for a few minutes before Jessa called her from the kitchen. She headed back up. A moment later, my brother rode back in. He went slow, kicking up no wake behind him.

His face looked ashen, his expression grim.

"What?" I said, my heart pumping.

"Cass," he said.

"What?"

"It's Delphi P.D." he said. "They've got two boats in the water. A couple of patrol cars up on shore. Cass, they found a body. The coroner took it away a little while ago, I guess. I talked to Len Savitch. He lives two houses down from the boat launch. The cops are still down there talking to the neighbors and looking for more evidence, I guess."

The air left my lungs in a whoosh. A body? No. Not here. Not on Finn Lake. Not this close. A shiver went through me, as if the hand of evil had just brushed my face and clutched my heart.

Vangie stood on the porch. Jessa leaned against her mother holding a pop tart.

"Go on back inside," Joe called out. Vangie knew something was wrong. They knew. They both knew. That same hand of evil had gotten far too close to them too. She pressed Jessa tighter against her and closed the door behind them.

"I have to go," I said. My voice didn't even sound familiar to my ears. It scratched out of me as I tried to remember to breathe.

"Cass," Joe started.

"Joe," I said. "This is ... I have to go."

"Where?" he asked.

It was a good question. One I didn't have the answer to. It was just, I knew in my heart what this was about. Delphi wasn't that big. Annie Liski was the only missing person in the county.

"Eric," I said. "He'll know what's going on."

"So, then we wait," he said. "What good is it going to do if you go racing down there?"

"Did you see? Was Eric down there?" I asked, not sure if I wanted the answer. "Tell me. Joe, I need to know."

"I couldn't see anything," he said. "They had a boat in the water keeping people from getting too close. Maybe it's not her. Someone could have gotten drunk last night. Drowned. Hell, you know that old man Mr. Moyer on the southern tip of the lake. Everyone on the lake expects him to fall in one of these days. He's joked about it himself. Said it's the perfect way to go."

His face fell as he realized he wasn't helping. "Yeah," he said. "Eric was down there. I saw him get into his car and leave though."

"Joe," I said quietly. Then I couldn't say anything else at all.

I got as far as my car before my cell phone rang. Kent Tucker's ID popped up. I took a breath and leaned against the door.

"Judge," I said.

"Is it true?" His tone was flat, distant. I didn't know what to say.

"I don't know anything yet," I said. "No one's called me. Has anyone called you?"

"The lake," he said. "You live out there, don't you? I have a police scanner. Don't ask me why. I got it as a gift."

"It's true there is a crew down there on the other end of the lake. That's all I know. We need to sit tight until we hear something. This doesn't have to mean ..." Lord. I sounded just like Joe and even less convincing.

"Judge, where are you? Are you at the courthouse?"

"I'm at home," he said. "I took time off like you wanted me to."

On the other end of the phone, I heard a doorbell. Kent Tucker let out a choked sound.

I knew what this was. He knew what this was. Everyone did. "Judge?" I said. "Kent. I'm ... I'm on my way."

I threw my phone in the car and climbed behind the wheel. Joe called after me. I slammed the car in gear. Gravel kicked up behind me as I left my white-faced brother shouting after me.

Chapter 16

JUDGE KENT TUCKER lived on a quiet cul-de-sac in one of
the newest neighborhoods in Delphi, three streets over from
Eric. I got there in less than ten minutes. My heart turned to
stone as I saw the judge sitting on his porch with his face in
his hands. Two uniformed Delphi P.D. officers stood above
him, one leaned in close resting his foot on the porch beside
the judge.

"Ma'am," the younger one said. He couldn't even be
thirty, I guessed. He had sandy-blond hair and a bodybuilder's
physique. His partner was closer to my age. I recognized him
but couldn't recall his name.

"They think they found Annie," Kent said, giving voice to
all our nightmares. "I have to go ... they want me to ..."

The older officer stepped away from the porch. He put a
light hand on my arm and led me down the driveway.

"You're his lawyer?" he asked.

"Um ... I was ... I'm his sister's attorney."

Chaney. The guy's name was Dale Chaney. His name-
plate jogged my memory.

"I think he's been drinking," Chaney said. "We were just

99

about to take him down to the morgue. We need him to identify his sister's remains."

"I mean, you're sure. It's her?"

"She fits the description," Chaney said with a hitch in his
voice.

I closed my eyes. "I understand. I'll drive him. May we
follow you?"

"I think that would be best," Chaney agreed. Best. There
was nothing "best" about any of this. But Chaney was right.
Judge Tucker looked ready to drop. As much as it horrified
me, I realized I was probably the one who would actually
make the identification.

Then I thought of Annie. If this was her, she needed me
too, as odd as that might sound.

"Give me one minute," I said.

"Of course," Chaney said. "We'll wait."

I left him and went to the judge. "Kent?" I said. "Do you
understand what we need to do?"

He looked up at me with red-rimmed eyes. "I can't."

"We'll get through this one together," I said.

It was somehow what he needed to hear. It occurred to me
how lonely he was just then. His parents were gone. He had
no wife. By virtue of his profession, he was isolated. At that
moment, there was just me. I held out my hand. Kent Tucker
looked at it as if he couldn't quite figure out what to make of it.
Then he rose to his feet. I led him to my car. He paused,
watching the Delphi P.D. patrol car back out. Then he slid
into the passenger seat.

Chapter 17

I DON'T REMEMBER the drive to the hospital. I don't remember parking or even how we got to the basement morgue. But I will never forget standing in that tiny hallway in front of a giant window covered by a dark-gray curtain.

Judge Tucker sat on a folding chair tapping his heel against the ground. Eric and Detective Megan Lewis walked down to join us.

Eric and I were at a point that just a simple look from him could tell me exactly what he was thinking. This time, he was questioning why I needed to be here. Then he saw the judge.

Eric pressed his lips into a hard line. "It's okay," I mouthed.

He shook his head in disagreement. But I wasn't moving.

"Judge," Eric said. "I'm so sorry. If there were any other way ..."

"No," Tucker said, rising. "I know. You don't have to explain. This is the quickest way. And I need to know. Annie needs me. Let's just ... let's get this over with."

Eric wasn't happy. But he knew me well enough not to

argue. The judge and I stood side by side in front of the window.

Eric tapped lightly on the glass. Judge Tucker grabbed my hand in a death grip. I squeezed back. He'd been drunk before. Now he was stone-cold sober.

There was movement behind the curtain. Wheels rolling over a tile floor. Squeaking. A rustle of fabric. The curtain swayed a bit and my knees went weak.

Then the curtain pulled back. The medical examiner, Amelia Trainor, and a second lab assistant stood on either ends of the gurney. Resting on top of it was a black body bag.

Dr. Trainor looked carved out of wax. She had pale skin and even paler blonde hair. She held a zipper at the top of the body bag in her purple-gloved fingers.

"No," Tucker said. "That can't be Annie. She's ... she's just a little thing. She weighs ..."

I squeezed my eyes shut. "Judge," I said before Eric could. "It's been a few days. She ..."

I couldn't say the rest of it. Later, in a courtroom, Tucker might hear Dr. Trainor's clinical description of what happened to the human body after five days and how long in the water.

Judge Tucker went still beside me but tightened his grip even more. My knuckles squeezed together. He gave Dr. Trainor a slow nod.

She pulled the zipper back.

We saw Annie's face and it was enough. She barely looked human. Her skin shone as if covered in oil. Her cheeks were engorged. The rest of her, the parts we couldn't see, were swollen to likely twice their normal size.

Her lips were white. You almost couldn't make them out. And her skin ... it was as if she'd been painted in purple, white, black.

But through all the horror of it, there was no question. No doubt. This was Annie.

She was dead. And she had died by violence.

"Annie." Kent choked out her name. He put his hand against the glass, letting me go.

Slowly, he slid down to his knees.

"Judge," I said. I went to him.

"Your Honor," Eric said. "I am so deeply sorry. But ... I must ask. I need you to say it ..."

"It's Annie," he said. "It's my sister. That's Annie."

I looked up at Eric and nodded, confirming what the judge said.

Eric tapped on the glass again. They zipped Annie back up and closed the curtain for good.

"He did it," Tucker whispered. "I'll kill him."

"Judge," I said. "I need you to hold it together for me for just a little longer, okay? I'm going to get you home."

His right fist was bandaged from where he'd punched a hole through my wall. His left was bruised but mostly healed. He looked ready to try his luck with the glass.

Finally, shakily, he rose to his feet and turned to Eric. "Do you have what you need?"

"Yes," he said. "And I am so sorry for your loss. And to have to put you through this."

"You don't have to be sorry," he said. "You have to do your job. The next thing I want to hear from you is that you've got that bastard in custody. He did this to her. I want him to pay."

"We'll be in touch," Eric said.

"Did he deny it?" Judge Tucker asked.

"Judge," Eric started. "I'm not at ..."

"Don't you say it," Kent said, his voice rising. "Don't you tell me you're in the middle of an investigation. This was my sister. You know who I am. I know who you are. No mistakes.

Do you hear me? If I find out you or anyone on this investigation didn't dot their i's and cross their t's and that little bastard gets away with this ..."

"Judge," I said. "It's time to go. Let Detective Wray do what he does best. Let him go to work for Annie now."

He was going to punch him. I could see it in Kent Tucker's eyes. So did Eric. But Eric knew it wasn't about him and to his credit, he walked away.

As soon as Eric and Detective Lewis disappeared behind the elevator doors, Judge Kent Tucker fell quietly and completely apart. He staggered back to the folding chairs as though he'd been punched.

In a very real way, he had.

I helped him into the chair and sat beside him. I don't know how long we stayed there. Tucker folded into himself, burying his face in his hands.

He didn't cry. He barely made a sound. But his grief enveloped him in wave after wave, hollowing him out.

Finally, he lifted his head and looked at me. He quite simply had no idea what he was supposed to do.

"Come on," I said. "Let me get you home."

Nodding, he seemed grateful for the direction. This time, when he took my hand, he held it lightly as we walked out of the morgue and went outside.

I could feel Annie's presence behind me. It took everything in me not to imagine what her last moments in life were like. And I knew I would always blame myself for not doing more to save her. For now, I would try to do what I could for her brother. Through that, I hoped Annie could forgive me.

Chapter 18

"When was the last time you spoke to Annie Liski?" Eric asked. But he wasn't Eric then. He was Detective Wray. I'd agreed to meet him in his office. Megan Lewis sat on the edge of his credenza, taking notes.

"I saw her on the tenth," I said. "We had an appointment in my office at eleven. She showed up exactly on time. We met for about a half an hour, maybe less."

"Can you tell me what you talked about?"

It was hard for me to do that. Attorney-client privilege survived the death of a client.

"I can't tell you the substance without a court order," I said, hating that I had to. "And Eric, it shouldn't be hard to get."

He leaned back in his chair and crossed his legs. "I think the interests of justice are pretty compelling here, Cass."

"I know," I said. "But I'm still going to need an order."

"Okay," he said. "But she filed for divorce from her husband." Of course he already knew all of this. Now my story needed to become part of his official report. The entire posture of Eric's job had changed. Before, he was trying to find Annie and save her life. Now, he needed to build a case against her killer. Everything mattered. And yet somehow it felt like nothing did.

"She did," I said; that part was public record. "And she also filed for a personal protection order."

I reached into my bag and pulled out a copy of the order. Annie's sworn affidavit was attached to it.

"This pretty much outlines what my client was afraid of," I said. "Judge Pierce also took her testimony when she entered it ex parte. So you'll have that preserved for the record as well."

Eric nodded to Megan; she wrote that down. "Thanks," he said. "That'll help a lot. What about Liski? I need to know about your dealings with him directly. That's not protected by privilege, he's not your client."

"No," I said. "It's not. Liski showed up at my office. I think it was on the fifth? So almost two weeks ago."

"What did he want?" Eric asked. He knew the highlights. He'd been there. But again, now he needed my formal statement.

"He had just been served with a copy of Annie's divorce complaint and the PPO. He wasn't happy about it."

"Cass," Eric said. "I need you to be crystal clear. Did Liski threaten you?"

"It was implied," I said. "I took it as threatening behavior. Did he ever say, if you don't stand down I'll hurt you? No. It was more of a general menacing nature. Like he wanted me to know he knew where to find me. And just his presence was threatening. But there wasn't anything illegal about it."

"You let me worry about that," he said. He was keeping his cool, but barely.

"What about anyone else Annie might have come into

contact with in the twenty-four hours before she went missing?" Eric said. "Can you shed any light on that?"

"Not really," I said. Without the court order, I couldn't tell him much else. When she was still missing and we thought she was in danger, I'd told him about the safe house. Anyone else she talked to would come forward, I hoped. Especially if Eric got a hold of Annie's phone records. She'd made calls to and from the safe house that day.

"Eric," I said. "The last thing I want to be is obtuse here. I want Annie's killer found more than anyone."

"I get it, Cass," Eric said. "And you're not saying anything that's surprising me. It's okay. We're working on the subpoena. You'll be covered. So, let's talk about something other than your communication with Annie."

"Good," I said.

"Judge Tucker," he said. "Have you met with him privately about Annie's case?"

It was an odd question. Eric kept his face neutral.

"I have," I said. "Though I've never discussed my confidential communications with Annie with him either. He came to me a few weeks ago expressing concern about her welfare. He told me there was a pattern of domestic violence with Brian as the aggressor. He was hoping I would reach out to Annie. I did."

"Got it," he said. "And Tucker came to your office."

"He did," I said. "After Annie went missing. He was distraught. We all were. I just wish I could have shared something that would have helped."

"She left your office about eleven thirty?" Eric asked.

"On the tenth, yes," I said.

"She was driving her own vehicle. Nobody dropped her off or picked her up."

"Uh ... to tell you the truth, I'm not sure. Miranda let her into my office. I saw her come into and leave the building. I assume she drove her own car, but I didn't look out the window to watch her or anything. I can check with Miranda to see if she remembers that."

"I'd appreciate it," he said. "I'm just trying to figure out who she was in contact with that day."

"Of course," I said. "And just let me know as soon as you have your court order. I'll tell you everything I can. But Eric, I don't think it'll be anything you don't already know from her affidavit and statement on the record."

"Okay," he said. "She was working at Bella Donna."

"Correct," I said. "And those women there, they're in each other's business. Make sure you talk to all of them. There's a receptionist named Reese. She had pictures on her phone of some of the injuries Brian caused Annie. Reese was concerned about her."

Eric nodded. "Got it. Thanks."

"Eric," I said. "Where is Liski now? I know you had to let him go after you questioned him a few days ago."

He folded his hands. His eyes pierced through me. "He's not getting anywhere near you. Don't worry."

"I'm not," I said. "I mean ... not really."

"You worried about Tucker?" he asked.

The question stunned me a little. "What do you mean?"

"Tucker shoved his fist through a wall at your office, right? And I saw him at the morgue. Do you have any concerns that Kent Tucker might try to settle this on his own?"

"He's grieving," I said. "His sister was brutally murdered. But I don't know him well enough to predict what he'll do."

"I'll keep an eye on him," Eric said. "Just ... stay out of it."

I let out a bitter laugh. "That ship has sailed. I'm about as smack dab in the middle of this as I can be."

"You know what I mean."

Megan rose. She gave a slight smile to Eric then excused herself from his office. So, the official part of this interview was over.

"You okay?" Eric asked. "You don't look like you've slept."

"I haven't," I said. "This is just ..."

"I know," he said. "But you're no good to Annie if you don't take care of yourself."

Though it was odd he spoke about her in the present tense, it fit my mood exactly. She did still need me. I had to do whatever I could to try and get her justice.

"The hardest part about this for you is going to be sitting on the sidelines," he said. "I know you."

"What do you mean?"

"I mean," Eric said, leaning forward in his chair, "you're not the prosecutor. You're not the detective. You're a witness. An important one. As much as it's going to kill you, you need to let the rest of us do our jobs."

"You've been talking to Jeanie," I said.

Eric's smirk gave me all the answer I needed. "You have," I repeated. "No fair."

"I'm not the only one worried about you."

"When are you going to officially arrest Liski?" I asked.

"Again, not your job," he answered. "Cass, I mean it. The main thing I need you to do is sit tight. No Nancy Drew stuff on this one."

"I do not do Nancy Drew stuff."

Eric laughed. "Okay. Just ... will you please take a couple more days off? Go out on the boat. Take an afternoon nap. Hang out with Jessa."

"I can't afford it," I said. "Haven't you heard? My practice is circling the drain."

I meant it as a lighthearted joke, but Eric's expression grew serious.

"Relax," I said.

"That's what I'm telling *you*," he said.

I rose from my chair. I did a quick check out the window of his office. Then I leaned in and gave him a peck on the cheek.

"I'm fine," I said. "And I'll think about taking some time off. Next week."

"Grr," he said. He sounded like a grizzly bear. "And if you see Liski ... if he tries to ..."

I waved a hand behind me as I grabbed the doorknob. "I know. I know. You're my first call."

"No," he said. "Your first call is 911. I mean it. And don't try getting in the middle of Tucker and Liski either. Tucker's not your project or your problem."

I stopped. "Eric, are you jealous?"

Eric rose. Lord, he was tall.

"Should I be?"

It was in me to tease him. But Eric wasn't joking. I swallowed hard.

"He's a friend," I said. "That's all. And he's alone. Annie was the only family he had. But I know my boundaries."

"Right," he said. "You have none."

"Hey," I said, smiling. "I'd say that's lucky for you or I'd have to steer clear of you. You've technically got me on retainer, remember?"

He opened his mouth to answer, then promptly clamped it shut. I laughed. "That's what I thought you said," I replied.

Chapter 19

ERIC WAS STILL SHAKING his head as I left his office. It was just a quick walk from the Delphi Public Safety Building to the county courthouse. I had a few filings to check on before heading home for the day.

I made a quick stop at the deputy court clerk's office on the first floor. Nancy Oleson sat behind her desk. She perked up when she saw me approach.

"I was hoping I'd see you today," she said.

"Well that's about as good a greeting as I'll ever get," I said.

Nancy reached into her desk drawer and pulled out a stack of thin files. She waved them at me.

"Court appointments?" I asked.

"Miranda said you're in the market again," Nancy explained. "How many you want?"

I swore if I stood still long enough, Nancy would be able to hear my stomach churn. I hadn't taken a court appointment in over a year. It wasn't great money, but it was steady.

"Beggars can't be chooser," I muttered. "No homicides."

"None in the bunch," she said. "DUIs mostly."

"Great," I said. "That oughta shine up my reputation." But I took the files. I tucked them into my bag and chit-chatted with Nancy for a little while. Once I'd gotten caught up on my courthouse gossip, I dropped off the rest of my filings and started down the hall.

"It's out of my hands right now!" Jack LaForge's voice echoed off the marble tile.

I turned to witness firsthand a new bit of courthouse gossip that would make its round by five.

Jack was Woodbridge County's busiest prosecutor. He stood at the elevator, red-faced. Around the corner, I saw Kent Tucker glaring at him, his face flushed.

"Damn," I muttered. I hurried over to the pair of them.

"I can't talk to you about this right now," Jack muttered. "Don't put me in this position."

"Judge? Jack?" I said. Jack let out a sigh of relief upon seeing me. I could pretty much guess what was up. Odds were Jack would catch the case when Annie's killer was charged. Regardless of the parts of this conversation I'd missed, Kent Tucker shouldn't be talking to him about it at all.

"Anything I can help with?" I asked, regretting it almost instantly.

Jack shook his head. "You're another one," he said.

"Excuse me?" I said.

"Maybe you can talk some sense into him. Take some more days, Your Honor. You look like hell." Jack batted a hand and turned on his heel. Tucker made a move to follow but I put a hand on his chest.

"If you're hounding him about Annie, don't," I said. "That's a good way to make it easy for someone to grant a change of venue when this thing gets litigated, Judge. I know you know that."

112

"I need to do something," he said. "I can't just sit at home."

"I know," I said. "What about arrangements for Annie?"

"The M.E. just released her," he said. "But as of right now, Brian's her next of kin. Cass, I'm going out of my mind. I don't even know what to do for her. We never talked about it. I can't ... I don't even know what ... I can't get into the house. Liski's family is trying to take charge of everything."

I took a breath. "It's going to be okay," I said. "If you'd like, I can help you out with some of that. We can get a court order appointing you at least the temporary personal representative of her estate. Brian's under suspicion of murdering her. These are extenuating circumstances."

"I don't even know," he said. The pleading look in his eyes tore at me. "I feel so helpless. But yes. If you'll help me. Her things ... they're at her house. Where Brian is. I need something for her. She needs her things. She needs ... something."

Lord. I hadn't even thought of that. I let my brain spin, trying to think of a solution. Then, cold reality sank in. There was no way he could be thinking of an open casket in any event.

I didn't say it. But maybe the look on my face was enough. My brothers always teased me for not having a good poker face.

I didn't get the chance to cover. Judge Tucker's phone rang. When he pulled it out, the color drained from his face. He took a step back and answered.

"Tucker," he said.

I watched his face go through several stages of pain. Finally, he put the phone down. He sidestepped and it looked like he was about to go over so I shot a hand out to steady him.

"It's starting," he said.

"Your Honor?"

"Liski," he said. "They've formerly arrested him and charged him with Annie's murder."

His words came out choked. Then he collapsed against me and sobbed.

Chapter 20

ANNIE AND BRIAN LISKI lived in a three-bedroom house about as far south as you could go but still be in Delphi. It was a starter home. One of thousands like it built for G.I.s and their young families in the first few years after World War II. All brick, with flowerpots in the windows and shutters painted green.

Judge Tucker parked in the street. Eric's unmarked sedan already sat in the driveway. We didn't need the court order after all. Eric ended up coming through for us on that. We'd have to sort through the legalities of Annie's estate later. For now, Brian himself gave permission to Tucker to get some personal items for Annie.

"I can do this for you, if you want," I said.

Tucker shook his head. "No. I need to do it. Or at least I need to be there when you do it. I don't know how to choose something like this."

I put a hand on his shoulder. "Today, it's just about one dress. I think the only way to really do something like this is one bit at a time."

He smiled at me. Judge Tucker had aged at least ten years

in the last week. Deep worry lines creased his brow. His eyes were permanently bloodshot.

We slipped out of the car and made our way up the cracked sidewalk. Grass grew over the edge and weeds through the seams.

"Brian was supposed to take care of this," Kent said, staring at the landscaping lapse. "Annie worked during the day and on the weekends too. He wouldn't let her hire anybody to take care of things like this. I tried to. She always told me it wasn't worth the fight."

Eric came to the front door. He had two patrolmen with him. A few nosey neighbors slowed their walks to stare. I pulled on Judge Tucker, not wanting him to notice. The last thing we needed was another scene.

"Thanks for letting us do this," I said to Eric. I knew he didn't think Annie had died here, but they were still executing the warrant on the house.

"Of course," he said. "I'm just sorry for the disruption."

Tucker nodded but didn't make eye contact with Eric. Eric gestured to one of the patrolmen as Tucker began walking down the hallway. I moved to follow him, but Eric caught my sleeve.

"How's he doing?" he whispered against my ear so no one else could hear.

I shrugged by way of an answer. "He's going over to the funeral home later this afternoon. I can't thank you enough for whatever hand you had in getting Annie released as soon as they did."

"I just know how I'd feel if this were my sister." He handed me a pair of latex gloves. I put them on.

Nodding, I started back down the hallway. Tucker stood in front of one of the doorways. It had to be the master bedroom.

"Maybe it doesn't matter," he said.

"What do you mean?"

"I mean, you saw her. We can't let anyone else see her. So what difference does it make?"

"It's just what we do, Judge. And I think Annie would have wanted to be buried in something nice. Something familiar. It's just a way to give her dignity. But if you don't want ..."

"No," he said. "You're right. And she really did look up to you. I think she'd love the idea that you helped with this. She wanted to be like you."

A lump formed in my throat. I didn't feel like I deserved Annie Liski's adoration right now. But it was just as I said to the judge. This was the literal least I could do.

I walked into the bedroom. I expected Tucker would follow, but he hung back, watching as I made my way to the closet.

It was mirrored. My own grim face stared back at me as I slid the door open and surveyed Annie's clothes. She had blouses and dress pants mostly, things she could wear to work while on her feet all day.

She didn't appear to own a business suit though that wasn't quite what I had in mind. Carefully, reverently, I slid each garment aside until I came to her dresses. Most of them still had the tags on them. In fact, a good half of the clothes in this closet looked like they'd never been worn. They were expensive labels.

There was movement at the door. Tucker moved aside as Eric came in. We passed a look that told me Eric had made a note of the price tags too. I hadn't gotten far into my forensic accounting for Annie's divorce, but I had a sneaky suspicion she might have had a shopping addiction.

I selected a simple blue silk dress with a high collar. It

would pair nicely with Annie's dark hair even if no one but God would ever see it.

I leaned down and found a pair of matching pumps, size seven. The shoes were even more expensive than the dresses.

Then I went to the long dresser against the wall. Annie had a jewelry box. I opened it slowly and my jaw dropped. We'd need an appraiser, but Annie owned at least a dozen diamond rings.

Eric was at my shoulder. He mouthed the words, "I know."

I turned to Tucker. "Judge, did Brian buy all of these things for Annie?"

He came further into the room. "Guilt presents," he said. "The more severe the fight, the bigger the gift."

"But how were they affording all of this?" I asked. "There are tens of thousands of dollars' worth of clothing and jewelry here, I'd guess."

"You think he might have been pilfering from the pawn shop?" Eric asked.

The judge shook his head. "Who knows. Brian thinks he's above the law. That the rules don't apply to him. Annie was property to him too. Don't you get it? She was a pretty trinket he wore on his arm when it suited him. He liked the attention he got when she was with him. Annie was special. People loved her. You saw it. It's why you're here."

There had to be some truth to what Tucker said. Annie Liski did have a quality about her. She was instantly likeable. Someone you wanted to have as a friend. Someone you wanted to protect ...

I picked out a teardrop diamond necklace that I thought would go well with the dress. It was such an odd thing to be concerned with. It just felt right somehow.

I held the things out for both Kent and Eric to see. Eric

wrote notes down on the little pad he kept. I accused him of being old school for that most days.

"Yeah," Tucker said. "That seems very Annie. She'd like that. I always liked her in blue."

He choked on the last word. I started to go to him, but the judge held up a hand to stop me. "I'm sorry," he said. "I need to get out of here."

And he did. He practically sprinted down the hall and crashed through the front door.

I waited a beat, then Eric turned to me. "You think he's going to be okay?" he asked.

"I really don't know. It's not like we were very close before all of this happened. I don't know what other kind of support he has. I think I told you before. There just doesn't seem to be any other family."

"Yeah," he said. "I mean, if he's calling you for this stuff."

I decided not to respond to the edge in his tone. It was possible he didn't even mean it the way it sounded. We were all a little raw.

"When do you think you'll be finished here?" I asked.

"By the end of the day," he said. The master bedroom was across the hall from a little home office. Since Brian and Annie had no children, the two other bedrooms weren't used as such. Annie had workout equipment set up in the third.

I watched as one of the patrolmen packed up the laptop from the office and bagged it.

"Oh," he said. "I got your court order for you." Eric slid a folded piece of paper out of his jacket pocket and handed it to me.

I scanned it quickly, not at all surprised by its contents. I was actually relieved by it.

"Thanks," I said. "This was just some C.Y.A. You know that."

"I do," he said. "And I didn't need your full statement to arrest Liski. But it'll help me a ton on some finer points and save me time. What I need most immediately is information on their financials."

I looked back in the bedroom. I'd left the jewelry box open and Annie's diamonds gleamed at me.

"Right," I said. "I was just starting to help her put that picture together. She brought me a recent credit card statement. I mean, you can subpoena all that, right? I've actually got one out myself."

"I can," he said. "And I am. But just having account numbers quickly makes it less a pain in the ass."

"No problem," I said. "You're welcome to anything I have now."

"Thanks. This is going to take me a few hours yet. How about I stop by your office first thing in the morning?"

"Sounds good," I said. "And what's the word on Liski?"

"He's still at the county jail," he said. "He put up a bit of a fight."

"Eric …" I said, narrowing my eyes at him.

Eric put his hands up in surrender. "Don't worry. I've done everything by the book with that bastard. Plus, he's got himself a lawyer already."

Once again, my gaze traveled to the jewelry box. "Something isn't right about all of that," I said.

"He's being arraigned tomorrow. I suppose I can't stop him, but I'd rather Tucker wasn't there for that. I get the strong impression the guy is hanging on by a thread."

"I'll talk to him," I said. "I'm sure Jack LaForge is going to prosecute this one. The last thing he'll want is grounds for a change of venue … whoever ends up defending Liski."

"My thinking exactly," he said. "For the moment, the less attention drawn to Annie's relationship to Tucker, the better."

"We're on the same page," I said. "I think I can convince him to steer clear if I volunteer to go instead. He trusts me."

Eric's eyes flicked down to the dress and shoes I held.

"Yeah," he said.

"Eric."

"I'm not jealous," he said. "I just ... you're taking this one personally. That worries me."

"How can I not take it personally?" I asked. "Annie was my client. She hired me to help her get out from under this guy. But all I managed to do is escalate it. And now ... she's dead."

Eric took a step back. "Cass, this isn't your fault. I need you to get that out of your head. You didn't cause this. You did the right things. We don't know what happened for sure yet."

"Yes, we do," I said. "Eric, we've both been at this way too long not to have seen this coming a mile away. The minute Brian realized she was leaving him for good, he made it so she couldn't. I just ... I can't figure out why she went to see him."

"Do you know for sure that she did?" he asked. He was back in investigator mode.

"I only know what I already told you. She left my office at eleven thirty that morning. She had a plan. She was going to get her things from her friend Maggie's house. We know she did that. Then she was going straight to the shelter Jeanie set up for her. If anything, she seemed hopeful about it. She didn't like feeling like she was imposing on Maggie and her family. It was a positive step and she knew it."

"Well," Eric said. "You did all you could."

"I should have stayed with her," I said. "I should have insisted on dropping her off at the shelter myself. I never should have let her out of my sight."

"She wasn't your sister," he said. "And if I recall, your own sister isn't always inclined to take your advice either and tends to resent it when you hover."

I wanted to argue the point further, but deep down, I knew Eric was right.

We were alone in the hallway. Tucker was still outside. The patrolmen carried out the rest of their bagged evidence. It was just Eric and me.

He slid his arms around me. "You know what you need," he whispered, sending a shiver of warmth through me. I looked up at him.

"You need a break. You need a night out. I should be off by five tonight. How about I take you out to dinner?"

"You sure that's a good idea?" I asked. "I mean, aren't I a key witness in a case you're investigating?" I meant it a little as a joke. But as soon as I said it, it mattered.

His grumble told me he knew I was right. "Just for a little while," I said. "Let's just not do anything that'll give whatever hick lawyer Liski's got ammunition."

"Hmm," he said. "See, *you're* my favorite hick lawyer."

"Damn straight," I said, tweaking his nose. Though I hated the idea of staying away from Eric, we both knew it was the safest bet right now.

"You better go then," he said. "I meant what I said about Tucker. Keep an eye on him. Just not ... too close an eye on him?"

I shook my head and laughed. As I walked out of Annie Liski's house though, my heart turned heavy once more.

Chapter 21

WEDNESDAY MORNING, June twenty-sixth, I walked into a
packed courtroom. Jack LaForge stood at the prosecution
table gathering his notes. At fifty-six, he'd been at this for over
thirty years, starting out as a court-appointed public defender
like most of us did, then rising in the ranks at the county prosecutor's office. He'd been on a short list for a few different
judicial appointments, but always shied away from the
headaches a later campaign would bring to retain such a seat.
He preferred working in the trenches while his direct boss,
Gary Hammond, managed the political arm of the office.

I'd known Jack since I was sworn into the Michigan State
Bar twelve years ago. I'd tried and won many cases against
him. He was tough. Fair. Sometimes infuriating. But now,
there was no one else I'd want prosecuting the case against
Brian Liski.

I took a seat behind him. Jack had a mass of silvery-gray
hair that always seemed a week overdue for a cut. He brushed
it to the side and pivoted so he was facing me.

"Is he coming?" he asked. I knew what he meant.

"No," I said. "I'm not going to lie. I may or may not have

tied him to a chair in his office, but Judge Tucker is sitting this one out."

He had had Annie's funeral the day before. It was a quiet affair and filled with the type of grief that had weight. No one from Brian's family came, which made things both easier and harder in some way.

"Good," he said. "And thank you. It's just ... one less thing."

"He understands," I said. "For now. I can't promise he'll be able to stay away if this thing goes to trial."

"I get that," Jack said. "And I'm going to want Annie's family out in full force for that."

"It's not much of a force," I said. "It's just Tucker. She had a lot of friends though."

Jack nodded absently. He wrote something down on his notepad.

"You heard who's representing him?" I asked. Before Jack could respond, I got my answer. Brian Liski walked into the courtroom. He looked far different from the last time I saw him.

Dressed smartly in an expensive black suit, Liski had gotten an equally expensive haircut. Though his face looked haggard, he'd clearly heeded whatever advice he'd been given to take today seriously. His red-rimmed, bloodshot eyes made him the picture of the grief-stricken husband.

Filing in right behind him was Dean Farnham, his defense lawyer. Dean had been around about as long as I had. He lived in nearby Chelsea and graduated the year before me in my brother Joe's class. They had been rivals on the football field. Dean took a gap year, so he entered law school the same time I did at U. of M. He started his own practice a few years ago after working for one of the bigger Southfield firms. To my knowledge, he did auto negligence.

"So, what the hell is he doing?" I whispered to Jack. "I think he'd be better off going with a public defender?"

"Beats me," he said.

"Hmm," I said. The defense lawyer in me bristled. I had no idea if Dean had ever handled a criminal case, much less a murder.

Dean caught my eye and gave me a barely perceptible nod of recognition. It felt bizarre, but I raised a hand back. Then Judge Mark Colton's bailiff came out and called us to attention.

Colton was one of the oldest judges on the Woodbridge County bench. He was set to retire in two years. Though I personally found him to be a nice guy, as a jurist, he was a train wreck. Luckily, felony cases only stayed in District Court through the preliminary stages before being bound over to Circuit Court if probable cause was found. For Annie, that would be a blessing.

"All rise!"

We did.

Colton liked to take the bench with a flourish, flapping his robes behind him, letting them settle like a bird's wings upon landing before he finally sat down.

"People of the State of Michigan versus Branislav P. Liski." The bailiff rattled off the case number.

Colton licked his finger while rifling through the charging documents. He then went through all the preliminary dialogue. Dean had a hand on Brian's shoulder and whispered into his ear. I'd been there hundreds of times myself. Most of the time, you just needed to remind your client that this wasn't some television show. You say guilty or not guilty when prompted. Nothing more. And no points were won with theatrics of any kind. Not at this stage of the game, anyway.

"Mr. Liski," Judge Colton said. "Do you understand the charges filed against you?"

"Yes, Your Honor," Brian said, leaning far over so lips nearly touched the microphone at the lectern.

"And how do you plead?"

"Not guilty, Your Honor. I did not kill my wife. This is a set-up ..."

So much for following directions. Dean got a hand on Brian's jacket and jerked it downward. Brian grimaced, but stopped talking.

Colton kept licking his fingers as he made notes and turned pages.

"Have you two come to any agreement on bail?" he asked.

"No, Your Honor," Dean chimed in. "My client has deep ties to this community. His support system, his family, and business are in nearby Taylor. He has never been in trouble with the law before. Not so much as a parking ticket in ten years. He poses no flight risk. We therefore request reasonable bail be set."

"Mr. LaForge?"

Jack rose. He'd perfected the art of looking befuddled yet deeply prepared.

"Your Honor," Jack said. "The defendant has a history of violence against the victim. The nature of this crime was heinous, brutal, and the defendant went to great lengths to conceal the crime by weighing her down at the bottom of Finn Lake. He has no real ties to Woodbridge County. As defense counsel has pointed out, Mr. Liski's cousins, his uncle, and closest family are in Taylor. They run a pawn shop. The owner of said pawn shop is the defendant's uncle, Peter Liski. He is a Ukrainian national and has a felony record himself. We have reason to believe that Mr. Liski has the means and method to leave the country and seek refuge with relatives in an Eastern Bloc country. As such, he most definitely poses a flight risk. And he owns a gun and has access to firearms through his employment."

"Your Honor," Dean said. "My client has been an upstanding citizen of this community. He has donated thousands of dollars to local charities including several food banks, children's funds, and St. Jude's Hospital. He doesn't even own a passport."

Judge Colton held a hand up. Dean took the hint and stopped talking. Colton made a great show of rubbing his forehead and rifling through paperwork. Jack saw it for what it was too and made a noise low in his throat that I was pretty sure only I could hear.

"Here's what I'm going to do," he said. "I'm going to set bond at two hundred and fifty thousand. Standard conditions apply. Mr. Liski, your attorney will go over those with you in more detail. No guns. No alcohol. No contact with known felons, that means this Uncle Peter of yours. And under no circumstances are you permitted to have contact with the victim's family. Do you understand?"

"Your Honor," Brian said before Dean could stop him. "I thank you."

"I'll leave you to work out the details of that within the boundaries of your bond conditions. I see from the paperwork that the defense has not waived prelim. Will set that for three weeks from today. Nine o'clock. That is all."

Dean banged his gavel and rose from his seat with the same flourish as when he sat down. Then he left the bench. Brian Liski collapsed into Dean Farnham's arms.

I was fuming. He'd be out. Liski's family likely had connections to several bail bondsmen and the means to post surety. I'd wager he'd be out on the streets by the end of the day.

Jack turned to me. "Can I count on you to break this news to Kent?" he asked.

I was speechless. "Jack ..."

"I've got my hands full with this. I'm meeting with the M.E. ten minutes ago. And I'd like to sit down and talk to you too in the next day or so. Can you make room for me?"

"Of course," I said. "Jack, you know he threatened me."

"I know," he said. "I've had more than one earful from Wray. He's another one I wouldn't mind you having a talk with. No cowboy stuff on this one. I need all of you to let me do my job now."

Though I appreciated the directive, at that particular moment I thought some cowboy stuff might be just what we needed. But I knew that ultimately wouldn't help bring justice to Annie.

"Wrangle the testosterone," Jack said, winking. "I've got a prelim to prepare for."

Nodding, I rose and started toward the back of the courtroom.

Testosterone indeed. Both Tucker and Eric would be livid. I knew I sure as hell was. If anything, Colton should have set bail for no less than a million. Though I wondered if the Liski family could have met it no matter how high the amount. And that was sort of the point. Luckily, if things went that far, Colton wouldn't be the one presiding over this case. More than likely, it would be assigned to Felix Castor. And we'd be in good hands.

Not surprisingly, I found Eric already waiting for me when I got to the office. No doubt the courthouse gossip mill had reached him about two seconds after Colton set bail. Eric was pacing in front of Jeanie's office. I swear there was smoke coming out of his ears.

"That imbecile," he muttered when he saw me. "Jack screwed the pooch on this one."

"He did his best," I said. "He raised all the valid points he could. And he can't control which District Court judge will draw a case. We were behind the eight ball the second Colton got pegged."

"I want you staying with Jeanie or Joe," he said. "Or ... me ..."

Jeanie wasn't in her office now. I tugged on Eric's sleeve and pulled him inside, shutting the door behind us.

"Cass," he said. "That guy is dangerous. You'll be a key witness in this case."

"And he would have to be the world's dumbest criminal to come after me now," I said.

"He doesn't have to come after you directly," Eric said. "This guy ... the more I'm finding out about him, the less I like. I'd feel a lot better if I knew you were safe."

"I won't take any chances," I said. "I promise. And staying with you is out of the question. Like you said, I'll be a key witness for the prosecution. You're the lead detective. Let's not give Dean Farnham any more help on cross-exam."

"Farnham?" Eric asked. "Isn't he a personal injury lawyer?"

"General practice," I said.

"He ever handle a murder trial?"

"Not that I know of. It's strange. But maybe Brian isn't as connected financially to his family as we've been afraid of."

"Maybe," Eric said. "But will you promise me not to be where Liski can find you?"

"I'm not going to be put out of my house," I said. "I did that for six months after the fire. I just got back. Send extra patrols around the lake if you must. I'll be careful not to leave the office alone. But I'm not letting this asshole disrupt my life."

Eric slipped his arms around me. "Why do you have to be so stubborn?"

"It's part of my charm," I said.

"Hmmm. You know I can't stand this."

"Good," I said. "So make sure the case against Liski is airtight."

Eric nodded. His temper had cooled. I just hoped Kent Tucker's would as well. More than Liski coming after me, I was more worried about Kent going after Liski.

As if my thoughts conjured him, my phone went off. I pulled it out of my bag. It was Tucker. No doubt I'd have to give the same speech to him about LaForge doing the best he could. Bail was set. I couldn't change that.

Eric saw the name pop up. He gave me a grave expression, but for once, no lecture. I took a breath, answered the call, and stepped into the next breach.

Chapter 22

"Thank you, Your Honor," I said. I stood in the middle of Circuit Court Judge Felix Castor's courtroom. He'd just denied defense counsel's motion for summary disposition on a workplace harassment case of mine. Michelle Stevens versus the Delphi Quickie Mart. The name alone would make a jury snicker. But for now, this meant barring settlement, my client's case against the convenience store owner she worked for would go to trial.

I gathered my things and stuffed them into my bag. "Let me talk to my client." Grace Eggert came up to my table. She was an up-and-coming attorney at one of those high-powered Southfield, Michigan firms. She reminded me of me a little, minus ten years. Grace had only been out of law school two years.

"I think that's advisable," I said.

"Let me come to them with a number," she said. "Where's your client at?"

"Three hundred thousand," I said. "Same as we were last week."

Grace blew a hair out of her eyes. "Cass, you know that's

not going to happen. Your client dated Paul Worthy for six months before this all happened."

"And that's a worse fact for your client than it is for mine," I said. "He was Michelle's supervisor. And I mean ... please don't tell me you're planning on using the 'she asked for it' defense."

Grace looked properly chagrined. The truth was, I really was looking forward to trying this case in front of a jury. But my client, Michelle Stevens, wasn't working right now on account of a high-risk pregnancy. Plus, the case had taken a toll on her marriage. Then there was the undeniable fact that I could really use a quick settlement for my own cash flow problem right about now. That said, I'd never take a low-ball offer to the detriment of my client no matter what it meant for me personally. I'd hang up my shingle and choose a new line of work before I ever let that happen.

"Give me a number I can sell," Grace said.

"Your sales pitch isn't my problem," I said. "The number isn't your issue. A jury is going to hear this case now. I like my chances a whole lot better than yours. Let me know what your bosses think."

It was kind of a cheap shot. And maybe it was a little beneath me. But it had already been an exceptionally long week and it was only Tuesday.

I gave Grace a polite smile, then left her in my dust as I walked out of Judge Castor's courtroom. Checking my phone, I had about a half an hour before I had to be in court downstairs for a DUI arraignment, one of my new court-appointed cases. With any luck, I'd be able to sell a plea deal and get my billings to Nancy before the end of the day. I stopped at the coffee shop on the first floor of the courthouse and ordered my lunch staple, a latte and a grilled cheese sandwich.

I put a twenty on the counter and told Ginger, the shop's

co-owner, to keep the change. I got two steps toward my favorite booth when I ran smack into Dean Farnham. I nearly spilled my coffee all over him. He was holding one of his own. There was no way around him, no escape.

"Hello, Cass," he said. "I was hoping to run into you."

Like hell, I thought. To my knowledge, Farnham had no other cases pending in Woodbridge County. The bastard probably checked the court docket and knew exactly where I was going to be.

"Dean," I said. "I'm getting ready for a hearing. Why don't you call my office and set up an appointment?"

"I just need a few minutes of your time," he said. "And let's be real. You were never going to take an appointment with me."

I had half a mind to not only tell him to go to hell but give him specific directions. On the other hand, maybe if I indulged him for five minutes, he'd go away.

"Fine," I said. I brushed past him and sat down in my booth. Dean hesitated for a moment, then joined me.

"I know this must be hard for you," he said. "Losing a client, I mean."

I set my coffee down and bit into my sandwich. "We're not doctors, Dean. We don't *lose* clients. My client was brutally murdered by the man she was trying to get protection from."

"He didn't do it," Dean said.

I stopped chewing. It was a singularly odd thing for a defense attorney to say. Our jobs didn't really depend on whether our clients were guilty. Our job was to ensure the system worked.

"Does that make it easier for you to sleep at night?" I asked. Just like I'd done with Grace upstairs, it was a bit of a cheap shot. I defended many guilty clients. It was never the point.

"We're on the same side," he said.

"No, Dean, we're not," I said. "Not this time. I'm on Annie Liski's side. And I know firsthand what your client is capable of."

"Not this," he said. "I've known Brian a long time. He's not ... he's not a murderer."

"Dean," I said. "What is this about? You're his defense lawyer. If you have questions about my testimony, fine. If you're trying to influence my testimony by whatever sob story Brian Liski is telling you, then we need to end this conversation right now."

"No," he said. "Hear me out. That's not what I'm trying to do."

I took another bite of my sandwich. Dean paused. He was clearly trying to regroup for a different approach.

"He's a monster," Dean said. "I mean, for how he treated Annie up until now. I'm not going to argue that. But he didn't kill her."

"Why do you care if I believe that?" I asked.

Dean worked the thumb of one hand into the palm of the other. I got the distinct impression that he didn't want to be here either.

"Did Liski send you here?" I asked, incredulous. "Did he ask you to come talk to me? To try to convince me? Of what?"

"He feels terrible about the way he treated you," Dean said. "He told me about that. He was desperate."

I shook my head. "Dean, I'm going to stop you right there. You can thank me later for saving you from yourself. This whole meeting is inappropriate. Whatever else he is, Brian Liski is your client. You're coming dangerously close to violating attorney-client privilege. And I can't believe I even have to tell you that."

"I know, I know," he said. "But I'm not doing anything my client hasn't expressly authorized me to. I'm not an idiot."

"You sure about that?" I sipped my coffee.

"Cass, listen. There's bigger stuff at play here than you realize. I'm telling you, Liski's innocent. He didn't kill Annie."

"Yes, Dean," I said. "He did. I saw her. I saw what he did to her the week before she turned up dead. He punched her in the face. Shoved her into a wall. He's done it numerous times before. She was terrified of him. She was making plans to leave him for good and get out from under all of this. So he made sure she never could. That's what I saw. That's what I know. That's what I'll be testifying to. You can read my statement to the cops. It won't change. And every second you spend talking to me about this is only going to make it even worse for Brian."

He looked like he was going to be sick. "He's not who you think he is."

"What if I just think he's an abusive, wife-beating asshole? You gonna tell me I imagined all that too?"

Dean rubbed his eyes. For the life of me, I couldn't figure out what he was trying to do here. Why in the world had Liski put him up to this? More than that, why had he agreed?

"Dean," I said. "Let me offer you some advice."

He dropped his hand and for a moment, he looked eager to hear what I had to say.

"Walk away from this," I said. "You're in over your head. You're not ready for a murder case. And not this one. Jack LaForge is going to eat you for breakfast."

Dean sat straighter. I couldn't tell whether I'd offended him or gotten through to him. Whatever I'd done, he looked even more miserable than when he first walked in.

"The Liskis have been good to me," he said. "Good to my firm. And Brian ... he ... just know that I'm telling you the truth."

"Why does Brian Liski care what I think?" I asked. "Why do you?"

"Because ... Annie trusted you. She looked up to you. And Brian believes in his soul she'd want you to know the truth. Even with everything he may have done to her."

"May have?" I said.

"Listen," Dean said. "You of all people should understand the position I'm in. Aubrey Ames, your sister, hell, even that psycho of a hitman you represented. These were imperfect people. But they were innocent people and you knew they deserved justice, even if it made you unpopular."

"Don't," I said. "Don't compare yourself to me. And don't drag my sister into your narrative. I don't need a lecture. Brian will have his day in court. Whether he takes the stand or not, he'll have due process just like every other criminal defendant. Do yourself a favor, no, do *him* a favor and turn this case over to someone who knows what they're doing. If you really care about giving him a real shot at acquittal, that is."

I was done. I couldn't stand looking at Dean Farnham for another second.

"Cass," he said. I didn't listen. I slid my plate and mug to the end of the table so it would be easier for the busser to reach.

"Cass," he said, louder.

I gathered my things. "We're done, Dean," I said. "I'll see you from the witness stand."

As I turned, Dean didn't just look miserable, he looked ill. He looked scared. A flash of worry went through me in spite of myself. What had him so frightened? Was it really just the

Imminent Harm

distaste of having to do his client's bidding? Or had Liski threatened him too?

As much as it piqued my curiosity, I knew it was time to walk away. So I did. And yet, the Catholic girl inside of me felt a pang of guilt. There was nothing I could do for Dean Farnham but pray.

137

Chapter 23

THREE WEEKS LATER, I met Kent Tucker in the hallway outside courtroom number one.

"You cannot go in there," I said to him, shocked that he'd even thought he should try.

"I can't stay away," he said.

"Judge Tucker ... Kent," I said. I tugged on his sleeve and pulled him down a short hallway leading to the stairs. "Mark Colton is your colleague. Among other things, Dean Farnham is going to ask that this case be transferred to another venue. If you're in there staring at Judge Colton, he might be inclined to grant it."

"I can't sit on the sidelines anymore," he said.

They say doctors make the worst patients. It turned out judges made even worse witnesses.

"I'll be there," I said. "I'll be your eyes and ears, okay?"

"Cass," he said. "I don't trust Jack LaForge with this case."

"What do you mean?"

"I mean I'm hearing rumors I don't like."

"You want to elaborate?" I asked.

"He's been off his game ever since you wiped the floor

with him in the Larry Drazdowski trial. He doesn't want to try this case. He looks tired. Worn out. He's hoping to force a plea deal."

I bit my tongue. A plea deal might still be in the state's best interests. Only I knew Annie Liski's brother didn't want to even consider it. It ultimately wouldn't be up to him.

"This is just prelim, Judge," I said. "Let's just get through the day. You know there's no way this doesn't get bound over for trial. You've done a thousand of these. Truly, there's no advantage to you being in that courtroom right now."

He clenched his fists but didn't argue further. "I'll be in my office," he said. "You find me right after."

"Of course," I told him, though I would have preferred if he'd just left the building for the day.

There were far more people in Judge Colton's courtroom than I liked. Though I didn't share Judge Tucker's sentiment about Jack LaForge, I did wonder whether this case would drain him. Delphi didn't need any more negative attention in the press.

I took a seat on his side of the courtroom. We were starting late enough in the day I wasn't sure he'd even get to my testimony if he decided to call me but wanted to be ready.

Jack acknowledged me with a small wave. Though I tried not to think about it, Tucker was right about something. Jack looked haggard. The doors opened behind me and Dean Farnham walked in with his client.

Once again, Liski sported an expensive suit. He fiddled with the button on his jacket as he took a seat at the defense table. If anything, Brian was avoiding my gaze.

Good.

Jonah Montri, Colton's bailiff, called court to order and the judge took the bench.

"You ready, Mr. LaForge?" he asked.

"We are, Your Honor," Jack answered.

"Mr. Farnham, have you explained the purpose of today's hearing to your client?"

"I have, Your Honor," Dean said. "He understands the Court's role in determining whether there is probable cause to bind this case over for trial. We submit that there is not ..."

"Stop," Judge Colton said. "Argument isn't appropriate right now, counsel."

Dean had the decency to look embarrassed. I almost felt sorry for him. Almost.

"Go ahead and call your first witness, Mr. LaForge," Judge Colton said.

"The state calls Amelia Trainor," Jack said.

Amelia Trainor made her way through the gallery to the witness stand. She stood tall and regal, almost as if she carried a wooden rod up her back. At sixty-eight, she'd served as Woodbridge County's Medical Examiner for seventeen years. I tried to push away the flashes I had of the last time I saw her, standing over Annie Liski's bloated body.

The clerk swore Dr. Trainor in, and she climbed into the witness chair. She was attractive with flawless, pale skin, but today looked almost ghoulish in the way she wore her silver-blonde hair pulled tightly into a bun.

"For the purposes of today," Jack started, "we've stipulated to Dr. Trainor's qualifications."

"Of course," Judge Colton said.

"Doctor," Jack said. "Can you please state your name for the record?"

"Dr. Amelia Penelope Trainor."

"Thank you," he said. "And can you tell me in what office do you serve?"

"I'm a physician, Chief Medical Examiner, and forensic

pathologist for the County of Woodbridge," she said. "I've served in that capacity seventeen years as of this past month."

"Thank you," he said. "And in that capacity, did you have occasion to examine the body of the victim, Anne Liski?"

"I did," she said.

"What was the scope of that examination?"

"I performed an autopsy including the running of toxicology reports and the corresponding tissue sampling."

"Before we get to the results of that analysis, can you describe for the court how you were called into this case?"

"Well, I was contacted by the Delphi Police Department on the morning of June fifteenth of this year. We were called to respond after a report of a body being found in Finn Lake."

"So, you personally responded to that call?" Jack asked.

"Yes. I and my assistant, Dr. Curtis Wellman, arrived on scene at about six a.m. that day."

"And what did you find upon arrival at the scene?" Jack asked.

"The lead detective in charge, Detective Eric Wray, had cordoned off an area near the boat launch on Finn Lake. It's my understanding that a body had washed up near one of the buoys on the north end of the lake. Upon my arrival, the body had been removed from the water and laid on the beach. There was an officer cataloging the scene. Taking photographs."

"Did you see the body?" Jack asked.

"Of course. Upon visual inspection, the body was that of a young woman, still partially clothed in a tee shirt and ripped bra. No pants though. I understand those were found in the water sometime later."

"Thank you," Jack said. "At that point in time, what were your observations about the condition of the body?"

Amelia Trainor took a breath. "The body was in an

advanced state of decomposition consistent with being submerged in water for several days. There were sandbags tied to her ankles but they had loosened and she floated to the surface. She exhibited significant bloating."

"Bloat?" Jack asked.

"Yes," Dr. Trainor answered. The body, upon death, builds up with methane and other gases. In this case, the victim was swollen to likely twice her normal size."

"I see," Jack said. "Were you able to determine a cause of death at that time, upon visual inspection?"

"Of course not," Dr. Trainor said. "I did observe significant injury in the form of bruising on the victim's arms and legs and quite significantly around her face and neck. Shortly after I arrived, I supervised the transfer of the body into an ambulance. At which point, she was brought back to the hospital so that I could begin my preliminary examination and prepare for autopsy."

"Were you able to positively identify this victim?" Jack asked.

"Yes," she said. "First, there was a visual identification from her next of kin, Kent Tucker. The victim's brother. We were then able to confirm that identification through her dental records and a DNA sample."

"Can you tell me when you performed that autopsy?" Jack asked.

"Later that day. It's in my notes, but I believe we began at 2:02 p.m., the afternoon of June fifteenth."

"And what were the significant findings of the autopsy?"

Amelia Trainor folded her hands in front of her. She looked at Jack and pointed to the stack of photographs on his desk. "May I?"

"Of course." Jack jumped. "Your Honor, we'd like to mark exhibits one through ten for identification."

"Any word from you?" The judge looked at Dean.

"No, Your Honor." Dean rose halfway out of his chair.

Jack went to an easel at the side of the courtroom and fanned out five photographs of Annie Liski as she lay on Amelia Trainor's examination table.

I turned my head to the side and retched.

"I cataloged thirty-seven different injuries to the victim's body," Dr. Trainor continued. "The majority of them were cuts and scrapes around her legs and torso. Likely, these were suffered post-mortem from the movement of the body from the place of death and into the lake, and the use of the sandbags as well."

"I see," Jack said. He had Dr. Trainor point out each cut and scrape corresponding with her testimony.

"Dr. Trainor," Jack continued. "Were you able to determine a cause of death?"

"Yes," she said. She picked up a pointer and circled the area of deep purple discoloration around Annie's neck in the photographs. "There is significant hemorrhaging and broken blood vessels around the neck of the victim consistent with manual strangulation."

"Manual?" Jack asked.

"Yes," she said. "The wounds cover a rather wide area of the skin. There are two deeper points of discoloration at the front of the victim's throat which suggests the perpetrator had direct contact with the skin. His thumbs were pressing against her windpipe."

"Objection," Dean said. "That is speculation. And also, the character of the perpetrator's gender."

"You'll have a chance to cross-examine," Judge Colton said.

"It's my job to speculate," Dr. Trainor offered.

"Can you tell me the results of the toxicology testing you performed?"

"Yes," she said. "We found no evidence of alcohol or illicit drugs in her system."

"Dr. Trainor," Jack went on. "Were you able to determine whether this victim was sexually assaulted as well?"

"No," she said.

"No, you weren't able to determine or no, she wasn't?"

"No, I wasn't able to conclusively determine that. We did conduct a rape kit. No semen specimens were recovered from the body."

"Thank you," Jack said. "Dr. Trainor, can you tell me how long it would have taken the victim to die from her injuries?"

Dr. Trainor leaned forward. "The victim would have expired in approximately three to five minutes once pressure was applied to her neck in this manner."

"Were there any defensive wounds?" Jack asked.

"We recovered tissue samples from beneath her finger-nails but were not able to identify who they belonged to. If you're asking me whether the victim put up a fight, I would say yes. She did."

"Thank you," Jack said. "I have nothing further."

Dean popped up. "Just a couple of quick questions. Dr. Trainor, is it your conclusion then that this victim wasn't sexually assaulted?"

"I'm saying I couldn't say one way or the other. I didn't find any bruising or injury to her genitals that would suggest sexual penetration. That said, I have to stress that my findings on this point were inconclusive. The body was too badly decomposed to say for sure."

"And you found no semen."

"I did not."

"And you found no other foreign DNA on this victim?"

145

"I'm saying I could not assemble a full foreign DNA profile. That was most likely due to environmental factors. The body was submerged underwater for several days, thus degrading any other DNA profile."

"You found skin under her nails, you said? But you don't know who it belongs to," he said.

"Correct," Dr. Trainor said. "I can conclude it was likely the victim clawed at someone. But no, I was not able to make a DNA match due to the factors I've already testified to."

"So, you didn't find the defendant's DNA on her anywhere, even though you say she put up a fight?" Dean asked.

"That's correct," Dr. Trainor answered.

"Thank you, I have nothing further." Dean sat down.

"None from me, Your Honor," Jack said.

"All right. Dr. Trainor, thank you. You're excused. Jack, who do you have next?"

Jack straightened his tie. "Your Honor, I'd like to call Cassiopeia Leary to the stand."

Chapter 24

"Ms. LEARY," Jack started. "How did you become acquainted with the victim, Annie Liski?"

Even with the court order ruling that my testimony served the interests of justice, it didn't feel good breaking my attorney-client privilege. The oath I'd taken had become such a part of my DNA it was hard to pull away from it. But I also felt Annie speaking to me from beyond the grave. She had no voice anymore. I had to give her one in the only way I could.

"I was first approached by Judge Kent Tucker, Mrs. Liski's brother. He had some concerns regarding Annie's domestic situation. Concerns I later came to share."

"How so?"

"I met Annie at her work, at the Bella Donna salon. I introduced myself. It didn't take her long to figure out that her brother sent me. She was very cagey then. Scared. She wasn't ready to go forward with any legal action against her husband."

"What did you do then?"

"I left," I answered. "But not before another employee at

the Bella Donna approached me. She showed me a photograph on her phone. One she'd taken of Annie."

"Is this the photograph you were shown?" Jack asked.

Good job, I thought. He'd tracked down Reese, the receptionist, and gotten her cooperation. I leaned forward and looked at the picture of Annie with her lip split and swollen eye.

"That's what I saw on Reese's, er ... the other employee's phone, yes."

"Did she tell you what happened to Annie?" Jack asked.

"Objection," Dean said. "The answer calls for hearsay. If Mr. LaForge wants to call this Reese person, he's free to do so."

"Sustained," Judge Colton said.

"Then what happened?" Jack asked, choosing a safer line of questioning.

I told him the rest. "Annie came to my office a few days later. She had obviously been beaten."

"Why obvious?" he asked.

"Her eye was almost swollen shut. Her lip was once again split. She had bruising on her arms where she said her husband had grabbed her."

"Did you document those injuries?" he asked.

"Of course," I answered.

Then Jack introduced the pictures I'd taken of Annie that day in my office. They showed a scared, tired, broken woman. She'd hated every second as I clicked my phone and photographed her injuries from each angle.

"Did you then have occasion to file legal paperwork on Annie's behalf?"

"Yes," I said. "We filed for an ex parte personal protection. Annie gave testimony to Judge Moira Pierce in Family Court. Judge Pierce granted her the order from the bench."

"Your Honor," Jack said. "We have the audio transcript of Annie Liski's testimony. I'd like permission to play it for the Court at this time."

Dean didn't object. He had no grounds.

So, I sat in stony silence as Annie's voice echoed through the courtroom.

"Your Honor," she said on the recording. "I'm in fear for my life. My husband has a volatile temper. He has warned me if I ever try to leave him, or if I go to court, it would be the last thing I'd ever do."

Judge Pierce's voice interrupted. "Mrs. Liski, are you telling the Court that the respondent, Brian Liski has expressly threatened to harm you if you file for divorce?"

"Yes, ma'am," she said. "Not harm. Brian said he'd kill me. He said he'd wring my neck."

"Ms. Leary," Jack said, stopping the recording. "When was the last time you saw Annie Liski?"

I told him.

"And that is the same day she disappeared?" he asked.

"Yes," I said. "I may have been the last person to see Annie alive before her murderer did. She left my office at approximately eleven thirty. She said she was going back to her friend Maggie Bonham's house to gather some things. She was supposed to show up at a battered women's safe house that my office had arranged for her. She never arrived."

"Ms. Leary, did you at any time become acquainted with Brian Liski?"

"I don't know if I'd call it acquainted. I arranged for service of the PPO and divorce pleadings. That was carried out by Deputy Jed Simons with the coordination of the sheriff's office up in Taylor, where Mr. Liski works. Deputy Simons can give more specifics. But the next day, Brian Liski showed up at my office."

"How's that?"

"When I left my office for the day, Mr. Liski was lying in wait for me in the parking lot."

"Objection to the characterization," Dean said.

"You can explore that on cross," Judge Colton said. "Ms. Leary, let's stick to the facts, not your impressions."

My jaw dropped. His ruling made no sense.

"What happened between you and Brian Liski in the parking lot of your office?" Jack asked, unfazed.

"He was angry. He got in my personal space and jabbed his finger at me. The defendant made it clear that he would protect what was his."

"Those were his exact words?" Jack asked.

"Yes."

"Ms. Leary, were you afraid?"

I paused for a moment. "Yes. I was afraid. It was entirely inappropriate for him to show up in the shadows, coming from the alley beside my building. I believed I was in imminent harm from Brian Liski."

"But he didn't touch you?" Jack asked.

"He did not. Detective Eric Wray was on his way to my office right then. Thank God. He saw Liski talking to me. He heard at least a portion of what Liski said. He grabbed Liski and pulled him away from me."

"I see," Jack said. "Then what happened?"

"Detective Wray and Brian Liski exchanged heated words. But Liski finally left. If Detective Wray hadn't arrived when he did, I believe Brian Liski would have become violent."

"Objection!" Dean shouted.

"Why do you think that, Ms. Leary?" This question came from the judge.

"Because I'd seen firsthand the physical results of Brian

Liski's temper when directed toward his wife. When he didn't get his way. Because, as I said, it was well beyond the bounds of social decency for him to have shown up like that. And because I believe he was lying in wait. I'd been in my office for almost two hours prior to leaving. He could have come in through the front door. He could have called me on the phone. He did none of those things, preferring to physically intimidate and threaten me."

Judge Colton nodded. I knew Dean Farnham probably wished he'd just left well enough alone.

"Thank you," Jack said. "I have nothing further."

Red-faced, Dean Farnham stepped up to the lectern. "Ms. Leary," he said. "You don't have any firsthand knowledge of Mr. Liski's alleged physical assault on his wife, do you?"

"Well, I mean, I saw her injuries firsthand, yes."

"Right. But you only have Annie Liski's word that her husband was the one who inflicted those injuries on her, isn't that right?"

Lord. Was he going with the defense that Annie had been lying about all of it?

"Did I see Brian Liski actually beat the living snot out of his wife? No. I only saw the aftermath."

"Ms. Leary," Judge Colton warned. "You're also an officer of the court. I expect a little more professional decorum from you."

"Yes, Your Honor," I said. I swear I could see his wheels turning. It was an old paranoia, but I half expected him to add, "despite your last name." My father, uncles, and brother had spent plenty of time in front of Judge Colton for various drunken infractions.

"Ms. Leary," Dean said. "Isn't it true that you actually didn't know Annie Liski well at all?"

"I'm sorry?"

"I mean, you stated that you first came into contact with her at the behest of Judge Tucker at the beginning of June?"

"Yes," I said.

"So, you'd actually known the woman less than a month. Correct?"

"That's correct," I said.

"And you're not claiming to know her on a personal level," he said.

"Well, I am claiming that. Practicing family law, especially in a domestic violence situation, is about as personal an association an attorney can have with a client."

Dean nodded. "But you weren't friends," he said. "You didn't socialize beyond the confines of your office?"

"We did not," I said. "Annie trusted me. She confided in me, but it was a professional relationship, yes."

"In fact, you never, ever saw her outside either your office or in Judge Pierce's courtroom when she gave testimony for the PPO, right?"

I thought for a moment. "Well, no. As I testified, I first met Annie when I went to her salon. She actually did my hair for me."

"Ah," Dean said. "But you didn't know her friends?"

"I knew she was friends with a Maggie Bonham because that's where she was staying. They were friends through the salon. I understand Ms. Bonham worked there too. I had begun to know some of her work relationships."

Dean shifted his weight from one foot to the next. I knew what he was trying to do. He was trying to make it look like I didn't really know Annie well. It wasn't the worst tactic in the world, but completely baffling to do at this stage of the litigation. Jack only had to prove that a crime had been committed and that the State had probable cause to arrest Brian Liski for it. Most defense lawyers either waived prelim altogether or barely put on a defense. Nothing could be gained from tipping one's hand to the prosecution as to which defenses you might present at trial.

In some small way, I almost felt bad for Dean Farnham. He was in over his head and seemed to know it. But instead of bowing out in favor of more skilled counsel, he seemed to be diving in with both feet.

"So, you know some of Annie Liski's acquaintances," he said. "But you don't know of any of her enemies, do you?"

I looked at Jack. It was barely perceptible, but he rolled his eyes.

"You mean other than her husband?" I asked.

Dean started to sweat. "What I mean to say ... isn't it true that you have no knowledge of any other adversarial relationships in Annie Liski's life?"

My mouth dropped open at that one. Had he just asked me what I thought he'd asked me?

"That's not entirely true," I said. "She felt isolated by Mr. Liski's family. She told me they weren't close and that they were against the marriage. But I don't know anyone else with a motive to kill Annie Liski besides your client, the defendant, Brian Liski."

Dean finally realized his mistake. Brian himself looked about ready to spit fire.

"Ms. Leary," Dean kept soldiering on. "Isn't it true that Mrs. Liski could have had enemies you just don't know about?"

"Objection," Jack said. "The question calls for baseless speculation."

"Mr. Farnham?" Judge Colton sighed. "Try one more time."

"Mrs. Liski never told you about anyone else she had a beef with, did she?"

I paused for a moment. "I don't know what you mean by beef. I just told you she didn't get along with her in-laws."

"Okay, Mrs. Liski told you about a problem she was having with the Bella Donna salon, didn't she?"

Jack started furiously scribbling notes. It was becoming quite painful to watch Dean.

"She mentioned that the owner was disinclined to renew her lease at the end of the month. Annie was upset about that, but it wasn't an adversarial relationship. She felt it was Brian meddling in her business affairs to further control her. And she wasn't scared of Donna Harris. And she didn't ask for a PPO against her."

I got a stern look from Judge Colton but didn't care.

"All right, that's fine," Dean said. "Let me ask you this: going back to the day you claim Mr. Liski waited for you outside your office, did you witness the altercation between him and Detective Wray?"

"Well," I said. "I was right there. So yes."

"Isn't it true that the detective threw Mr. Liski against a wall?"

"He pulled him away from me," I said. "I don't know that I'd characterize it as throwing him against a wall."

"And isn't it true that it was in fact Detective Wray who did the threatening that day? Specifically, he told him he'd kill him if Brian ever so much as looked at you again. Is that correct?"

"Yes," I said. Anger rose in me.

"I see," Dean said. "What is your relationship with Detective Eric Wray?"

My stomach tightened a bit. The jerk was trying to set Eric up now. This was exactly what I'd been afraid of. Maybe Dean Farnham wasn't as dumb as he acted.

"Detective Wray is one of the senior homicide detectives

in Delphi. I'm a criminal defense lawyer. We have had multiple occasions to communicate on cases we had in common. He graduated from Delphi High School in the same era that my brother and I did. I've known him socially, as I know most people in Delphi, for a few decades. Beyond that, I consider him a very close friend."

"Are you sleeping with Eric Wray?"

Jack rose from his seat and shouted. Brian Liski's face broke into a smile.

I didn't so much as blink. I leaned far forward into the microphone. "No," I said.

Dean blanched.

"But isn't it true you are romantically involved with Detective Wray?"

"Objection," Jack said.

"Overruled," Judge Colton said.

"Detective Wray and I are close, yes," I said.

"Kissing close?" Dean asked.

I rolled my eyes. "What is this, fourth grade?"

"Ms. Leary," the judge admonished me again. "Mr. Farnham, I'm going to ask that you rephrase your question."

"Your Honor," I said. "I believe I've already answered it. Detective Wray and I are personally close, yes."

"Move on, Mr. Farnham," the judge said.

Dean made a great show of shuffling his papers at the lectern.

"I don't think I have any more questions for this witness."

"You don't think, or you know, Mr. Farnham," Judge Colton said, his irritation plain.

"I'm finished with her for now," Dean said. He wore a smug smile on his face that I had the overwhelming urge to smack off.

"Anything else, Mr. LaForge?" the judge asked.

Jack's skin had paled. I didn't like it one bit. This was a sideshow. A distraction. It made no earthly sense why Dean Farnham indulged in these theatrics now. When it came to trial, we'd all wipe the floor with him.

"I have no other questions," Jack said.

The judge dismissed me from the witness stand. I walked past the lawyer's table. Brian Liski sneered at me and licked his lips. He might as well have just called me a slut to my face. I clenched my fists and kept on walking.

At my back, Judge Colton said, "Okay, it's four o'clock. We'll end for the day. Who's up first thing tomorrow, Mr. LaForge?"

Through gritted teeth, I heard Jack say, "Detective Eric Wray, Your Honor."

Terrific.

Chapter 25

"You THINK he's going to gain any traction with it?" Jeanie asked. I sat in her office at seven o'clock the following morning. I'd given her the highlights of Dean Farnham's cross-examination yesterday.

"With Judge Colton?" I asked. "Not really. I can't figure Farnham out. I mean, from a defense attorney standpoint, it's not a bad strategy. Raise the suspicion that the victim's lawyer and the lead detective in the case are in cahoots. Try to cast doubt over every step said lead detective made as some grand plan to impress his girlfriend. Maybe you get enough dumb ones or those who have some inherent mistrust of cops that didn't come out in voir dire to think all the evidence was tainted."

"Hmm," Jeanie said. She chewed the end of her pencil and sat with her feet up on the desk. "But why do that at preliminary examination? Jack LaForge is too damn good at what he does. All Farnham's doing is giving Jack lead time to prepare for that strategy at trial."

"That's what I can't figure out," I said. "I mean, we know Farnham's green. He's never tried a murder case."

"He's not stupid though," Jeanie said. "And lord, he could probably read about the perils of showing your hand at prelim in any basic law practice manual. I mean, this isn't that hard."

"I don't know. I really don't."

Jeanie let her feet drop. She stared hard at me. "Uh oh."

"What, uh oh?" I asked.

"I know that look. Your wheels are turning."

"I don't know, it's just got me thinking."

"God help us all," Jeanie said.

I laughed. "No, it's just. Why Farnham? From everything Annie told me, Brian Liski's family has some money. But it hasn't been without grief. That pawn shop in Taylor was almost shut down a few years ago. One of his uncles was charged with dealing in stolen property."

I'd finally gotten a call back from Agent Lee Cannon. He would neither confirm nor deny whether the Liski family was part of any ongoing federal investigation. But his omissions made one thing clear. Brian Liski's family wasn't entirely on the up and up.

"But he beat it," Jeanie said.

"Yes," I said. "Miller Lafferty was the defense firm." It was another detail Lee Cannon supplied. These were all things I could have tracked down on my own, but Cannon saved me the time and resources. With Tori sitting for the bar, I appreciated it.

Jeanie scrunched her nose. "Big guns," she said.

"Exactly," I said. "So, Brian's got access to family money. And they're connected to a heavy hitter defense firm. So, why go with someone like Dean Farnham? It just doesn't make a whole lot of sense."

"You sure his family is paying for his defense?"

"No," I said. "I'm not sure of anything. But I have to admit, I'm curious."

"You need to stay out of this," Jeanie said. "Jack's capable of prosecuting this case without your help."

"I know. It's just ... I may have access to resources that he doesn't."

"No," Jeanie barked. "No way, Cass. I'm not going to let you go down that road. Do I need to remind you what happened the last time you tried? You almost got yourself killed."

I bit my bottom lip. There was no point in arguing with Jeanie. She wasn't wrong. I'd spent over a decade as a mob lawyer in Chicago. I'd cut those ties for good, but I still knew how they operated. And something smelled decidedly fishy about what was going on in Annie's case.

"You talked to your Fed friend," she said. "That's far enough."

"Is it?" I said, though I shouldn't have. I could call in another favor. I could reach out to the Thorne family and see what they could dig up on the Liskis. Only then I'd be in a position to owe them again. The last time, I'd almost paid with my life.

"Jeanie, I just want to know more about Dean Farnham," I said. "That's all."

"Don't go poking bears," Jeanie said. "I'm warning you."

"He's not a bear," I said. "He's barely a hamster."

"Why don't you just tell Jack what's got you curious? Let him decide whether he wants to use county resources pulling at that thread. The best thing you can do is tell the jury what you know about Annie's last days."

I scratched my chin. "I just hope it's enough. What if we've overlooked something?"

"We haven't. And Dean Farnham is just trying to rattle your and Eric Wray's cages. And it's working. When does Eric testify?"

"This morning," I said.

"Please tell me you haven't talked to him since you left the stand. You shouldn't. Steer clear of him on anything to do with this case; don't give Farnham any more ammunition."

"What, that I'm tampering with witnesses?" I asked, incredulous.

"Just ... Eric's temper can be a problem. And it's at its worst when he thinks someone is messing with you. All I'm saying is Farnham's going to keep using that. And Eric doesn't do much to help himself in that regard."

"He hasn't done anything wrong and neither have I," I said.

"Eric never should have gotten into it with Liski in front of witnesses."

"I don't disagree," I said. "But I was scared of him that day, Jeanie. I honestly don't know what might have happened if Eric hadn't shown up when he did."

"Fair enough," she said. "I'm just saying ... I've got a weird feeling about all of this. Like there's some other shoe about to drop. I just don't want it to be on your head."

"Me either," I said. I picked up my phone from where I lay it on Jeanie's desk. It was nearly eight o'clock.

"Annie's hearing is going to restart soon," I said. "I want to be there."

"You plan on sitting in on Eric's testimony?"

"Haven't decided. I've got my own hearing in Judge Castor's court at nine. I just ... I don't know. I just feel like I should be around, you know? For Annie."

Jeanie gave me a sad smile. "I know," she said. "I can't stop thinking about that kid either. I just don't like seeing you get sucked in."

"It's too late," I said. "It was too late for that the second I met her."

"Yeah," Jeanie said. "Same here."

I came around the desk and gave her a hug.

"Son of a bitch," she whispered. When I pulled away, Jeanie had tears in her eyes. "I just want that bastard to get what's coming to him. I should have seen it. You know?"

"I know. Me too," I said. I hugged Jeanie again, then headed off to court.

Chapter 26

My hearing in Judge Castor's courtroom took longer than I expected. It was almost eleven by the time I headed down to the District Court hallway. I got there just in time to see the last of Eric's cross-examination.

I knew him. To anyone else, Eric might have just looked calm or neutral. To me, I saw the fury hiding behind his eyes.

"You saw the victim's body," Dean asked.

"Yes."

"You communicated with the M.E., Dr. Trainor. You read her report. You know what she testified to during prelim?" Dean asked.

"Yes. Yes. And I wasn't in the courtroom for that," he said through tight lips.

These were tame questions. It meant Dean had likely already pushed his buttons asking the same things he did of me yesterday. I took a seat in the back, right next to Detective Megan Lewis.

"Detective," Dean went on. "Did you find any bruising on the defendant's face when you picked him up for questioning?"

"Not that I recall," Eric said.

"No scratches, no claw marks?" Dean asked.

"Not that I recall."

I pulled out a pen and scribbled a quick note, then turned it so Megan could see. It read, "Did he get personal?"

Megan's nostrils flared and she gave me a quick nod. She took the pen from me and scribbled an answer.

"Started by asking if you've slept together. Then asked whether he *wanted* to sleep with you. Then took a few cheap shots about Eric's wife."

Oh boy. I was surprised Eric hadn't launched himself across the witness stand. Brian was frantically scribbling his own notes. Yesterday, he seemed smug. Today, he just looked agitated.

"Detective," Dean continued. "You testified on direct exam this morning that you can't pinpoint where Annie Liski was murdered, can you?"

"That's correct," he said, settling.

"Her cell phone was never recovered," Dean said.

"It was not. As I also stated, we subpoenaed her phone records. We have a general idea where she might have been up until approximately one thirty the afternoon of the tenth."

Dean shuffled through his notes. "Right. You said her phone pinged the tower near Mackenzie Street in the south end of town."

"Yes," he said. "Her car was still parked in front of her own house. Her belongings were in it. Those things she'd packed up to presumably take with her to the shelter later in the day. But her phone and her purse weren't among them."

"So, you're saying she just vanished off the face of the earth after one p.m. on the tenth of June?"

Eric gave Dean that sly smile. I held my breath, knowing he was about to go in for the kill. "No, I'm saying she made a classic, fatal mistake, and went home. Her husband met her there. When he realized she was leaving for good, he did exactly what he'd been threatening to for years. He beat and strangled her to death and dumped her in Finn Lake with sandbags tied to her ankles so we wouldn't find her for five days."

"But you searched Brian Liski's car. You found no physical evidence of a struggle."

"Hair and clothing samples were found in that car. They matched the victim's."

"But you have no way of knowing when those samples were left. I mean, that was her husband. She had to have been in that car hundreds of times, right?"

Eric sighed. "Yes."

"I mean, she didn't bleed in there," Dean said.

Eric leaned forward. "She had the life choked out of her," Eric said. "She didn't bleed to death, counselor."

"All right," Judge Colton said. "This is getting repetitive, Mr. Farnham."

Dean looked crestfallen. He recovered quickly. "Yes," he said. "I have nothing further, Detective."

Eric pushed the microphone aside. Color rose in his cheeks as he charged through the gallery, not even seeing me. He burst through the courtroom doors, fists curled. I gave Megan a look, telling her I'd handle this one. She looked relieved. I went after Eric, catching him in the stairwell. He was livid.

Shit.

"That piece of ... that little ..."

"What happened?" I asked, though I could already guess.

"He pretty much just accused me of planting evidence."

"What? How? What evidence?"

"Does it matter?" he said.

"You have to calm down," I said. "Don't let Farnham rattle you."

No sooner had I said it than Dean Farnham opened the stairwell door and ran smack into the furious stare of Eric Wray.

Farnham's face went white. "Uh ... excuse me, Detective."

I put a death grip on Eric's arm and pulled him away.

"You need to watch yourself," Eric said. "You pull that kind of crap too many times, you'll never get a decent plea deal again. See how many of your criminal defense clients drop you."

"Stop," I whispered through gritted teeth.

Dean was speechless. He wisely chose to scurry down the stairs.

Eric whirled on me. I knew better than to argue with him at this point. Jeanie was right about his temper. She was also right that most of this was because of me. I knew Eric didn't give two shits about some two-bit defense lawyer trying to rattle his cage on the witness stand. He cared about the potential blowback on me.

"Is it over?" I asked. The stairs Dean Farnham had just run down led straight to the parking lot.

"No," he said. "LaForge wants to call one more witness. That girl you met at the salon. The one who took the picture of poor Annie Liski's face bashed in. She's late getting here, and Colton had another hearing he wanted to squeeze in. He's going to go back on the record on this one in an hour or so."

"Eric, none of this matters," I said. "This is prelim. You know this will get bound over for trial and Jack will have a strategy."

"Farnham's not as dumb as he looks," Eric said. "He's angling for a plea deal. That's all this is."

"Right," I said. "And he's also trying to see how far he can push you and what kind of witness you'll make."

There was an accusation in my tone. Eric's jaw clenched. To his credit, he blew a breath out and shook his head.

"I know," he said. "Dammit. I know."

"Good," I said. "It doesn't help that Farnham saw us congregating here."

"He can go to hell!"

"Right. I know. I just ..."

Eric put his hands on my arms. "Dean Farnham doesn't dictate how I live my life. I'm not afraid of him. And we haven't done anything wrong."

I had more to say, but Eric stopped me with a hard kiss on the mouth that made my knees a little weak.

Then he gave me that trademark smirk of his and bounded down the stairs two at a time. I couldn't help but laugh. And hope Dean Farnham had the good sense not to hang out by the door down there.

I brushed a hair out of my eye and walked back out the door, heading for Colton's courtroom. It was empty though. Colton must have wanted a break before calling whatever hearing he wanted to squeeze in.

Jack LaForge was nowhere to be found either. No doubt he was off trying to wrangle Reese from the salon. I knew Jack. It would have irritated him no end having to break between calling witnesses like this. I decided it wouldn't do me any harm to try and help him find her.

I went down the hall and stopped at the women's restroom. I checked my lipstick in the mirror, and sure enough, Eric's kiss had left some evidence behind. I grabbed a tissue and blotted. I fished through my giant bag for a tube of lip gloss.

As I pulled it out, my ears exploded with the shrill, sharp sound of the fire alarm.

"You've gotta be kidding me," I said to no one.

The lights flashed in the bathroom, a backup in case there were any hearing-impaired litigants. I checked the stalls. No feet.

I threw my tissue away and shoved my lipstick back in the bag then readjusted its weight on my shoulder.

"Mercy," I said, covering my ears. The siren echoed off the tile floors in the bathroom. I hoped it would be better outside.

As I turned toward the door, the lights went off. It became instantly pitch black.

"Great," I muttered.

I waved my hands in front of me, feeling for the counter so I could make my way to the door. I made it three steps, then felt something hard at my back, just below my ribcage.

"Don't try to scream," a male voice whispered in my ear. Then a strong arm came around me, pressing me back against him.

"Walk," he said. "Don't run. And if you make a sound, I'll kill you right there."

Cold terror gripped me as I recognized Brian Liski's voice. Then he shoved me forward into the blackness.

Chapter 27

THE BLARING alarm was even louder in the hallway. Brian Liski pushed me hard, pressing the gun deep beneath my rib cage.

I could have screamed, but nobody would have been able to hear me over that noise. Besides, there wasn't a soul around. With Judge Colton's court in recess, most people had already cleared out. When the fire alarm went off, anyone milling around would have headed for the exits.

I thought that's where we were going too. The restroom was just down the hall from the stairwell where Dean Farnham exited maybe fifteen minutes ago.

Was he in on this? Did he help Brian?

I started moving toward the stairwell, but Brian grabbed my shoulder and turned me the other way.

"Go straight," he hissed against my ear. It was the only way I could hear him over the chaos.

He led me to a different corridor past the records office. I tried to slow my step as we passed the window where the clerk sat. But there was nobody in that office either. Brian opened an unmarked door next to the clerk's office and shoved me through it. I nearly lost my footing and pitched forward down a small flight of stairs.

Brian was there, catching me with a hard grip on my arm. "In there," he said.

The alarm wasn't so loud there. He had me open a second steel door. He pushed me forward into the darkness.

I'd only ever been in this part of the courthouse once before. The clerks called it the "Dead File" room, an ominous distinction at the present. It's where they kept archived court files until the county started the process of digitizing everything. Now, most of the dusty old paper files were gone, relegated to some off-site storage facility or destroyed altogether.

All that remained were two long, metal tables and a row of empty file cabinets. I heard they were planning to convert some of this space into more offices for a legal clinic, but were waiting on grant money from the state.

So, for right now, Brian Liski might have just pushed me through the portal to Narnia. Nobody else was coming down here.

"Get up against the wall," he said, giving me another shove to help me along the way. Hands up, I did as I was told. I suppose I should have been scared. Terrified. I don't know. The assault on my senses from the fire alarm hadn't waned. It was all too surreal.

The room was windowless. Now it felt airless. It occurred to me that if there were a real fire, this might be the worst place to be in the entire building.

I stood with my back pressed to the wall, hands still up. Brian turned one row of lights on in the back of the room. Two of the panels were out, so only one flat rectangle of fluorescent light came to life in the ceiling behind him.

As Brian walked toward me, I felt the first chill of panic crawling up my spine. Maybe it was just the weird lighting, but Brian Liski's face was pale with a waxen cast to it. His eyes remained cold and focused straight on me. The barrel of his gun never wavered from its target straight at my face. We stood like that for a moment. An eternity. Brian stayed still as a statue. He didn't seem nervous or panicked. My heart beat so fast I started to get a little lightheaded. It was the last thing I needed right now.

"Brian," I said, my voice cracking past a dry throat. "What do you think ..."

"Shut up," he said. I saw the first tremor of nerves go through his arms. Definitely not something I needed right now as he kept that gun trained on me.

"Was this you?" I asked, not heeding his warning. "The fire alarm? Because if there's a real threat ..."

"There's no fire," he said. "If there was, that's the least of your worries right now."

"Okay," I said. "But there's no other way out of this room besides the way we came in. You know that, right? And if you're the one who pulled that alarm, they're going to start doing a sweep of the entire courthouse as soon as they figure out there's no fire."

"I'm not worried," he said, his mouth turning up at the corner in an odd smile.

"Okay," I said. "So, what's the game plan? Are you just planning on pointing that gun at me? Or did you want to tell me something? You've got my attention."

Brian laughed. "You should have listened to me before. You think you have this all figured out. You think you know me."

"No," I said. "I don't know you at all. I only knew Annie ..."

"Shut up!" he yelled. I flinched and brought my hands up even higher.

"You only think you knew Annie," he said. "Nobody really did but me."

"Okay," I said. "That's fair."

"You wouldn't listen to me before. None of you would. Now you will."

"Yes," I said. "Now I will. But my hands are getting tired."

"Are you afraid of me?" he asked.

Such an odd thing to ask. There was no malice in his voice when he said it. I was beginning to wonder if perhaps Brian Liski was far more mentally unstable than any of us realized.

"Of course," I said. "I'm afraid of you, Brian. You're holding a gun at my head."

"Sit down," he ordered. The table nearest to me had four metal chairs around it. Slowly, with my hands still up, I made a move toward the closest one. Brian kept his gun steady as I pulled the chair out and slowly sat down.

Brian nodded. He came toward me and sat at the opposite end of the table. He rested the gun on the table but kept it pointed at me.

"Okay," I said. "What do you want to talk about?"

My head pounded. My ears still rang. Outside, from the hallway, the fire alarm still blared. I'd been through safety drills in the courthouse before. There was an evacuation plan, floor by floor. Everyone would be instructed to file out the front and side entrances. Courthouse employees would act as marshals and herd members of the public with them to the administration building across the street. Then they'd start a headcount.

It would be impossible to account for all the civilians in the courthouse that day. There was every chance nobody would realize I wasn't among the evacuees. Had Eric still been in the building when the alarms went off?

Even if he'd already left, he'd hear about them. He knew I was waiting for Annie's prelim to resume. He'd come looking.

"Give me that," Brian said; he made a gesture with the gun toward my bag. I thought of throwing it at him. The thing was heavy, more than five pounds without anything in it. Impractical, unwieldy, but a part of me.

Brian grabbed it from me, nearly tearing my shoulder off with it. He dug through it, finding my phone. He was nimble and quick as he ripped it out of its case and pulled the battery, bricking it. Now I couldn't use it, and no one could ping it to try and figure out where I was.

My cold fear grew as I began to realize how far ahead Brian must have planned all this.

"I didn't kill Annie," he said.

"Is that what this is? You're trying to convince me you didn't murder your wife by holding me at gunpoint?"

"I didn't *kill* Annie!" he shouted and slammed the butt of the gun against the table. I jumped.

"What exactly do you want me to do with that information?" I asked.

"I want you to know it," he said.

"I'm not the one you need to convince," I said. "And I'm not your lawyer. You're getting your day in court, Brian. That's how this process works."

He ran a hand through his hair. Brian Liski wasn't what I'd call an attractive man. He had a wide face with his eyes set too closely together and a beakish nose. His lips seemed constantly pursed. He had thinning brown hair that he used too much product in, making it stand up in spikes. Right now, in this light, I could see clear through to his glistening scalp as he began to sweat.

"He won't help me," Brian said. "Farnham isn't ... he can't help."

ROBIN JAMES

"He was doing a pretty good job last I saw," I said. Maybe if I could convince Brian that his case wasn't hopeless, he'd come to his senses.

"I can't trust him," Brian said. "Not anymore."

I had no idea what that meant. "He's trying to do his job," I said. "You know he came to me. He told me you wanted me to know you didn't kill Annie. Why?"

"It matters to me," he said. "I didn't kill Annie. I loved her."

Brian squeezed his eyes shut. When he opened them again, they shone with unshed tears.

Good lord. Was he actually going to declare his love for her now?

"This is your fault," he said. "You put ideas in Annie's head. Those papers ... that wasn't Annie. That was you putting her up to it."

I didn't know what to say. Arguing with him didn't seem wise.

"Brian," I said. "She was afraid of you. She was afraid *for* you."

"She loved me," he whispered.

I took a breath. "Yes," I said. "She did."

The corner of his mouth curled up. Hatred filled his eyes as he looked at me. My God. He did blame me for Annie's actions before he killed her.

I realized with cold clarity this wasn't about convincing me he was innocent. This was about him punishing me for what he thought I'd done.

I sat frozen in front of him. I had to buy time. What could I possibly say that he'd believe? That would work?

"Brian," I said. "I know you don't want to go to jail. I meant what I said about you having a fighting chance against the murder charge. I'll be honest, I wasn't so sure at first. But

174

Dean's doing a good job for you."

"You think I did it. You think I killed her," he said.

"And I already told you, I'm not the one you need to convince of that. But right now, you did do something that could send you to jail. Coming into the courthouse with a weapon is a felony. Kidnapping me and holding me at gunpoint is a felony. They're going to catch you for that."

He glared at me.

"Unless you let me go right now," I said. "I'll walk out of here. That'll be the end of it."

It was his turn to freeze. Another eternity went by then Brian Liski started to laugh.

"You think I'm dumb or crazy," he said. "I'm neither one. No. This ends when it's finished. Not a second before."

"Fine," I said, my anger rising. "So, what now?"

Brian opened his mouth to answer. As he did, the alarms in the hallway finally ceased. For a moment, it made my ears ring even louder. I pressed my thumb and forefinger to the bridge of my nose.

"Your clock is ticking now, Brian," I said. "They're going to figure out we're in here. There are security cameras all over the courthouse."

He shook his head. "No. They aren't."

I meant to ask him what he meant. Instead, I heard a moan coming from behind me and jumped. In doing so, I pushed my chair away from the table.

I looked at Brian. He didn't move. I turned back to the source of the sound. There, in the shadows between two of the empty file cabinets, I saw the tips of two black dress shoes.

There was a man lying on the ground.

Another moan. I acted without thinking; leaping out of the chair, I went to him.

Jack LaForge lay on his side, slumped against the wall.

Blood trickled down from a gash on the side of his head. I didn't need to be Dr. Amelia Trainor to know what made that kind of a wound. Brian had pistol-whipped him.

"My God! Jack? Can you hear me?"

Jack opened one swollen eye. Relief flooded his face as I came into focus for him. I took off my suit jacket and bunched it beneath Jack's head.

"He needs a doctor," I said to Brian.

"He needs to stay quiet," Brian said. He'd moved from the table and stood over us, pointing the gun at Jack this time.

Jack's eyes widened with new terror as he tried to sit up. The effort of it drained the color from his face.

"Get him up," Brian said. "Sit at the table. Both of you. It's time for us all to have that talk."

I was about to argue that Jack was in no condition to move. But Jack *did* move. I helped him, draping his arm over my shoulder. Slowly, with great effort, he got to his feet.

I led him to the table. He sat down with a thud as more blood poured out of the wound on his head. I turned to Brian, ready to beg for help. But Brian only smiled.

"I told you," he said. "He's just fine."

And I knew Brian Liski had jumped off a cliff taking me right along with him.

Chapter 28

JACK WAS ANYTHING BUT FINE. His color was wrong. I pressed my jacket against the wound on the side of his head.

Brian had taken to pacing in front of the door. His footsteps echoed, making it impossible for me to hear anything that might be happening out in the hall. I didn't have my phone and had no idea what time it was now. We'd been in here for what seemed like an exceedingly long time. It had to be well after one o'clock. Surely.

It would have taken at least an hour to sort everything out after the fire alarm. It wasn't a drill so the fire department and sheriffs would have to make sure there was no threat before they let anyone back in. It would take maybe a half an hour for the deputies to make a sweep of the courthouse. Probably a couple of hours before everyone was allowed back in. The few fire drills I'd been caught up in here always seemed to take an eternity and those were planned. This wasn't.

Then what? Eric would at least try to call me. It would go to voicemail but that wouldn't mean much. I'd told him I planned to sit in on the rest of Brian's hearing and handle a few other things in court today. I had nothing on the docket.

177

"They're going to resume your hearing after all this settles down," I said to Brian. "How long do you think you have before everyone figures out that you and the lead prosecutor are missing, Brian?"

He didn't answer, but just kept pacing.

Jack started to cough. I pulled my jacket away from his head. The bleeding had stopped. Thank God. Still, I really didn't like his color.

"You don't know her," Brian said. "Not like I do."

Annie? His use of present tense disturbed me. Just how much of a psychopath was I dealing with?

"She wouldn't have done any of this unless you put her up to it," he said.

"Maybe not," I said. "But she was scared, Brian. Of you. And her brother was scared for her. He loved her too."

Brian's jaw twitched. "You have no idea what you're talking about. You profit off other people's personal problems. You twisted everything around. That shit you wrote. That you made Annie sign. That wasn't her. You put words in her mouth."

I took a slow breath. "It was Annie's choice," I said.

"Shut up!" he shouted. I flinched as he charged toward the table. Beside me, Jack gasped.

"Okay, okay," I said. "You're right. I didn't know Annie the way you did. But do you think she'd want you to be doing this right now? She did love you, Brian. I think, maybe, despite everything, she wouldn't want you to get hurt."

He made a choked sound. His grief was written plainly on his face. Had he really convinced himself this was all my fault? Was he so twisted that he believed killing her was his only option?

"Son," Jack said, his voice ragged. "You've got options

here, still. But the longer you keep us here, the fewer you'll have."

"I don't want to hear anything from you," Brian said. "There's only one thing you can do, and I already told you."

I shot Jack a look.

There was movement outside. Voices. I recognized one of the deputy sheriff's voices giving an all-clear further down the hall.

Brian moved lightning quick. He grabbed me around the neck and pointed the gun at Jack.

"Not a word," he said. "Not a sound."

The footsteps drew closer. They came down the stairs and stopped just outside the door. My heart exploded as someone tried the doorknob.

"Bo, you gotta key for this one?"

"Not a sound," Brian whispered.

I couldn't move, not even to turn my head. Brian had his arm so tightly around my neck I saw black spots. I thought of Annie. God help me.

"Shit," one of the voices said. "Not on me. They changed the locks in this hallway. Dammit."

"We'll circle back," the other deputy said. "Stop by the clerk's office."

Jack jumped as one of the deputies pounded on the door.

"Anybody in there?"

Should I try to scream? Would Brian really go so far as to shoot one of us? If he did, he'd never get out of here alive either.

But I wasn't willing to risk Jack's life, let alone my own. I stayed silent.

"We'll just come back," one of the deputies said. Then two sets of footsteps retreated down the hall and up the stairs.

Brian held me against him for another minute with his

ROBIN JAMES

gun pointed at Jack. Then slowly he let me go. I gasped for air and rested my head on the table. When I raised it, anger roiled through me.

"So now what?" I bit the air with my words.

"Now?" Brian said, looking at me as if I were the insane one. "Now?" he said again. "Now, you two fix this mess and do the right thing."

I looked at Jack. His expression had gone stone cold.

"How are we supposed to fix it?" Jack asked, panting through his words. I didn't like it one bit.

"You need to drop the charges against me," Brian said, as if the answer was obvious.

"What?" Jack asked.

"You need to drop the charges against me. And you"—he pointed the gun back at me—"you need to stop lying and tell him the truth."

"Son," Jack said. "You've been charged with murder and misuse of a corpse."

Brian pressed the side of the gun to his head as if he were in pain. "Stop saying that! I didn't kill Annie!"

"Fine," I said. "So who did?"

Brian sat back down at the end of the table and lay the gun in front of him. The barrel was still pointed at me, but his fingers were at least off the trigger.

"That's what you're for," he whispered. Now he was looking at me like *I* was crazy.

My throat felt thick. My brain felt like it was coated in tar.

"Brian," I said. "I'm sorry. I don't understand what you want from us."

"I want a deal," he said. "You tell him the truth. You made all that stuff up about me and Annie. You get the word out that I've been loyal. And he drops the murder charges. I'm an innocent man."

"How do you expect me to do all of that sitting inside this damn room!" Jack asked, his voice rising. Then he erupted into another fit of coughs. I patted him on the back until Jack held up a hand, waving me off.

"Brian," I said. "I know things were complicated between you and Annie. They always are. But she told me you hit her. I saw her face. She came to me the day after you hurt her."

Brian scrunched up his face. "I didn't mean to hurt her."

"I know," I said.

"You have no idea the kind of pressure I'm under. I try to do everything right. They expect me to ..."

"It's hard working for family," I said.

"She had everything," Brian said. "She didn't have to work at that salon. I was going to get her her own place. She could set her own hours."

"She told me," I said.

"But then she wanted a bigger house too. She bitched at me how late I worked. Every time. She didn't understand and neither do you."

"Bigger houses, her own salon," I said. "Those things take a lot of money. And making more money takes a lot more work. I run my own business too, Brian. I can't even imagine how frustrating that is. I don't have a spouse at home nagging me about it."

He sneered at me. Under the table, Jack squeezed my knee.

"Don't pretend you understand anything about me," Brian said.

"I'm saying I understand how you could get frustrated. And you're right. There are two sides to every story. I only heard Annie's. So, tell me yours now. We're here. We're listening. It's what you wanted, isn't it?"

For a second, I thought we were getting somewhere. Then

ROBIN JAMES

a dead look came into Brian Liski's eyes. He moved away from
the table and went back to the door. When he had his back
turned to us, I looked at Jack.

I mouthed my words slowly, keeping an eye on Brian. "Do
you have your phone?"

Jack carefully raised his arm and patted his lapel. I saw
the faint rectangular bulge in his breast pocket. My heart
soared. Brian had taken mine. Why hadn't he searched Jack
for his?

"They can't run that business without me," he said. "But
I'm not their favorite son. My father was weak. He was
dumb."

"You're smarter than all of them though, aren't you?" I
asked. "Your uncles. Your cousins. And you do all the work,
but they take all the credit."

"Did she tell you that?" Brian asked, his expression
brightening.

"Yes," I said. "Brian, yes. Annie was proud of you. She
knew you weren't being treated fairly."

"I didn't make her work at the shop like all my cousins'
wives. Do you know how much grief I've gotten for that?
Keep it in the family. That's our way. I risked so much for
Annie. Did she tell you we had to elope?"

"No," I said. "But that sounds romantic."

"I kept all the ugly stuff from her. She never would have
listened to it anyway. She just wanted all the nice things.
Expensive cars. I tried to protect her. All I've ever done is try to
give her the best life. You know how hard my cousins' wives
work? They treat them like slaves. They don't get paid.
They're just expected to pitch in and not complain. And you
know what? They do it. Because that's what family does. She
never wanted to be part of it. You know what she called them?"

"No," I said. "I don't."

Brian snarled. "She told me she didn't want to be like my gypsy cousins."

Brian spit on the ground as he said the word. I winced. It was a racial slur and I had a hard time believing Annie Liski would have uttered it. But you never know what someone might say under duress when no one else can hear. There was no doubt Brian pushed Annie to her breaking point over and over again. And I still had no concrete idea how deeply the Liskis might be involved in criminal enterprises. Even so, Annie didn't deserve the abuse she suffered at this man's hands. And she didn't deserve to die.

"That's awful," I said. "People say things they don't mean in the heat of the moment sometimes. And they do things they don't mean."

He waved me off. I stayed silent. Brian leaned against the door and stayed that way for what seemed like forever. I was dying to get a look at Jack's phone. Judge Colton would have readjourned Brian's hearing by one thirty, two at the latest. Was it that time now?

In some ways, it felt like I'd been here an eternity. In others, it felt like no time had passed at all. But it had been hours. I felt sure of that.

Brian slid down the wall and sat in front of the door. His head lobbed up and down. I stayed still as stone. Would he pass out? Fall asleep?

I waited a minute. Two. Brian just stared straight ahead, glassy-eyed. The room had a tomb-like quality. We had no fresh air from outside. No window. Just the dank, musty smell of the basement in a hundred-year-old building.

Brian turned. He curled into himself. His shoulders shook as he silently wept.

I tapped Jack under the table. "Your phone," I whispered as lightly as I could.

He didn't respond. I turned to him. Jack's head had lolled back. His mouth fell open and drool spilled out the corner of his mouth.

"Jack?" I said, my voice rising with alarm. Brian Liski was no longer my immediate concern.

I shook Jack's shoulder. He slumped over and fell to the ground.

"What's the matter with him?" Brian asked.

I slid off my chair and knelt beside Jack.

"Turn more lights on!" I shouted.

He didn't.

I loosened Jack's tie and shoved my jacket beneath his head.

"Jack! Jack!"

Nothing.

I pressed my ear to Jack's chest. His heart was beating, but his pulse was so fast. He was drenched in sweat.

"Is he breathing?"

I held my face above Jack's. It took far too long, but he finally drew in a labored breath. His eyes opened but took longer to come into focus than I liked.

"Jack?" I said, gently tapping his cheek.

"Can't," he whispered. "Can't feel my arm."

"Brian!" I shouted. "You have to let me get help. I'm a lawyer not a doctor, but I'm fairly sure he's either having a stroke or a heart attack. If you don't let us out of here, he's going to die, and it'll be on your head. And it won't matter what you did or didn't do to Annie!"

Chapter 29

I ROLLED Jack to his side. He started coming around and coughing into his fist.

"Do you have a heart condition?" I asked.

He nodded. It explained so much. Jack had looked so haggard lately. In his last trial, I'd thought him off his game. This was serious. I wished I remembered what to do. Should his feet be over his head?

"Can you breathe?"

He nodded again. The coughing subsided a little.

"Brian," I said. "He needs help. And he needs it now. If this is a heart attack, every second is going to count. Do you understand what I'm telling you?"

Brian looked back toward the closed door. Sweat poured down his temple.

I was sweating too. We'd been in here at least a couple of hours. Why hadn't the deputies come back? Someone had to have figured out Jack and I were missing by now.

Jack leaned heavily against me. I guided his head to my shoulder. While Brian had his back turned, I reached inside Jack's jacket and slipped out his phone.

"Here," I said. "We need to get this jacket off you. Can you move your arms?"

"Yeah," Jack said. Relief flooded through me. It was good he could talk.

As we jostled with his jacket, Jack put his index finger on the home button of his phone. I quickly swiped up.

No bars. In the bowels of the courthouse, we were surrounded by steel. He had about thirty percent left on his battery.

I quickly dialed 911 anyway. The call immediately failed. When I got the chance, I'd see if moving to a different part of the room would help.

"You don't get to die," Brian yelled to Jack. "You got that? You don't get to worm your way out of this that easily."

"Brian," I said, trying to make my voice even. "Exactly how is Jack supposed to help you if he's sick or dying? He can't very well drop charges against you if he isn't alive to give the order."

"Make him comfortable," Brian said.

"How the hell am I supposed to do that?"

"I don't know," Brian said, waving the gun. "Make him a bed. I don't care."

I wadded Jack's jacket beneath his head. The floor was at least carpeted, though not exactly plush. I had no idea if it was the right thing to do, but I vaguely remembered reading somewhere to elevate his feet. Something about making the heart not have to work as hard.

I supposed at this point, nothing I did could make things much worse. I propped Jack's feet up on a nearby chair. He gave me a weak nod.

"It's not so bad," he whispered. "Don't worry about me."

"Move away from him," Brian said.

I rose to my feet. Anger bubbled up. "What's your move,

186

Brian?" I said. "You're out on bail. You didn't show up for your hearing this afternoon. That means there is a warrant being filed for your arrest as we speak. I have client appointments this afternoon. I never miss those. People are looking for Jack and you and me."

"I need time!" he shouted. I had him rattled. Brian started pacing again. On the next pass he made away from me, I pressed redial on Jack's phone. For half a second, I got hopeful the call would go through. Then it failed once more.

The time on Jack's phone read five thirty before the screen went dark again. I had fleeting thoughts of murdering deputy Bo and whoever else had checked that door. They never came back. It seemed as though no one would figure out we were in here anytime soon. Most of the courthouse staff would already be leaving for the day. Woodbridge County was small. Not much happened here. As far as I knew, they didn't staff the building with night security.

"Fine," I said to Brian. "Why don't you at least sit down? You're making me nervous."

Miraculously, Brian listened. He threw himself into the chair opposite me and met my stare.

"You didn't think much past bringing us here, did you?" I asked.

Brian didn't answer.

"Okay," I said. "So let me help you with that. You want me to believe you didn't kill Annie? Is that it? Okay. Fine. I believe you. Jack believes you too. Why would you go to this extreme unless you were telling the truth? Right, Jack?"

Coughing, Jack nodded.

"I loved her," Brian whispered.

"Okay," I said. "What did you love most about her?"

"She was so beautiful. And she believed in me. Nobody ever did that before."

"It was hard for you," I said. "Like you said, your father wasn't the favorite son. Not the smart one like his older brother. Right? Your Uncle Peter? So, all your cousins got a bigger piece of the family business. And you did most of the work. But it wasn't going to matter. Right? Unless you were Peter Liski's son, you were always going to be second class."

"You know my uncle?" he asked.

"I know a little," I said. "Annie told me. She was ... because I asked her about your business."

"Because you were getting to screw me over with alimony, is that it?" he snarled.

I jutted my chin out. "Screw you? No. But I was damn sure going to do my job. I'm good at it, Brian. That's why your brother-in-law recommended me to Annie. I never lose. Ask Jack."

Jack watched us through red-rimmed eyes. But he was still conscious. Thank God.

"Jack's never beaten me in court," I said.

"I know," Brian said.

"I'm the best there is, Brian."

He rested the gun on the table but kept his hand over it. It took great effort to keep my eyes on Brian and not on it.

"That's what I'm counting on," he said.

"What do you mean?"

"You have to show them. Dig for the truth. That's what you do. And I know who you are. What you've done."

"That's right," I said. "So you know where I came from. I mean, before I came back to Delphi. I worked in Chicago. For the Thorne Law Group. You've heard of them? One of my biggest clients was Killian Thorne."

Brian narrowed his eyes. The name held meaning for him. "I said I know exactly who you are. That's why you're here. That's why you're the one who's got to help me."

The trouble was, I didn't know enough about who Brian Liski was. We were just getting started when Annie turned up dead. But maybe I knew enough. He worked for the family business and Uncle Peter fit a profile I was more than familiar with.

A thought hit me straight in the chest, making my heart race. I ran with it.

"They hung you out," I said. "Is that it? When your cousins run into trouble, Peter takes care of it. That's why I've never seen their name in the papers. If they need it, Peter sends a hired gun from Miller Lafferty to clean it up. They're probably the top criminal defense firm in the state. But you? They gave you Dean Farnham."

Brian's lip twitched.

"He owes your family something. That's it, isn't it? He's working for free as a favor to Uncle Peter. Except he's in over his head and you've known that since day one. I sure have."

Brian slammed a fist against the table. "For once I need you to be as smart as you think you are."

"Oh," I said. "I'd say I'm doing all right. So, the family wants you out of the way. They send you a mediocre defense lawyer who's been bungling your case."

"What would you have done differently?" Brian asked. "I thought you said he was doing a good job."

Lord, it was an odd question. He'd backed off proclaiming his innocence.

I sat back in my chair. Jack's labored breathing filled the room. I chanced a look at him. He gave me the slightest nod to tell me he was doing okay. I knew it was a lie.

I decided to tell the truth.

"For you?" I said. "I'd have pushed for a plea deal. Second-degree murder. A crime of passion. You'd get twenty years, maybe less. But with a strong possibility you'd be out even sooner if you kept out of trouble. You're what, thirty-five? So, you'd be no more than fifty when you got paroled. You'd have a life. A path to start over. Am I wrong, Jack?"

Jack shook his head. "No. She's right. And ... I can still make that happen." He tried to sit up but the effort of it made him nearly pass out.

Brian got quiet. For a moment, I thought maybe I'd finally gotten through to him.

"Fifteen years," he whispered. "I'd never live that long."

"You would," Jack said. "I'd make sure of it. There are things I can do. I have some pull."

Slowly, Brian raised the gun and pointed it right at Jack.

"Stop!" I shouted.

Brian looked at me but kept the gun trained on Jack.

"I could just put you out of your misery. It hurts, doesn't it? My old man died of a heart attack. I was with him when it happened. He turned the same color as you. Gray. Almost green. Said it felt like a truck was sitting on his chest. He lived for a while in the hospital. He begged me to kill him. The pain was so bad. Do you feel like that now? It would take me less than a second. All gone."

"Stop it," I said. "You're not a killer. Remember?"

Smiling, Brian lowered the gun.

"What do you mean, you wouldn't live that long? Are you saying your family wouldn't arrange for your protection inside either?"

Brian's eyes held the answer. I'd hit on something.

"They set you up," I said. "Is that what you're trying to tell me? All of this?"

It seemed impossible to believe. But could it be true? Or was I just starting to lose my mind as well?

"I told you," he said. "I need you to be as smart as you think you are."

"Fine," I said, my anger rising. "Then I need you to be half as smart as *you* think you are. You want me to help you? I can't do it from in here. And if Jack dies on that floor, I'll be the first one lining up to help them charge you with another murder. If you're so worried about dying in prison, you're doing just about everything wrong, Brian. So, be smarter."

He popped up out of his chair so quickly, my breath left me. Sweat trickled down the center of my back. My stomach growled.

I stole a quick look at Jack's phone. My heart leaped as I saw one tiny bar. But the phone screen had locked again. I didn't know the code.

I turned to Jack and tried to transmit my thoughts to him with just my eyes. Shielding the phone with my body, I showed him the screen.

Jack's nostrils flared. He was too far away from me for him to unlock the phone with his finger. As I kept an eye on Brian at the door, Jack flashed four numbers with his fingers. Two. Four. One. Two.

Brian turned back toward me and sat down. I put the phone between my legs on the chair, ready to sit on it if need be.

"You have to prove I didn't do this," he said. "You have to make them understand I've been loyal."

"Then why don't you start telling me the truth," I said. "You're dancing around it. If you didn't kill Annie, I think you know who did. Was it one of your cousins? Someone your family has crossed?"

He hissed through his teeth. Then Brian rested his head on the table. "I'm not a rat. You know what happens to rats. I'm loyal. I got the message." He choked out the last sentence. Loyal. He'd said that over and over.

Great. So now Brian Liski had a moral code. I quickly

looked back at the phone. The bar was still there. This might be my one chance to dial 911 and give the cops a clue where we were.

My finger hovered over the screen. Just as I was about to dial, Jack's notifications came up. Several texts in quick succession. Mostly from his secretary Tricia, asking where he was. But the fourth one to pop up made my blood turn to ice.

"Jack. Call back. They found Farnham shot dead three blocks from the courthouse. We need you back here."

I looked up at Brian. His head was still on the table. My fingers trembling, I punched in 911. An eternity passed. Three little dots. The phone was still on silent from when Jack was in Colton's courtroom. But the second counter popped up. The call had gone through.

Chapter 30

I PRESSED the volume button down so Brian wouldn't hear the dispatcher answer. Then I put the phone on speaker. From his vantage point on the floor, Jack saw it all go down. He curled into a fetal position and began to cough uncontrollably. I was certain he was doing it to provide a bit of a distraction, but if anything, his color had gotten even worse.

"Shut up!" Brian shouted.

"Mr. LaForge needs help, Brian," I said, as loud as I dared. I kept the phone on the chair, trying not to muffle the speaker with my legs.

"You've kept us here at gunpoint for hours," I said. "No water. No food. What's the point of all of this? What do you want?"

"I want him to shut up!" Brian said, pressing his free hand to his head.

"Mr. LaForge needs medical attention," I said, praying the dispatcher could pick all of this up. Praying the call hadn't dropped again. I didn't dare shift my position to check.

"He's having chest pains. He's barely conscious."

"That's not my problem," Brian said.

"It is your problem. It became your problem the second you forced him down here against his will into this back room in the bowels of the courthouse. There's no way out of here except through that door. Do you want to go somewhere? I'll go with you. I won't fight you. I promise. You and I can walk out of here together, right now. Leave Jack here. Give him a chance, at least. You haven't eaten or slept or had anything to drink either. It's been hours."

I let my words tumble out. At first, I'd just wanted to relay as much detail about our situation as possible so the dispatcher could inform the police and a medical team for Jack. But now that I'd said it, the plan made sense.

"You don't need him," I said. "If Jack's going to do anything for you, he can't do it from right here. And he can't do it if he's dead. Take me anywhere you want. We can talk. I want to know everything there is to know about Brian Liski. I want to understand."

Brian turned on his heel. My idea was making him think. I stole a quick glance down at the phone. The counter showed two minutes and thirteen seconds. Thank God! We'd been connected. Had the dispatcher heard it all?

At a minimum, he or she would be able to see the number I'd called from. It would take all of about five minutes for them to determine it was Jack's phone. His office was already aware he was AWOL. It was enough. It would have to be enough.

Two seconds later, the call fail message came back up. I shoved the phone back under me. I could try later. With any luck, I wouldn't have to.

"You're lying," Brian said. "You don't care about what happens to me."

"I do," I said. "I care because in spite of it all, I know

Annie wouldn't want a bad end for you. She did love you. So if you didn't kill her, then tell me who did."

Then Brian Liski started to cry. It wasn't great, wracking sobs. No, it was slow, silent tears as he leaned against the door and fingered the trigger on the gun.

"I'm no rat," he whispered. "They'll kill me. I got the message. Tell them I got the message. You don't understand."

"So make me understand," I said. "You're afraid of your family. I get that. You *want* me to know what really happened. If you want me to figure it out, help me. Give me a clue."

Brian shook his head. He was hanging on by a thread. I wasn't sure how hard to push him, but time was running out for Jack.

"You need to believe me," he said, sobbing.

"You brought me here to tell me your story," I said. "So tell it."

The room fell silent. The words from Jack's text replayed in my head. Dean Farnham was dead. Shot outside the courthouse. And here I was, trapped in a room with the man who had to have killed him.

I was a fool to think I could get through to him. I just wasn't done trying.

"Brian," I said. Maybe the lack of food and water had finally driven me insane, but I rose from my chair. The seat was still shoved under the table. Brian wouldn't be able to see the phone even if he walked right next to it.

"Brian," I said. He crumpled against the door then slowly sank to his knees.

"Brian." I made my voice soft. "There's a way out of this. You have to know that."

He shook his head. "No. You can't bring Annie back. Nobody can."

"No, I can't."

He looked up at me. His whole posture shifted. He'd loosened his grip on the gun.

A thought crossed my mind. Could I disarm him? If I kicked him hard and fast enough, I could get the gun out of his hand.

And then what? No. That only worked in the movies. I wasn't strong enough to overtake him. He was a man. He outweighed me by at least seventy pounds. At least right now, I was on my own.

Slowly, I lowered myself to his level. We were just a few inches from each other.

"I just needed time," he whispered. "I told her that. A few months. A year at most. I was going to get us out from under it all. I just needed her to trust me a little bit longer. That was always her problem. She trusted the wrong people. She believed everyone but me. Now I can't even make them pay for what they did to her. I didn't kill her, but it's my fault. They took her from me."

"Make who pay? Brian? Tell me who you think killed Annie."

He went very still. I could see the wheels of his mind turning. He was desperate to tell me something.

"You might be the one," he said. "Did you know I told her that? Months ago. I said I knew who you are. Who you really are."

"What do you mean?" I asked.

He shifted, facing me full on but with his back to the door. I could feel his need to confess something. What? Was it about his uncles? Something his family was deep into that started to make trouble for him? Yes. I'd had run-ins with that type before. Only at the Thorne Law Group, my role had always been to protect the family businesses like the Liskis. Not the other way around.

"Your family," I said. "You've been trying to get out from under them, haven't you? And they started to suspect. Brian, did your family have Annie killed to punish you? Are they trying to frame you for it? They know, don't they? Whatever you're trying to do against them, they found out. It would be easy. With your history. She's on record with you threatening to kill her. They used it. Am I right? And they gave you an inexperienced defense lawyer."

Good grief. If I was right about all of that, why didn't Peter Liski just kill Brian outright if he were the weak link? The moment I thought it, I knew the answer. Because Brian was family. You don't kill family. Not directly, anyway.

Brian ran a hand over his face. "Brian, you said you know who I am. I know about families like the Liskis. I know you don't get out from under them. You know too much, don't you? You can tell me. If you ... if I were your lawyer, anything you tell me would be confidential."

He laughed.

"I'm not kidding," I said. "You could give me whatever money you have in your pocket. Consider this our initial consultation."

Brian paused. "It's not confidential if someone else is here." He gestured with his chin toward Jack. He'd gone so quiet, for a second, I'd almost forgotten he was there.

He'd gone so quiet ...

Heart racing, I scrambled to my feet and went back to Jack. Brian rose along with me and followed.

"Jack," I said, breathless. I checked for a pulse. At first, I didn't feel one. I ripped at Jack's shirt, popping off the first three buttons. His chest wasn't moving. I pressed my ear to it.

Slowly, faintly, I heard his heart beating. It didn't sound right though.

"Jack!" I tried to shake him awake. Nothing. His eyes rolled to the back of his head. His lips had gone grayish and dry.

"Brian," I said. "Enough of this. Jack's going to die. Not in a few hours or days. Right now. He needs to be in a hospital!"

"You said you could help me!" Brian shouted.

"There's no more time for that!" I said, matching the volume of his voice. I leaped to my feet.

"Dammit, Brian! No more games. No more stalling. You've backed yourself into a corner. I'm offering you the only way out there is. Take it. It's through that door."

There was a moment. Brian's face fell. For the first time in hours, I think the truth finally sank in for him.

But then, two things happened.

Jack's phone began to vibrate on the chair. The buzz echoed through the room without my body to muffle it. It tumbled right off the chair and onto the floor.

"You fucking bitch!" he yelled, then dove for the phone. He threw it against the wall.

"You have to answer it," I said. "It'll only get worse if you don't."

Instead, Brian turned, raised his gun, and fired once. I screamed as the shot thundered through the small room and obliterated the phone into chunks of metal.

I covered my ears and crawled next to Jack, covering him with my body.

"I wasn't going to hurt you!" Brian shouted. "You stupid, stupid bitch. I wasn't going to hurt you."

"You already have!" I shouted, my patience and common sense wearing thin.

"Here!" he yelled. Charging me, he threw a wadded-up

twenty-dollar bill at my face. "I'll take my initial consultation now."

I tried to compose myself. If I didn't keep my head, Jack would die. Brian had killed twice. I was a fool to think I could talk my way out of this.

"It's too late for that," I said. "If Jack dies, it's too late."

"You *will* help me!" Brian hissed. He got right in my face, grabbing me roughly by the jaw.

"How?" I said, defiant.

Brian stared straight at me. His pupils had narrowed to pinpoints. His breath reeked and his body odor grew pungent from hours of sweat. I supposed I didn't smell too great either by now.

He let go of me. "By being as smart as everyone thinks you are."

"Why do you keep saying that? What the hell does that even mean?"

Brian regained some of his composure. He went to the table and sat down. He checked the sights on his Glock and pointed it at me again.

Jack stirred. His eyes snapped open. He tried to sit up. I got my arms under his shoulders and helped roll him to the side just as he vomited all over the floor.

"Brian, please," I begged.

For the first time since he'd brought us down here, Brian looked concerned. Had he thought Jack had been faking it this whole time?

"They're coming," I said. "That phone call? It was probably the cops. First, they'll bring in a trained negotiator to try and talk to you. They've probably figured out where we are. If they hadn't, you just helped with your little temper tantrum." My ears were still ringing from the gunshot. I knew Brian's were too.

Still, I heard nothing outside that door. It had been easy to hear the two deputies before. Now it was just dead silence.

Brian went silent again.

"Jack," I whispered, cradling him on my lap. His skin felt so cold, but he was sweating. "Jack. Can you hear me? I need you to stay with me."

His eyelids fluttered, but he couldn't focus. Jack LaForge had gone to some dark place and it shook me to my core.

"Don't you dare," I said, my temper and panic rising. I did the only thing I could. I slapped Jack on the cheek.

He sputtered awake. "That's it!" I shouted. "You stay the hell away from whatever light you see. You hear me? Not yet!"

Fear spiked through me as thunder cracked against the door.

"Liski?" I didn't recognize the voice.

Brian rose to his feet. There was no panic in his eyes though.

"Is everyone okay in there? This is Andy Gunther. I'm with the Woodbridge County sheriff's office. Mr. Liski, we know you're in there. We want to help you, but you're going to have to let us know everyone is okay."

A beat passed. Then another. I squeezed my eyes shut as Brian Liski raised his gun and pointed it straight at the door.

Chapter 31

THE POUNDING on the door started up again. I jumped higher than when Brian fired his gun. "Mr. Liski?" Deputy Gunther said. I knew him. In his mid-forties, he had a calm, authoritative demeanor that made him perfect for negotiating.

"Mr. Liski, we know you're in there. I'm going to need you to let me know what's going on."

Brian pointed the gun at me. "Don't you dare," he whispered.

"Then you better dare," I whispered back. "If you don't start talking, they're going to blast their way in here and anything you hoped to have accomplished with this will be for nothing, Brian."

"Liski!" It was Eric's voice. I heard a scuffle outside and could guess at what was happening. Worried about me, Eric would be coming in hot. But this was the county courthouse. The sheriff's office had jurisdiction, not the Delphi P.D.

"I'm okay!" I shouted on instinct. Dumb, maybe. But I couldn't help feeling that if Brian Liski wanted to just shoot me, he would have done it already.

"Cass!" Eric yelled out.

"Not another word," Brian said. He changed the angle of the gun, but his eyes filled with fire. My throat ran dry. I recognized that look. It was one I knew in my heart Annie Liski had seen just before her husband brutally beat her. Was it also the last thing she saw before she died?

"Talk to them," I said, my heart pounding. "Do it now."

"I'm going to need you to leave," Brian said, shouting it loud enough for the cops to hear.

"We can't do that, Brian," Gunther said. "You have people in there we're pretty concerned about. We're concerned about you too. A lot has happened. That's got to be hard on you."

"I. Just. Need. You. To. Leave!" Brian shouted.

There was silence on the other side of the door. They would reassess. The biggest issue the police had was blindness. There were no windows in here. No security cameras. The only way out now was straight past them.

"Look, Brian," Gunther said. "Tell us who's in there with you."

"Don't pretend you don't already know."

"Fine," Gunther said. "We're worried about Mr. LaForge. Tell us what's wrong with him."

"You've heard enough," Brian said. He started pacing again, going faster with each pass.

"Let me talk to them," I said. "The longer you stay silent, the more on edge they're going to get. If they know I'm okay, they'll back off a little. It's your best play."

He didn't answer. So, he didn't stop me.

"Andy?" I called out. "This is Cass Leary."

"Cass?" Andy said. "There's a whole lot of people out here worried about you."

"I know," I said. "I'm okay. Brian hasn't laid a finger on me. It's Jack I'm worried about though. He's not doing so great."

"I didn't hurt him!" Brian shouted.

I clenched my teeth. It was in me to point out that he'd only just pistol-whipped a defenseless almost sixty-year-old man with a weak heart.

"What's wrong with Jack, Cass?" Andy said. "Talk to me."

"I think he's had a heart attack," I said.

There was more movement outside. No doubt they'd brought in medical support.

I went over to Jack. His eyes were still opened. He focused on me.

"I've got you," I whispered. "I'm going to try and get you some help. Hang in there."

Jack shook his head. "Too late, honey."

"Stop," I said. "You're not dead yet, LaForge. You're too stubborn for that, anyway."

He managed a smile and it lifted my own heart.

"Can you tell us what's going on, Cass?" Andy asked. "Tell us how Jack is."

I looked at Brian. He looked toward the ceiling. "Tell them."

"I'm here, Andy," I said.

"Can you talk to us, Jack?" Andy called out.

Jack tried to sit up. The effort of it made his eyes roll back.

"Shh," I said. "Just stay put. Andy? I'm with Jack. It's kind of hard for him to talk right now. But he's conscious."

"Okay, how's his color?"

"Not great," I said. "He's ... a kind of ashen." I looked closer. Jack licked his lips. They were cracked, dry, and had a bluish tinge.

I had to be careful what I said. As much as I needed the medical team to understand what was going on and maybe talk me through this, I knew instinctively that upsetting Jack wasn't going to help.

"His lips are a bit blue," I said.

There was silence on the other side of the door. I knew what it meant. Jack knew what it meant. Did Brian?

"Can you check his pulse rate for us?" Andy asked.

None of this mattered. I think Andy was just trying to keep me talking. To distract Brian as much as possible. Jack LaForge was dying. I knew the longer he went without medical attention, the worse his chances of surviving this.

I pressed two fingers beneath his chin and rooted around until I found his pulse. It was strong. But fast.

"Okay," I said. "I'll count the beats. You tell me when to stop. I don't have a timer."

"Will do," Andy said. He paused. I made sure I had a good feel for Jack's pulse.

"Start," Andy said.

Jack gripped my free hand. He kept his eyes locked with mine. I was in every sense of the word his lifeline right now.

"I've got you," I whispered. "I won't let go."

It seemed like an eternity passed. Finally, Andy called to me. "Stop."

I swallowed hard. Brian's eyes were fixed on me. So now he was concerned about Jack's status?

"What do we have, Cass?" Andy asked.

"One hundred and forty-eight," I said.

"Okay," Andy said, keeping his tone neutral.

"Brian?" he said. "Jack needs our help. I want you to let us give it to him. Okay? Is that something we can work out?"

Nothing from Brian. I didn't like his stillness. He kept his back to the door. Was it possible Andy understood how physically close he was to him at that moment? Just a few inches of steel separated them.

"Brian," I said. "Let Jack go. At least Jack. I'll stay here with you. We'll keep talking."

"It won't matter," he said. "Not for Annie."

"No," I agreed. "Not in the way you want. But I still believe Annie wouldn't want things to end like this for you. She'd want you to go on. Live your life. Find peace. You can still do that. And you can help bring her justice if you just tell me the truth."

"She wanted to have a baby," he said. "We were trying. Did she tell you that? Even this last month. We were waiting to test. Was she ... did you hear if they found out ...?"

"No," I said. "I don't know if she was pregnant, Brian."

"I want to know. I think I have a right to know."

I looked down at Jack. "Jack? Can you hear me? Did you hear what Brian asked?"

Jack's whole face reminded me of a fish out of water. His gaze was fixed. His cheeks puffed in and out as he struggled to keep breathing. He squeezed his eyes shut.

"I can find out for you," I said to Brian. "But what good does that do now?"

"Because I'd like to say a prayer for my son. If she was pregnant, I bet it was a boy. They run in my family. All my uncles, my father, my cousins. They all have sons. Firstborns, most of them."

"That's amazing," I said.

"Why couldn't she have just waited like I asked her to?" he said. His eyes filled with tears as he finally met my gaze. "I just needed a little more time, and everything would have worked out just like I promised her."

"What did you promise her, Brian?" I asked.

"Brian!" Andy cut in. "What can we do for you? What would make you feel comfortable? There isn't a soul out here who doesn't want to help you. But you gotta help us do that, okay?"

"Brian," I said. "He's right. We can keep talking. I'll stay here with you as long as you like. I'll stay with you out there too when you're ready to leave. But Jack can't. He needs help right now."

The single fluorescent light flickered above us. I was drenched in sweat. The room smelled of body odor and where Jack had gotten sick a while ago. A part of me wondered if this was what hell smelled like. If I let myself think too hard, panic began to blur the edges of my vision.

No. It was hunger. Lack of sleep. The press of my bladder. Those were all things I could shut out. I focused on Brian as Jack held my hand in a death grip.

"Brian," I said. "They'll come in here one way or another. Soon. They've been able to do it whenever they wanted. They have barricade rounds. Do you know what that does? They can melt that doorknob with them. You can't keep them away forever."

"They aren't going to risk your life," he said.

I snapped. "What the hell do you want from me?" I yelled. "If you wanted to kill me you would have done it by now. You keep saying you want me to be as smart as I think I am. Help me. What did you promise Annie? What is it you want us all to know about you? I'm listening. They're listening. But if Jack dies, if I die ... they won't. You'll just be the monster who murdered his wife and went out in a blaze of glory. Your family? Your cousins? Your uncle? They'll have won. They'll be able to paint any picture of you they want."

Brian vaulted to his feet. He snarled and raised the gun at me.

"Brian!" Andy pounded on the door. "What's going on?"

More movement, rushed footsteps outside. This thing was escalating. Now.

I raised my hand, slipping the one out of Jack's grip. He'd gone limp. Passed out.

"I'm better than they are," he said. "Smarter."

"So, prove it," I said. "You can start by letting Jack go."

"You don't see it!" he shouted. "Why don't you see it? I know you're not that dense."

"See what?"

He tore at his hair. Something shifted inside of him. His tears stopped flowing and he went silent. Andy Gunther pounded on the door.

"Okay, okay, okay," Brian said. "I'll tell you. I'll tell you. Make them go away and I'll tell you. Just you. Get him up," Brian said, waving the gun at Jack.

"He can't ..."

"Get him up!" Brian shouted.

I leaned down and slipped an arm around Jack's waist. "Can you stand?" I whispered. He grumbled and started to come around.

Brian came to us. Slipping his arm around Jack's other shoulder, he helped me get Jack to his feet. Jack tried to take a step, but his feet dragged on the ground. We got him to the front of the room. Brian let go and I eased Jack to the floor. Then Brian snaked his arm around me and pulled me to the back corner of the room into the shadows.

"Go," Brian said to Jack. "Get the hell out of here."

Jack was slumped against a file cabinet. He started to reach for the doorknob.

"Jack's coming out," Brian shouted. "The door is going to open, and you can grab him. You got that? But Cass stays. I've got a gun to her head."

He did. Brian Liski was using me as a human shield.

Moaning, Jack found the strength to lift his hand to the door-knob. I heard shouts outside as Andy's men got into position. He would have told them to fall back in case this was all a trap.

Sweat poured down my back. I couldn't breathe.

Jack disengaged the lock. Two arms came through the door and grabbed Jack LaForge. He disappeared as if he'd been taken by some unseen, tentacled monster.

"Don't come in here!" Brian said. "Not another step. I'll kill her. I swear to God."

"It's okay!" I shouted. "I'm okay. We're just going to talk. Don't hurt him. Don't hurt me."

"Brian!" Andy shouted. The door was open about four inches. A metal snake with a light on the end appeared. It was a camera.

"It's okay," I said to Brian. "It's going to be okay. We'll talk. I'll listen as long as you need me to."

"No," Brian said. "They'll keep coming. I can't breathe. I can't breathe! They'll keep coming! You can't save me. Nobody can! They'll keep coming!"

"Yes," I said. "So, let it be on your terms. Not theirs. Let me help you."

"You promise you'll listen?" he said.

"Yes!"

"I didn't kill her. I swear to God. I'm loyal. If this was a test, I passed it. You let them know."

"I'll make them believe," I said, though half of it made no sense.

"Swear it to God."

"I swear it," I said.

"Okay," Brian called out. "I'll send her out first."

"Okay, Brian," Andy said. "We're going to open this door very slowly. Let Cass go. Put your weapon down and raise your hands where I can see them. We won't hurt you. Nice and easy."

Brian gave me a shove forward. I stumbled. I put my hands in the air. It felt like my feet were encased in cement. The door was twenty feet away. Ten. Five.

It cracked open. Andy Gunther stood there in full protective gear. A helmet. A Kevlar vest. He reached for me. Behind him, at least a dozen members of the Woodbridge County SWAT team waited at the ready.

From the corner of my eye, I saw Brian Liski raise his hands.

Andy grabbed me hard, jerking me forward by the arm. I fell. Another set of arms encircled me and yanked me forward like a ragdoll.

I turned. Brian took a step forward. All around me, a cacophony of shouts rose, telling Brian to drop his weapon.

He didn't. He looked at me and shook his head. "They'll keep coming," he whispered. Then Brian raised his gun and pointed it straight at Andy Gunther's head.

"No!" I shouted. "They'll ..."

A split second. A scream. Mine. Then Brian Liski took the full force of about a dozen rounds from at least one twelve-gauge shotgun and two semi-automatic ARs.

It made him dance for a grotesque moment. Then he sank to the ground as if he were a marionette whose strings had been cut, all in a cloud of smoke and blood.

Chapter 32

ERIC CLIMBED in the back of the ambulance with me. Another one had just raced off with Jack inside of it. I could only pray there was still time left to help him.

I was numb. I was there, but ... not. A kind, soft-spoken EMT took my vitals. My blood pressure. My pulse. He shined a light in my eye and had me track it. Something about the bump on my head.

I didn't remember that. Eric said I'd landed hard against the wall when the SWAT guys pulled me out. I couldn't feel the fingers in my left hand.

I just felt ... nothing.

I heard the medical personnel radioing into the emergency room.

Caucasian female. Mid-thirties. Vitals good. Blood pressure, slightly elevated. Oriented to date and time.

We pulled into the ambulance bay and waited. Jack needed attention first. Of course. The heavy double doors opened in the back of the truck.

Chaos. Racing. Shouting. The young girl I'd seen helping intubate Jack now sat on the gurney with him, administering chest compressions. He'd crashed on the way here. It was bad. I said a prayer knowing it was all I had left to give.

"Cass," Eric said.

They lowered me out of the vehicle. Eric held my hand.

"I can walk," I said, trying to pull myself off the moving stretcher.

"You just stay put, ma'am," the EMT said. "We're going to take care of you."

"I'm fine," I said. "I've been through worse."

Eric said something to them in hushed tones. I didn't like being wheeled through the hallway. I wasn't sick. It was too much fuss.

They pulled me into an exam room with sliding doors. Eric pulled up a chair beside me. There were other emergencies. Far worse injuries. Sickness. Death. I just wanted them all to leave me alone.

"Your brothers and sister are on the way," Eric said.

"No," I said. "Don't. I don't want the bother."

Eric's face changed. Worry lines creased his brow. "Cass," he said. "We've been worried to death about you. I thought ..."

"I'm fine," I said. "Really. Nothing hurts."

"I think you might be in a little bit of shock," he said. "You need to let them check you out. Then I'll take you home."

"I'm fine!" I said, my temper flaring. It was odd. I didn't feel angry. But the moment the words came out, I felt the need to hit something. To hurt something.

Eric was there. I didn't know I needed it, but he pulled me against him. I started to shake uncontrollably. The moment that started, my shoulder screamed in pain. Feeling flooded back to my fingers. I wished it hadn't.

When Eric pulled away, I saw the blood on my sleeve. Little drops of it. My face felt sticky. The wash station beside me had a metal paper towel holder, shiny as a mirror. I looked at myself.

There was blood spattered all over my cheek. Calmly, Eric went to the sink and wet a towel. I sat still, feeling a bit like a child as he tenderly wiped Brian Liski's blood off my face.

Slowly, trembling, I started to come back into myself. Eric sat beside me as another detective came in and took my statement. It felt like there was so little to tell. And oddly, I felt embarrassed.

"I should have done something," I said. "I shouldn't have let him corner me like that."

"Cass," Eric said after the other detective left. "He had a gun. He caught you by surprise. And he'd planned everything out. This is my fault. I should have insisted on having someone by your side the whole time. Hell, I never should have left your side."

"Don't," I said. "Not now. Maybe never. I just want to go home. I want to take a shower."

A doctor came in after that. I barely remember what she asked me. I remember answering her questions. She tested my reflexes, probed my shoulder. They brought in a portable X-ray machine.

Nothing broken. A slight concussion if at all. Nothing ice and rest wouldn't cure.

My siblings showed up. I hugged Matty and Vangie. Vangie held back her tears but I saw the worry on her face.

"I'm fine," I said, finding the tone and the humor she was used to. "Things just got too boring around here, so I thought I'd mix things up. Just take care of the dogs for me. I probably won't get back to the house until dawn or later. I don't know."

Matty had no words. He just held me for a moment,

assuring himself I was there, and I was whole. Then I convinced Vangie to take him home.

Joe was another matter. He waited for the rest of them to clear out.

"Can I talk to my sister for a second," he said to Eric. "Alone?"

I saw the protest rise in Eric's expression. I put a soft hand on his shoulder. "Just a few minutes," I said. "Then come back. Find out what you can about Jack's status and come tell me."

Eric worked a muscle in his jaw but didn't argue. He gave a quick nod to my brother then disappeared out the glass doors.

"You sure you're okay?" Joe asked. "You look like hell."

"I'm okay," I said. "I mean, I think. I just spent the last six hours held at gunpoint, but I mean other than that."

Joe rolled his eyes. "You need to quit doing that."

"Noted," I said. "But will you do me a favor? I just ... I don't want a crowd at the house. Really. I just need some peace and quiet tomorrow. I'm not sick. I'm not broken."

Silence settled between us. My brother stared at me for a long, hard minute. Then his face split into a smile.

"Nice try," he said. "But you act like this is your first day in this family."

My mouth dropped open. I meant to argue with him. Instead, I couldn't help but laugh.

When my brother came to me, his arms open, I fell into them and let myself cry. But just a little. Joe kissed my head. The nurse came back in with my discharge papers.

"That was fast," I said.

A look passed between Joe and the nurse.

"What time is it?" I asked.

"It's just past six," she said.

"In the morning?" My heart raced.

"You were a little out of it when they brought you in," she said. "That's pretty normal considering the excitement you had. Glad to see you're feeling better. We've got your belongings in a bag out in the hall. Let me bring them in."

I didn't remember having any belongings. I'd left everything back at the courthouse. But she came in with a giant white plastic bag. In it, I saw the outlines of my battered messenger bag. She placed it on the bed beside me and quietly left the room.

I slid off the gurney and went to Eric. "I'm okay," I said.

"Don't," he said. My brother cleared his throat. I'd almost forgotten he was standing there. I shot him a look and he followed the nurse's cue.

"I'll be right outside," he said.

I touched Eric's face. "I'm okay."

"No," he said. "You're not. Cass, I was there. I saw what you looked like when they pulled you out. If they hadn't ... God. They pretty much had to sit on me to keep me from getting to you."

"I'm glad they did," I said. "You of all people know that team knows what they're doing."

"If they hadn't ... he was going to kill you."

"No," I said. "That's the thing. He wasn't. It's hard to explain. I know you're going to think I'm crazy, or that I have Stockholm Syndrome or something. But Brian trusted me. I told him I was going to help him, and he believed me. I think it's the whole reason he did all of this. It's just ... it didn't matter. Something changed in those last seconds. That was suicide by cop."

Eric frowned. "Trusted you to what?"

I didn't even want to say it. I knew exactly how Eric

would react and I was just too damn tired to argue. I also knew he'd never let it go.

"He trusted me to prove his innocence," I said.

Eric flinched like I'd slapped him. "What?"

"The whole time, all he cared about was convincing me he didn't kill Annie."

"Well," Eric said. "Let me save you the trouble. He was lying."

"I'm just telling you what he said," I said. "And what I promised him."

Eric shook his head. He picked up the bag on the end of the bed and took my bag out of it. He looped the strap over his shoulder.

"Come on," he said. "I think you've had enough for a while. Time to get you home."

"I can take that," I said reaching for the bag. The effort of it sent pain shooting through my shoulder. It was just some bad bruising, but Eric made his point. I wouldn't be carrying anything with it today. "I'll drive her home," Eric said to Joe as we walked out of the exam room.

"Wait," I said. "What about Jack?"

Eric turned to me. "He's up in surgery. He had a massive heart attack. They thought they lost him in the ambulance. His sister's married to a retired cop I know. They're up there with his wife right now. He promised to give me a call when Jack gets out surgery."

"Joe," I said. "Can you just go meet everyone at the house? I want to go up there. I want to sit and talk to Jack's wife for a minute."

"Cass," Eric and Joe said it in unison.

"Stop," I said. "Yeah, I'm tired as hell. And hungry. But I made some promises to Jack too. I just want his family to know ... I don't know ... it's just something I want to do."

"I've got this," Eric told Joe. For once, my brother didn't argue. Eric handed him my bag. I'd need a new phone. For the moment, I was glad mine was gone. I didn't want to talk to anyone else.

My brother took the bag and gave Eric a hard, decidedly male stare. Then Eric led me toward the elevators.

"Third floor," he said as I went to punch in a number.

"What about Dean Farnham?" I asked.

Eric sighed. "We're still trying to piece the timeline together."

"You're not on that?" I asked.

"Not lead," he said. "I'm a witness. I'm pretty sure you and I were the last to see him alive. Plus ... er ... everyone figured I'd want to stay pretty close to you."

"Thanks," I said. "I do appreciate it. I don't know why he killed him. As far as I know, Dean was the only other person who believed Brian was innocent of killing Annie."

The elevator stopped and we waited for the doors to open. Eric had a gentle hand at the small of my back as we stepped out.

"He never said why?" Eric asked.

"I don't know," I said. "I mean ... he said repeatedly he's not a murderer. He never once denied hurting Annie. Like he was fine with me thinking he beat his wife, but not fine with me thinking he murdered anyone. I never got a chance to ask him about Dean. I wasn't supposed to know. That was something that came through on Jack's phone before Liski knew I had it."

Eric froze. "Cass ... that was a really dangerous risk you took."

"And it's over," I said. "I'm okay. Remember? I just need to know that Jack is too. He was ... Eric, he was in tremendous pain. For hours. I've never seen anyone so brave. The thing with the phone? How did I possibly have a choice? I needed you to know where we were."

Eric stood with his fists curled. "Dammit, I'm so sorry. I should have waited for you. I tried to get back in there after Liski pulled that damn fire alarm. It took a bit to figure out that's what happened. They were supposed to sweep every floor!"

I hesitated. I hadn't yet mentioned the part about the two deputies who came to the door early on. If Eric found out now, I couldn't trust that his response would be rational. Heck, I wasn't sure mine would be. For now, it was enough to just see that Jack was okay.

"Later," I said. Sensing my train of thought, Eric nodded and the two of us made our way to the cardiac waiting room.

I'd only met Liza LaForge a few times. She was a pretty, plump woman who made the most amazing pastries and sent them to the courthouse staff every holiday. She and Jack never had any kids. Liza sat on a couch in the waiting room chewing her nails. Beside her sat a woman who had to be Jack's sister. She had the same thick, white hair and straight nose.

"Cass?" Liza said. She leaped to her feet when she saw me.

"Oh, don't get up," I said. But Liza LaForge lunged for me. She pulled me into a bear hug that nearly choked the life out of me.

She sobbed against my good shoulder.

"Jack was worried," she said. "That's the last thing he said before they took him in for surgery. We told him you were okay. That they got you out. But he kept forgetting. He was really out of it. Thank you for staying with him. You kept him alive. I know it."

"I didn't do anything," I said. "Do you know anything?"

"Not yet." Another man appeared bearing a tray of coffee

in Styrofoam cups. He seemed to know Eric, so he had to be Jack's brother-in-law. Plus, he had that cop look about him. "He's been in for a few hours. The doctor said they'd come out when it was all done."

No sooner had he said it when they did. A doctor in scrubs followed by an intern and a third woman who I instantly recognized. It made my blood run cold. She was the hospital social worker. A bereavement specialist. The grim expression on the surgeon's face told me everything I needed to know.

Liza LaForge collapsed against me as she heard the words that would change her life forever. They would change mine too.

"We're so sorry, Mrs. LaForge."

Chapter 33

Jack LaForge and Brian Liski were buried on the same day, an oddly chilly Saturday in late July that felt far more like fall. After a sweltering summer the year before, Delphi was now smashing records for cool temperatures. Michigan can be like that. I could even see the first hint of changing colors on some of the trees across the lake.

A hundred people lined Jack's graveside service. Four times that number had attended mass at Saint Cecelia's this morning. The lieutenant governor, a man who'd gone to law school with him, delivered a touching eulogy. He told an old one L joke that made me wince. If you don't know who the class jerk is by week three, it's you. The lieutenant governor claimed he was the one who didn't know, and Jack had clued him in. Jack had graduated first in his class at U. of M. Law School. I never knew that. And he'd served twenty-five years as a reservist in the National Guard. That I knew. He was given full military honors.

Now, Liza LaForge sobbed as she hugged the folded American flag that had draped her husband's coffin. I sobbed plenty myself.

The entire Woodbridge County bar had shown up in full force for Jack LaForge. His loss would be felt by all of us for years to come.

"They don't make them like Jack anymore," a hoarse voice came from behind me. I turned to face Judge Kent Tucker. It was the first time I'd seen him since Brian's shooting. He looked as if he'd aged twenty years. I felt like I had.

He pulled me into a light embrace. I kept my body stiff. It was too much. Too fast. If I let myself feel anything, I was afraid I'd fall apart.

"I'm so sorry," he said. "It's because of me this happened to you."

"Shh," I said. "It isn't."

"I'm sorry," he said. "And here I go trying to make you comfort me. I didn't mean for this to happen. Not any of this."

Of all the victims in this awful mess, somehow Kent Tucker seemed one of the saddest. Liza LaForge had her family around her. She had Jack's family. I had mine. Kent was all alone.

He straightened. Before I could offer him any more words of comfort, he gave me a sad smile and walked down the hill to his car.

"This wasn't your fault," Joe whispered beside me. I knew it, but I still felt guilty. I was the only one who made it out of that room alive.

As we headed back to our cars, I let him hold my hand. I don't think we'd done that since we were kids. But it was good to have him here today. Though I'd left the hospital a week ago, he hadn't yet left the house. I wanted to think he stayed out of mere concern for me. But, as each day passed, I was beginning to think there was something deeper going on between him and my sister-in-law Katie.

"I know," I said, leaning on the driver's side door of my Jeep.

"No," he said. "I know you. You don't. You think if you'd been more convincing or smarter, quicker. I don't know. You think you could have gotten Jack out of that room faster than you did."

I smiled. I touched my brother's cheek. "Yeah. Well, you don't know everything."

"Neither do you," he said, reaching around me to open my car door. It had been my idea to drive separately. I hoped Joe wouldn't offer to follow me home. If he knew my plan, he'd fight me.

"I'll see you back at the house?" he asked. Ah. So, he *was* concerned about my plan. Two could play at that game.

"Isn't it about time you checked in on your own?"

Joe smiled. Checkmate.

"If you're nice to me," he said. "I'll make some of Grandma Leary's potato soup. Emma wanted to know if she could come over. She's got a new boyfriend and wants to go water skiing."

I laughed. "Well, it's a good sign if she's bringing him over to meet the both of us. Though they'll freeze their butts off."

"They're teenagers," he said. "They won't care. We never did."

Joe was right. We never passed up a chance for water sports at Grandma and Grandpa Leary's, even if our lips were blue. The image of that stopped me short. I saw Jack LaForge's lips as I held him in my lap. I squeezed my eyes shut and tried to force it from my mind for now.

"Fine," I said to my brother. "I'll see you back there. I've got a few things I need to take care of today."

I held my breath, waiting for Joe to interrogate me. He didn't. He just smiled at me, then pulled me into a hug. I forced back a fresh round of tears as I pulled away and got behind the wheel.

No one eulogized Brian Liski like they had Jack LaForge. He didn't even have a church service, as far as I knew. I only knew this thing was happening today after a phone call to Amelia Trainor's office. His body had been released to the family for burial in a small cemetery outside of Taylor.

After an hour drive and a few wrong turns, I arrived at the cemetery and even then wondered if I'd come to the wrong place. As I walked through the gate, a young man approached.

"Are you with the Liski family?" he asked.

"I ... what? Um ... no. I'm just ... an acquaintance."

He looked distressed. Wearing a black suit, I knew he had to be the undertaker. He spoke with a heavy Ukrainian accent.

"You're here for Branislav Liski?"

"I suppose I am," I said.

The man nodded. Man. He looked fresh out of college, rosy-cheeked with thinning blond hair. There were no rolling hills or streams through this cemetery like there were at Saint Cecelia's. This was a small church cemetery attached to a Ukrainian Orthodox congregation. Brian's plot wasn't hard to find. A small seating area had been set up, though every chair was empty.

"I'm from Koval's funeral home. I'm John Koval. You can call me John," he said. "We were told to start promptly at two." It was almost two thirty now.

I followed him to the back of the cemetery. Two other men from the funeral home stood back. They looked as uncomfortable as John.

"We thought there would be more," John said. He had two rows of ten chairs set up on green carpeting. He'd set up a tiny pulpit. Brian Liski's simple casket hovered over his open grave.

Not knowing what else to do, I took a seat.

"Should we start?" John asked.

I meant to answer that it wasn't up to me. Instead, my eyes fell on the headstone right beside Brian's grave.

It was Annie's.

"What?" I said, hyperventilating. "What's she doing here? I was told …"

"Oh," John said. "I don't … this was a marital plot. The headstone was purchased some time ago. I understand the wife passed away recently and was actually buried some-where else. I'm so sorry. The family didn't mention …"

"Who buys a headstone when they're in their thirties?" I asked.

"I don't … I'm sorry … this is the family's plot. That's why I thought …"

I looked around. Sure enough, I was surrounded by dead Liskis. It was the living Liskis who were strangely absent.

"It's close to three," John said. "I really do have to wrap things up. We have another service at four."

"By all means," I said.

John walked to the small lectern he'd set up. Clearing his throat, he began a generic service that sounded just Catholic enough to be familiar. Then he said a few prayers in Ukrain-ian. I made the sign of the cross.

"Would you perhaps like to say a few words?" he asked.

"Me?"

Just then, another car pulled in behind mine. I recognized it, but its driver didn't come out. Poor John kept staring at me with a pained expression.

"Right," I said, rising. I smoothed my skirt and walked to

the casket. I felt nothing. Not fear. Not sympathy. Not even anger. I folded my hands in front of me.

"May God have mercy on your soul," I said. It was the only thing I could think of. John answered my prayer, though I didn't understand his words. An affirmation, perhaps. I crossed myself one last time and got the hell away from there as fast as I could without running.

I didn't wave or acknowledge the other late-arriving mourner as I walked around the vehicle. I simply opened the passenger seat and slid inside.

Jeanie gave me a tight-lipped smile and kept her hands on the wheel.

"Coward," I teased. "You had to have seen I was the only one here. How did you know to come?"

She shrugged. "A little bird at the coroner's office told me. Plus, it didn't take much doing to figure out the Liski family pretty much owns this place."

"Yeah," I said. "Except, where are they? All I ever heard from Annie was how close they were. How big. It was all Brian talked about too. He orbited his uncles, his cousins. And not one of them shows?"

"Yeah," she said. "So why did you?"

"I don't know."

"Bullshit. I know how you get when your wheels start turning. They've been spinning so hard on this one, I swear I can see smoke coming out of your damn ears."

I laughed. It was in me to argue with her and deny it all, but I no longer saw the point. "I don't know why I came. That's the truth. It's just ... Jeanie, I've never hated anyone like I hate Brian Liski. For Annie. For Jack. For me. I thought maybe ..."

She smiled. "Forgiveness."

"It's not okay," I said. "What he did."

"And you're still Catholic enough to know that's not what forgiveness means, honey. It's about letting go and letting peace back into your own heart before the hate eats you alive. Did it work?"

I looked back at Brian Liski's grave. I wasn't sure at all. I felt numb and I felt sad. I supposed that was a start.

"Come on," she said, sighing. "I also know this isn't going to get any better for you … for the whole office … until you get it out of your system."

"Come on where?" I asked.

"Get in your car and follow me back to the office."

"It's Saturday," I smiled.

"Maybe so," she answered. "But a whole stack of discovery just got delivered. I figured you'd want to see it. I knew you'd be here. And I was curious enough myself."

"Discovery?" I asked.

"Yeah," she said. "The Liski divorce. All those financials you subpoenaed. Somebody forgot to tell the bank the case was closed."

Chapter 34

Two hours later, Jeanie and I sat in the conference room surrounded by stacks of bank statements and tax records. It was everything I'd promised to get for Annie over a month ago.

"So," Jeanie said. "Are you going to make me ask?"

"Ask what?" I said as I picked up the first stack. So far, nothing jumped out at me. Annie and Brian Liski had all the normal bills that married couples have. I'd known when I first met with her that a forensic accounting would be necessary as Brian worked for the family business. We assumed he'd try to hide assets and income to reduce or eliminate the amount he'd have to pay her.

Now I had an inventory of everything they owned. Every piece of furniture in the house. The cars. Annie's income from the salon. And a picture emerged about all the debt they owed. The outlines of it took the shape of two people living far outside their means. The house was in Brian's name with his mother as joint owner, not Annie. I never had the chance to sort all of that out. It had been on my to-do list for Kent

Tucker. Now it looked like I might not have to. There was nothing in Annie's name.

Jeanie came around the table and stood beside me. She crossed her arms in front of herself.

"What?" I asked again.

"You don't think he did it, do you?" she said. "You don't think he killed Annie."

No one had come straight out and asked me that since the day Brian died. They'd tiptoed around me. Now that Jeanie was sure I wouldn't break, she gave it to me with both barrels.

I let out a breath. "I don't know," I said. "That's the truth. I think he probably did it. It's just ..."

"Just what?" Jeanie said, lowering herself into the chair beside me.

"He went to an awful lot of trouble to try and convince me he was innocent. And he wanted something from me. It wasn't revenge. It wasn't to hurt me. He said repeatedly he just wanted me to be as smart and good a lawyer as everybody thinks I am. He wanted me to know he was loyal. He said that multiple times too. Near the end, he said he was going to tell me the truth. He'd wanted me to figure it out for him though. He was worried about someone thinking he was a rat. Jeanie, he seemed to care more about that than people thinking he was a murderer. There was something going on with his family. If that wasn't clear before, it sure was today. Not even his mother showed up to bury him. And he told me he'd promised Annie he was going to get them out from under it. Those were the words he used. He was plotting something. I know it. But maybe it wasn't Annie's murder."

"You think it was them?" Jeanie asked. She started pawing through some of the records. "We both know the rumors about that family. They are connected to some shady stuff.

Ukrainian mob ties. You think what happened to Annie was part of that?"

"Maybe," I said. "Or maybe someone just wanted it to look like Brian killed his wife. As a way to get him out of the way. I asked him that. He didn't admit it, but he didn't deny it. I think … I think Brian believed his family killed her. Or at least he wanted me to believe that's what he thought. If we'd just had a little more time. If Brian's locked up for murder, he can't really cause problems for the family business, right?"

Jeanie furrowed her brow. "Maybe. But don't go down that road. If you'd spent more time in that room with him, you might be dead too, Cass. Forget about Liski's family. They aren't your problem."

"They sure weren't trying to help Brian," I said. "That's another thing I asked Brian and he didn't deny it. Dean Farnham wasn't qualified to represent him. And Dean was scared of something. The Liski family wasn't bending over backward to provide Brian with the right kind of legal help, that's for sure."

"So why did Brian kill Farnham then?" Jeanie asked. "Whether he was good at it or not, Dean was the one person actively trying to help Brian. And I gotta be honest. He wasn't totally horrible at it. He drew some blood with Eric at that prelim, Cass."

I threw up my hands, baffled.

"Come on," she said. "It's getting late. Joe made me promise to get you home for dinner. Potato soup. I'm crashing."

"Joe? How the hell did he know I was with you?"

It dawned on me then why my brother didn't push me on where I was going after Jack's funeral. He already knew. He tagged Jeanie to follow me instead.

She smiled and it was as good as an admission. I waved in surrender. "Fine," I said. "I don't have the energy to fight the both of you."

Chapter 35

"ANYTHING?" Miranda asked.

For the second day in a row, Jeanie and I were elbow deep in Brian and Annie Liski's financial records.

Miranda was antsy. She had a right to be. The Liskis weren't exactly paying clients.

"There's something," I said. Jeanie sat with her chin resting on her hand. Her job had been to reconstruct Annie's salon business. She was underwater on it, spending far more on overhead than she brought in.

"Whatcha got?" Jeanie asked.

"Well, they did a lot of online shopping. Every week."

"Why is that unusual?" Miranda asked. She picked up one of the statements I'd been looking over. "Somebody had a vinyl record collection, huh? Terrible taste though. Led Zeppelin. Highly overrated."

Jeanie and I exchanged a look. Miranda was dead serious.

"It's not that," I said. "It's that starting about a year ago, most of their purchases were made using gift cards. And he ... or she ... is refilling the balance on these things starting about six months ago. Every Monday. Only I can't find the funding source for any of it. And I can't find a record of any of the purchases for all that jewelry and clothing I saw in her bedroom."

"He's probably getting under-the-table payments from the pawn shop," Jeanie said. "And maybe he's skimming off the top, giving Annie diamonds other people pawned. Maybe even stealing from his cousins. Especially if he didn't think they were paying him fairly."

"I think that was one of his main beefs," I said. "His father started the business with his brother. But his cousins and uncle were all partners. After his dad died, they started trying to freeze him out. It doesn't look like his father, Jan, had a formal partnership with his brother."

"Hmm," Jeanie said. "Well, Annie made twenty grand last year. It was dropping off this year. And she was spending it as fast as she made it."

"Except for these gift card balances," I said. "It's just odd. And like I said, they start about a year ago and I'm not seeing a corresponding withdrawal from the checking account. They're buying a ton of stuff online and paying for it with these cards. Only where's the money to buy those coming from?"

"Always five hundred a week?" Miranda asked.

"Almost always," I said. "Over the last six weeks, before Annie died, it goes up to six hundred. Then there's one for seven hundred and fifty. The last one is a thousand."

"You think he was putting the squeeze on his cousins?" Jeanie asked.

"Well, it would be consistent with what Brian kept saying. And he kept saying something about having a plan to get out from under all of it."

"What do you think?" Miranda said. "Blackmail?"

"Yeah," I said. "So, Brian knows about whatever shady

crap his cousins are into. They'd been in trouble for receiving stolen goods before. Or it wouldn't be a stretch for the shop to be engaged in some sort of money laundering enterprise. Maybe Brian doesn't like how he's being treated. He threatens to go public with it or make trouble for the family if they don't cut him in."

"The family isn't going to take too kindly to that," Jeanie said. "But they throw Brian a little extra sugar every week just to get him to shut up. But it's not enough. He wants more and more. Then he starts causing problems, drawing attention because he's taking it all out on Annie."

"She pushes him to his breaking point," Miranda says. "Brian snaps. Kills Annie, expects the family to take care of it for him like they do every time old Uncle Peter, or the cousins run afoul of the law. Only they don't, because they see it as the perfect opportunity to rid themselves of Brian once and for all."

"Right," I said. "But they have to be careful because Brian might try to use what he knows about the family to cut a deal with the cops."

"So, they do like they've always been doing," Jeanie said. "Throw him a bone. Or make him think they're throwing him a bone in paying for Dean Farnham to represent him. Only Dean's not qualified to really do him any good."

"Brian figures it out," Miranda said. "Offs Dean. Then completely snaps and figures he's going to take matters into his own hand by forcing Jack LaForge to drop the charges by pulling that stunt at the courthouse. You just happened to get caught in the middle of it. Or not, but he's angry enough with you anyway because of Annie."

"It's just ... Brian kept saying over and over again that he wasn't a rat. It was a point of honor with him. He wanted me to get the message that he was loyal. He even said something about making sure I told them he passed the test. He said that right before he died."

"He was crazy, Cass," Miranda said.

I tapped my pen against the table. It made a certain degree of sense. I couldn't say it, but I'd seen similar scenarios play out on a much larger scale when I worked for the Thorne Law Group. I was never directly involved with anything illegal but wasn't naive.

"You gonna bring all of this to Eric?" Jeanie asked. "Or your contact at the FBI? What's his name? The cute one with the blond crew cut. Gunn?"

I smiled. "Cannon. Lee Cannon. And I don't know. Not yet. I need to sit with it for a little bit longer. I still don't know exactly what it was Brian had over his cousins."

Jeanie pushed herself away from the table. "It's not your job to know. Let Cannon handle it. You've sacrificed enough of your life and sanity to Brian Liski."

"I know," I said. "It's just ... Jack LaForge and Annie Liski sacrificed more. If their deaths could be the catalyst that brought the Liski family down? Well, maybe it wouldn't feel so pointless."

"But it was," Jeanie said. "Any death like that is pointless. They didn't deserve what happened. And I know neither one of them would want you to stick your neck out any further on this. We don't know how dangerous the Liski family is or how deep their connections go. Walk away from this one. Give what we have to Wray or Cannon or whoever, and let's get back to our own shit."

"Go on, you two," I said. "Quitting time." Miranda put her arm around Jeanie and the two of them scooted on out. It was getting late. I promised Joe I'd pick up some carry-out on the way home. Chinese sounded good.

I locked up and walked out to the parking lot. Jeanie

pulled out first, followed by Miranda in her cute little Volvo. I looked to my right, waiting for traffic to clear. As I edged out, a silver sedan crossed over into my lane but heading in the opposite direction. The driver, a blonde woman, looked straight at me and rolled down her window. She came so close, she blocked me from getting out.

I rolled down my window, ready to let my Irish out. Something made me stop.

She wore a pair of dark sunglasses. Slowly, she slid them down. "Brian Liski," she said. "He was ... is it true he is really dead?"

I froze, gripping the steering wheel. Her words were clipped. Fear lit her eyes. And her voice ... her accent matched John Koval's from the cemetery. Ukrainian, without a doubt.

Chapter 36

I scanned the street. At nearly eight in the evening, downtown Delphi was eerily quiet. There were only government buildings in the surrounding blocks. Everyone had gone home for the day long ago. My car and hers were the only traffic. She pulled closer so only two feet separated our windows at most.

"You were with him," she asked. She was alone in the car. She kept her hands on the wheel. If I had to, I could slam on my gas pedal. It'd take my mirror off at the very least, but I had the means to escape.

"I read it on the internet," she said. "You were with him? You're Cass Leary?"

"I am," I said. "And yes. I was there when it happened. He's dead. I watched it happen."

She considered my words, maybe translating them for herself. I saw her face go through changes. Some of the fear left it, but she wasn't at ease.

"Can I help you?" I asked. "Do you want to tell me who you are?"

She took a breath, then settled. "I am Tatiana," she

answered. The way she said it made me think she expected it to mean something to me. I considered whether I should pretend it did.

"Okay, Tatiana. Why don't you tell me what you want?"

She blinked rapidly as tears came to her eyes. This woman was scared to death. "I thought you would call me," she said. "I've been waiting."

"I'm sorry," I said, deciding on the truth. "I'm afraid I don't know who you are."

She narrowed her eyes in confusion. "I told you. I'm Tatiana."

"You knew Brian Liski," I said. I took a closer look at her. The woman was supermodel gorgeous. She had flawless pale skin and professionally applied hair and make-up. I could only see her from the waist up, but she had curves for days.

"You ... *worked* for Brian," I said. I didn't want to make assumptions, but she had a look about her. I'd seen the type. She might have been a working girl.

She looked straight ahead. "I thought ... she said she would tell you about me. She said you could help."

"She?"

Tatiana's eyes snapped to mine. "She said you were her lawyer and that you could help someone like me."

My heart jumped into my throat. "Annie? Are you talking about Annie Liski? Did you know her? Did you talk to her?"

My mind raced, trying to make a connection. "Tatiana," I said. "She didn't tell me your name. She didn't know it. But you called her, didn't you? You were Brian's mistress."

Her face fell. I thought I'd hit on it, but she looked disappointed.

"He hurt you," I said. "Brian hurt you like he hurt Annie. Is that it? Is that what she told you I could help you with? I can."

She shook her head. "You don't know anything. This was a mistake. Please forget I even came."

"No!" I shouted. "No. Please. Tell me. When did you speak to Annie?"

This made no sense. Annie never said anything about meeting or talking to this woman. My heart went hollow. Was it possible Annie never had the chance?

"Tatiana," I said, my voice growing sterner. "When did you speak to Annie Liski?"

"I'm sorry," she said, putting her car in gear. "It's not safe for me here. I gave her proof. I thought ..."

"Who are you afraid of?" I asked. "Brian can't hurt you anymore. Is it his family? Do you know something? You gave her proof of what? You mean to use in her divorce? I *can* help you. Please, come inside with me. I can get you in touch with ..."

She shook her head. "No," she said. "I have to go. I'm sorry. I thought you knew. You don't. I can't trust you."

She looked over her right shoulder for traffic. As she turned, the light hit her neck. It was so faint, if I hadn't been looking straight at her, I would have missed it.

But there was no mistake. Tatiana had bruising around her neck. Faded, but recent, maybe a few weeks old. Three lines on either side of her throat. Just like the ones the medical examiner found on Annie Liski's body.

I yelled to her to stop, but Tatiana's tires squealed as she pulled away from me and sped down the street, disappearing around the corner.

Chapter 37

I CALLED my brother to tell him I wasn't coming home anytime soon. Eric agreed to meet me at his office.

"You're sighing before I even walk in the door?" I said as we met each other in the hallway. He unlocked his office door and ushered me in.

"Don't," I said, putting a hand up to cut off what I knew he was going to say. "Don't tell me you know my look."

He gave me about a quarter of a smile then sat behind his desk. "Well," he said. "I do. Sit down. What are you planning on driving me nuts with tonight? You know how hard it's gonna be for me to get overtime approved?"

"Well," I said. "You may know my look. But the problem is, I always know what you're going to say. So, hear me out before you rip my head off."

"Cass."

"No," I said, lifting a finger to silence him. "You first. Swear it. No judgment until you let me get this all out."

"You can't control what I think," he said.

"Well, no. No, I can't. Just what you say. And maybe that eye roll thing you do. And also, your smirk."

This got the first genuine laugh out of him I'd heard in a while. He reached across the desk and took my hand in his. "Maybe if you'd stop giving me reasons to smirk. And roll my eyes."

It got hard to think straight when he touched me like that. With everything that had been going on with the Liski case, and Jack's funeral, I realized it had been weeks since Eric and I had been alone. I was about to burst with the news I had to share.

"You haven't promised me yet," I said.

Eric lifted his hands in surrender. "Okay, I promise not to roll my eyes."

I pointed at him. "Or smirk."

He crossed his arms in front of himself. "Christ. What? What was so urgent it couldn't wait until tomorrow morning?"

"Brian Liski," I said. "There's more to the story. I had an unexpected visitor tonight while leaving my office."

He frowned. I took a breath, then told him everything that happened with the mysterious Tatiana. I put a piece of paper on his desk. I couldn't make out all of Tatiana's license plate, but I hoped what I *did* have was enough.

"You should have called 911," he said. "Dammit. I'm sending a crew to sit outside your house and your office, Cass."

"You don't need to. Brian's dead. He can't hurt me anymore. But this girl? She's still scared of something. You have to try and find her," I said. "She knows something about Annie. I think she might have even been the last one to see her alive. She said Annie promised her I could help her. She'd been beaten, Eric. Just like Annie. I think Brian was abusing her too."

"That's a lot of assumptions," he said.

"Eric, something just doesn't sit right with me about all of this. Brian was desperate that I figure it all out. It really mattered to him that I believed he was innocent in Annie's murder. What if he was telling the truth?"

He looked at me, then broke one of his promises. He rolled his eyes. "Cass ..."

"Eric, I think ... no. I know. You have to reopen Annie's case. Something doesn't add up. I just ... I know in my heart Brian was telling the truth. He didn't kill Annie and we owe it to her to find out who did."

He dropped his fist to the table. "Cass, I want you to take some time off. Maybe talk to someone. You've been through hell. Not just this last time. I mean, come on."

"I don't need a shrink," I said. "I need a promise. From you. That you'll take another look at Annie's case."

I reached back into my bag and pulled out the financial records Jeanie and I had secured. I organized them with colored tabs. I put them on Eric's desk.

"I think Brian was blackmailing someone. It's all right here. See for yourself. I think if you can figure out who it was, it'll lead you to the truth about what really happened."

He squeezed the bridge of his nose.

Eric turned his attention to the files I'd given him. He thumbed through some of the records then looked up at me. "Cass, I know you've heard of Occam's Razor."

"Right," I said. "The simplest solution is usually the correct one. Yeah. I know. But there's also Leary intuition. And face it, I'm usually right. Eric, listen. This woman, Tatiana. I need you to look at Annie's phone records again. Annie told me at that last meeting that she'd suspected maybe Brian had a girlfriend. She said the woman had called her. I don't know if any of that is connected to Tatiana. But you have to look into this. I'm serious. What if she *was* the last person to see Annie alive? I mean that very day! Tatiana seemed shocked that I didn't know who she was. She said something about giving Annie proof. Proof of what? And I know in my bones that Annie wouldn't have kept their meeting a secret from me. I think she was murdered before she could tell me. What if that meeting was the reason why? You have to reopen her case."

"You're not going to let this go," he said.

I crossed my arms and stared at him. I expected another lecture, but something hard came into Eric's eyes. My heart went cold.

"What?" he asked.

"You already have been," I said.

"Cass."

"No," I said. "I know *your* look. What's going on? What happened?"

Eric let out a resigned sigh. "Fine," he said. "I was going to call you tonight and tell you anyway. It'll probably hit the news by morning."

"What?"

He ran a hand through his hair. "Dean Farnham."

"What about him?"

"Liski didn't shoot him."

"What?" My heart started to race.

"Ballistics came back. The bullet they found in Farnham's body didn't match Liski's gun. And he didn't have time to do it in any event. Farnham left the courthouse alive. We got him on two security cameras leaving the parking lot right when Liski would have been busy pulling that alarm and muscling you out of that bathroom. It wasn't him."

"Son of a ..."

"Exactly," Eric finished for me.

"I'm right," I said. "I told you. I'm right."

Then Eric broke his third promise. He smirked.

Chapter 38

EVERYONE KNOWS EVERYONE. It's one of the best things about living in a small town. It's also one of the worst. But Sunday night, four days after my meeting with Eric, I got a call from a friend of a friend of a neighbor at two o'clock in the morning. There was trouble at Brian and Annie Liski's former house.

No one bothered to call the police yet. It hadn't gotten that bad, but the reason for my phone call was standing with his fists curled at the back gate looking ready to throw the first punch.

"Kent!" I called out. It felt odd to call him that, but I didn't see the point in broadcasting his status all the way down the street in case there was at least one person who didn't already know who he was.

Judge Tucker squared off with an older couple. The man had a ready stance just like Kent's. The woman was shorter, rounder, and wore her dyed jet-black hair in a giant pile on top of her head. She was yelling something to the man in what was most certainly Ukrainian.

"Kent," I said, racing to his side. "What's going on here?"

It was at that point I saw the opened boxes strewn all over the side yard.

"He's trespassing," the man said. As I met his eyes, a shiver of terror went through me. Though older, with deeper lines in his face and less hair, he was the spitting image of his nephew Brian.

"Mr. Liski," I said. "Let's calm down, shall we? Let me talk to the judge for a moment."

I grabbed Kent by the sleeve and led him a few feet away. He was snarling, nostrils flared; he reminded me of a rabid dog.

"They're stealing everything."

"There's nothing to steal!" the woman said. "This was my son's home. It is my home."

"Please," I said to her. "Just give me a minute."

"We've put up with enough," she said. "Lies. Insults. Slander."

"Those are my sister's things!" Kent yelled.

"Shhh," I said. "Keep your voice down." But the spectacle had already drawn somewhat of a crowd.

On one side of the driveway, it appeared the Liskis had rented one of those large trash yarders. I couldn't see all the way over the top, but it appeared they'd already hurled a few boxes inside of it.

"They're the ones trespassing," Kent said.

I took a measured breath. "Well, technically, she owns the house. I've seen the deed."

"They don't own my sister! They have no right to throw her things away."

"We got a call," Peter Liski said. "One of the neighbors said this man was trying to break in!"

"Why do you even care?" I muttered and looked straight at Brian Liski's mother. "You didn't even bother to come to your own son's funeral. But now you want to protect his things."

The moment I said it, a new sense of urgency went through me. There was something in that house perhaps the Liskis didn't want us to see.

"Cass," Kent said. "You have to do something!"

Before I could answer, a police car pulled slowly into the driveway behind us. I supposed it was a small blessing they hadn't come in blaring lights and sirens.

I recognized the officer, a young kid who graduated with my sister, Vangie. Dillon Beach.

"Hey, Dillon," I said. "You wait here and don't say a word," I warned Kent.

Dillon looked about as miserable as I felt. No doubt he'd already been tipped off Judge Tucker was in the center of this little domestic squabble.

"Cass," he said. "I need to talk to the judge. We've had a report ..."

"I know," I said, putting up a hand. "I'll get him to leave. I just need a second."

Mrs. Liski charged forward. "He's a burglar. A thief. My son was living here. We own the property."

Poor Dillon looked to me for guidance. I had the distinct feeling he'd drawn some sort of short straw on the dispatch of this.

"The property is listed as owned by Mila Liski," he said.

"Yes," I said. "But there's some dispute about some of the personal effects inside."

Dillon shook his head. "Cass, I'm sorry but this is a civil matter."

"I know," I said.

"You have any paperwork?" he asked. "Showing who's got authority to act for the estate?"

"Not yet," I said. "Things have been ... um ... complicated since Annie Liski's death."

"Murder!" Kent shouted.

"Liar!" Mila Liski shouted back. I saw some lights flashing at a house across the street. Great, they were probably live streaming as we spoke.

"Kent," I turned to him. "I want you to get in your car." I looked at Dillon. He shrugged.

I poked a finger at Kent. "Whether you like it or not, the Liskis have a right to be here. You don't. Just give me some time and I'll figure out a way to sort this out."

"I just want my sister's things," he said. "Her clothes. Pictures. I don't know. I have nothing left, Cass."

Dillon gestured toward me. I gave Kent a sharp look and walked over to Officer Beach, out of earshot of the others.

"I can't let him take anything, you know that. Not without a court order."

"I know," I said, then pointed to the giant dumpster. "But at the moment, the stuff is in danger of being thrown out."

"What are we talking about there?" Beach asked.

"These are her clothes," Peter Liski said, pointing to the discarded boxes. "We are donating them to a battered women's shelter."

"That's not your decision!" Kent shouted.

"They were left behind in my house!" Mila Liski yelled.

"Oh boy," Beach sighed.

"I'll tell you what," I said, turning to both the Liskis and poor Officer Beach. "What if I take custody of them? I'm an officer of the court. I'll open up an estate first thing in the morning."

Judge Tucker stuffed his hands in the pockets of his jeans. I decided to call that progress; at least he wasn't making any more fists.

"All right, fine," Officer Beach said. "If everyone agrees to it. But Judge, you can't come out here anymore. This isn't your property. I'm so sorry."

He was fuming, but not arguing.

"I'll take care of this," I told him. "I'll get things sorted out with the probate court."

"I just want to have something of hers," he said, his voice faltering.

"I know," I said. "And this is the best way to help ensure that you do."

Incredibly, the Liskis backed down. Mila Liski threw up her hands and went back into the house.

"I want to go in there," Kent said. "I don't know what else there is."

"Judge," Officer Beach said. "That's not happening without a court order."

He walked over to the boxes on the driveway and pulled back the lid.

"It's just clothes," he said. "A couple of photo albums."

He went to the dumpster and shined a flashlight in. "Broken furniture. Rotted food."

I stepped up beside him and peered down. He was right. There was a dresser, I recognized it from the spare bedroom. It was chipped and broken, the drawers all pulled out. But it was empty.

"Come on," Beach said. "You got room in your trunk for what's left?"

"Yes," I said.

"Give them to me!" Kent said.

"No can do, Your Honor," Beach said. "You let your lawyer take them or they're staying here until the court sorts this out."

Kent's face went through several shades of purple. He

looked at me, then the officer. Finally, his shoulders dropped, and he stepped back.

Five boxes. That's all there was. It squeezed my heart thinking about Annie. Beach and I put three of the boxes in my trunk, the other two in the back seat. I thanked Beach and thought he'd leave. Then I realized that wouldn't happen until Kent did. I walked over to him.

"Go home," I said. "I'll call you in the morning. I'll file paperwork and I'll try talking to the Liskis again. You'd be surprised how much the light of day and a neutral third party can accomplish."

"Neutral?" He let out a bitter laugh. "After everything that monster put you through, you're not neutral."

"You're right," I admitted. "But I still intend to act as Annie's advocate."

Kent Tucker hung his head. "I should have been her champion."

I touched his sleeve. "Go home. Get some sleep. Take some time off. I'll call you. I promise."

Defeated, Judge Tucker got in his car and drove away. I thanked Dillon Beach profusely.

"It's okay," he said. "We all feel terrible for the guy. And ... for you too. Those guys at the courthouse."

I gave him a weak smile. I knew he was talking about the courthouse deputies who'd failed to come to mine and Jack LaForge's aid sooner. They'd been put on administrative leave pending the outcome of a full investigation. But I knew they'd likely never work for the sheriff's office again. It was hard for me to feel sad about that. I couldn't shake the thought that if they'd been more thorough, Jack might have had a chance.

To his credit, Officer Beach wasn't about to let any more Liskis give me trouble on his watch. He waited in the driveway, hands on his hips, until I drove away.

Chapter 39

"THIS IS ALL THERE IS?" Miranda asked.

I'd just finished bringing the last of Annie Liski's personal belongings into the conference room. Later in the afternoon, I planned to head over to probate court to open her estate and have Kent appointed her personal representative. With Brian dead, and no other relatives, there would be no opposition. He was eager to take possession of whatever meager belongings his sister had left.

"Yes," I said. "The house. The cars. Brian and his mother owned everything."

"Do you think she knew?" Miranda asked. She'd opened one of the boxes and pulled out a Joan Jett tee shirt. My breath caught. I recognized it as the one Annie had been wearing when I met her at the salon that first day.

"I'm not really sure," I said. "I mean, she knew about the bank accounts. Brian was already living in that house when they got married. She made some of her own money at the salon, and there were all those gifts he bought her, so I don't think it was of great concern to her until Donna started threatening to end her booth rental."

"This is a one-day probate, Cass. Small estate," Miranda said. She walked to the last box.

"Except for that one," I said. Miranda pulled out the wooden jewelry box I'd seen on Annie's dresser. I winced, thinking of the necklace I'd chosen to bury her in.

She set it on the conference room table. "Her wedding and engagement rings are in here," she said. "She stopped wearing them?"

Miranda held up the simple gold band.

"I think it was mostly that she didn't wear them when she was working," I said. "At least, more that than a statement on the state of her marriage."

Miranda opened the three little drawers. I'd already had a look inside. The expensive bracelets and rings I'd seen in there a few weeks ago were gone. It was something I'd need to do discovery on once I got the estate opened. There were just a few costume pieces left. But likely, the jewelry I'd seen in that box never belonged to Annie in the first place. In any event, this wouldn't be a simple, small estate filing.

"Well," she said. "Her brother should have all of this. Someday ... I mean, he might have a wife. Or a daughter. It'll mean something to them."

"That was pretty much his point," I agreed.

"Those awful Liskis were just going to throw all of this away?"

"I don't know," I said. "There was a dumpster, but these boxes weren't in it. I think they already took anything she had of value. I think ... well, they're doing their best to try and erase Annie's existence from their minds."

"Their son's too, maybe," Miranda said. She started closing the little drawers. The third one gave her trouble. It wouldn't go in all the way. She gave it a shove, then tried to reposition the bracelets inside of it. Miranda's poor hands had become gnarled from arthritis after decades of using traditional typewriters.

"Here," I said. I took the box from her and gently pushed in the drawer. Something shifted inside. I pulled the drawer all the way out. A piece of metal dropped down.

"Cheap thing," Miranda said. "That's barely more than plywood. My grandmother used to have this great big jewelry box made of mahogany. She hid her cigarettes in it. Oh, but she had the most fantastic, colorful, gaudy costume jewelry ..."

I pulled out the piece of metal and held it in my palm. It wasn't part of the jewelry box at all. It was a flash drive.

"Miranda," I said. "Can you get Eric Wray on the phone?"

Miranda tilted her head. "I mean, sure ... why ..."

She saw what I did. I walked over to the end of the table and opened my laptop. Miranda went silent mid-sentence then walked into my adjoining office and picked up the phone.

I slipped the flash drive into my USB port. Ten seconds later, its directory popped up. There was only one thing on it, a .mp4 file. The title of it sucked the air right out of my lungs. *Tatiana*.

Her words echoed in my brain. Proof. She gave Annie proof. I knew. I just knew. Shaking, I hovered my finger over the touchpad for a moment, then pressed play.

It was grainy, dark footage. For a moment, I couldn't make out anything. Then a hand obstructed the camera and repositioned it.

Laughter. Grunting.

A face came into view. Blonde hair tossed over one shoulder. My throat ran dry. It was Tatiana.

"He's out on a search warrant," Miranda called out.

Keeping my eyes glued to the computer, I grabbed my cell phone and hit Eric's private number on speed dial. It went to voicemail. I hung up and called again.

Onscreen, Tatiana was fully naked. She lay on a bed in a hotel room. I could tell from the fire escape plan taped to the door. Eric could work with that. It would mean something. The camera was positioned on the floor, angled up. If I had to guess, it was placed inside a closet or something.

There was a man on top of Tatiana. Kissing her. Light-brown hair. Broad shoulders. I couldn't see his face.

His voice though.

I called Eric's number again. Voicemail. Again. I punched it a third time. Same. I tried a fourth.

Tatiana went up on all fours. She knew the camera was there. She stared straight into it. Then she moved to the side so the man's face behind her became visible. Proof. Oh God. *Proof!*

Miranda stood at my side now and covered her mouth.

"Is that?"

Judge Kent Tucker flipped Tatiana over. His face changed. My lungs burned. The air in them seemed to turn to ash as Tucker raised a hand and struck Tatiana hard enough that she flew off the bed.

My phone rang. I didn't even need to look at my caller ID to know it was Eric. I was breathless when I answered.

"Eric," I said. "I need you to come to my office. Right now. I have something you're going to want to see."

"Your ears must be burning," he said.

I couldn't answer. On screen, Tucker stuck Tatiana again. This time, she stopped crying. Tucker reached down and wrapped his hands around Tatiana's neck.

"What?" I said.

"I'm on my way," Eric answered. "There's something I need to tell you too. And Cass, you're never going to believe it."

Chapter 40

THE WHOLE BUILDING shook as Eric bounded up the stairs to the conference room. Miranda quietly excused herself and shut the door.

He was breathless, cheeks flushed. I stood with my hand covering my mouth while staring at my now dark laptop screen.

Eric's face fell. "What is it? Are you okay?"

I shook my head. My hand went from my mouth to my stomach. I wanted to throw up. He came to me. Concern flooding his face, he put his hands on my shoulder.

I took a step back and pointed at the laptop. I did my level best to make sense.

"Trouble at Annie and Brian Liski's house last night. His mother and uncle were trying to throw out all Annie's things. Judge Tucker showed up. I got ... I took ... it's here. It's all here."

I pointed to the boxes. Slowly, I sat down in a chair and gestured to Eric to join me. "Come here."

He did.

"We found this flash drive in her jewelry box. I mean ...

you searched through all of this, right? I was *there* for part of
it. Her necklace. You saw me take it out."

He nodded.

"Well," I said. "Your guys missed something."

I hit play on the screen again. I could only watch the first
few seconds. Eric's jaw dropped. I flinched as I heard Tatiana
scream, then go silent. That wasn't even the worst part. That
came later as Kent Tucker delivered the next blow to her
unconscious body and wrung her neck.

"Tucker," he whispered. "Son of a bitch. Do you recognize the woman?"

I nodded. "That's her. That's Tatiana. The woman I met
with."

Eric clenched his jaw. "That's what I came here to tell
you," he said. "You know we never found Annie's phone. We
of course subpoenaed her cell phone records."

"I know all of this," I said. "You pinged her phone at my
office. Then her house. Then it fell off the grid."

"Right," he said. He pulled out the crumpled piece of
paper I'd given him with the partial license plate. "About two
weeks before she went missing, there was an incoming call to
Annie's phone. We called it. It was just a travel agency. It
seemed meaningless. There were two other calls from it a
couple of weeks before that. It didn't really trip anyone's
radar. Then everything else that happened ... it just didn't
seem important. But that plate, Cass, we traced it. That car is
owned by the same travel agency. It's a front. It doesn't exist.
At least, there's no physical office."

"What is it?" I asked.

"Best guess," Eric said. "It's a front for the call girl service
Liski was probably running. We're scrambling to set up a sting
operation. I've worked on dozens of operations like this

before. Hopefully, we can track down your Tatiana again that way."

"It'll be too late," I said. "She'll already be in the wind."

"Maybe not," he said. "Cass, I'd bet my badge this girl has been looking for a way out. That's probably why she took a risk and reached out to Annie. I've seen this kind of thing before. Most of the time, these girls wind up dead. I'd bet money Brian is the one who made this tape. You said Liski kept saying he'd found a way out. That he just needed more time."

"Those payments," I said, following his line of thought. "All those gift cards. I assumed they were from his family. But what if they were from Kent Tucker?"

Eric smiled. "I just have to figure out how to prove it."

I rose. My whole body tingled with fear and perhaps a little bit of excitement.

"Eric," I said. "I think I have an idea."

He slowly looked up. His face fell. "Shit," he said. "Cass."

I held up a finger. "Don't say it. The hell with my look. You're not gonna like it. I know. But I also know you won't have a better idea, and we're out of time. Tucker's made a point of going to that house at least twice while I was there. He's looking for something. He's trying to cover his tracks."

Eric ran a hard hand over his face and growled, sounding not too unlike a grizzly bear.

Chapter 41

I PULLED into Judge Tucker's driveway. The five boxes in the back of my Jeep were all that physically remained of Annie Liski.

I said a prayer for her as I waited for her brother to come out.

When he did, he was wearing a blue golf shirt and a pair of khaki shorts. Tanned. Athletic. The breeze lifted his hair and he smiled at me with that row of perfect, straight teeth.

"Thanks for meeting me out here," he said. "I just ... I didn't want to come to your office. It's so close, it might as well be part of the courthouse. I've drawn enough attention over the last few days."

"Right," I said. "I think you were smart to finally use some of your bereavement days. Clear your head. Things will look different in a few weeks."

I kept my smile as natural as I could. Cold sweat broke out along my spine and that could be a big problem. I couldn't keep Tatiana's bruised face out of my mind. Kent Tucker's smile had always been infectious, charming, charismatic. The District Court was only supposed to be a stepping stone.

"Come on inside," he said.

"Annie's things," I said, stepping back. "Nothing's very heavy."

"Oh," he said. "I'm so sorry. Lord. I should have sent someone to your office to pick them up. I didn't mean for you to haul all this here."

"It's fine," I said. "I really don't mind."

"Cass," he said. "Thank you for all you've done. I really mean that. These past few weeks ... and everything you did for Annie before ..."

I smiled. A tear came to my eye. "It wasn't enough though. Not from either of us."

Tucker walked up to the garage and punched in his code.

I picked up the first of Annie's boxes and set it down on a bare space along the wall. Tucker came in close behind me. I drew in a sharp breath and tried not to startle.

He put the second box next to mine. I turned back to get the third.

"Come on," he said. "It's a nice day. You have a few minutes to sit and talk? We can go out back if you'd prefer. I've got a pitcher of iced tea by the pool. I was actually just about to swim a few laps."

I smiled. "I'm more of a lake girl," I said.

Kent scrunched up his nose and shivered. "Never liked the lake," he said. "Don't like swimming where I can't see the bottom."

"To each his own," I said. I repositioned my purse over my shoulder. There was still some soreness there and I must have flinched. Tucker came in close and put a hand on my arm.

"You sure you're okay?" he asked.

"I'm fine," I said. The door at the back of the garage was open. Paving stones led to the deck in the backyard. I hesitated. His posture was easy, his smile light. I jumped off another cliff and followed him.

Kent Tucker had a luxury pool complete with a grotto and a small waterfall on one end. It was the kind you see on those designer pool building shows on HGTV.

"Wow," I said. "I guess you really are a pool guy."

True to his word, he had a small bistro table on one end of the pool shaded by an umbrella. A large pitcher of iced tea sat in the center on a tray surrounded by empty glasses.

I joined him at the table. He poured me a glass.

"What's next for you?" he asked.

"Same as always," I said.

"I heard a rumor you had a big settlement go through."

I nodded. "Mediation award. Michelle Stevens versus the Quickie Mart on M-50. Both parties accepted."

"Ah, the Quickie Mart case," he said. "Word's already gotten around. You know what I heard?"

"What's that?"

"Defense counsel is scared of you now. They're calling you a hero for standing up to my sister's killer. It got your name in the paper again and nobody wants to take their chances with you in front of a jury for a while. Congratulations."

"It came at the right time," I admitted. My office would end up with a nearly six-figure contingency fee. No more court appointments for a while. I made a solid job offer to Tori and she'd accepted.

"Good," he said. "So just don't take any more cases representing your family members and you won't have to worry about tarnishing your reputation again."

"Kent," I said, ignoring the joke. "I want to talk to you about Tatiana."

I didn't know a smooth way to say it. I decided on the drive over, abrupt would probably work best anyway.

"Tatiana," he said. "Who's that?" He sipped his iced tea and looked out at the pool. He had a small koi pond on the north end of it.

"Well," I said. "I'm assuming she wasn't your girlfriend."

He set his glass down. "Where did you hear that name?"

I ran a finger through the condensation on my glass. "Kent," I said. "I know you know who I am. Who I work for. The Thorne Group has an exceedingly long reach. And you know how close I am with Killian Thorne. It's come to their attention that certain business dealings they have with the Liskis may be in jeopardy. I've been led to believe you might be able to help clear some things up about that. Do you understand?"

I worried I wouldn't be able to hear him over my own heartbeat. I waited, praying he'd buy my bluff.

His smile faded. "Yes," he said. "What is it you want to know?"

I put my glass down and turned to him. "I thought that's why you came to me in the first place. You said you did your research. Kent, the Liski family is small-time compared to where I come from. Did you think I wouldn't ask around about you? About Brian?"

Kent Tucker's charming smile turned grotesque. He looked around, nervously. I said nothing. To Kent Tucker, it spoke volumes.

"I'm not looking to change anything," he said. "You tell the family that. You tell the Thornes that. Will they be taking over?"

I raised a brow. "It seems like you are trying to change things," I said. "You know I had occasion to go through Brian and Annie's financial records. There were a lot of interesting payments coming in. Two hundred a week. Then five hundred. A thousand. That came from you, didn't it? Tatiana told me as much."

He turned in his chair. "I don't have anything else I can give. It's over."

"Is it?"

"I've kept my mouth shut," he said. "I did everything Peter told me to. I told him. Brian was the problem, not me. If they would have helped me when I asked for it instead of leaving me twisting in the wind. He made promises. Big ones. It didn't stop though; Annie was never supposed to get hurt."

He slammed a fist on the table. My eyes went to it. It took me back to that day in my office after Annie went missing. He punched a hole in the wall. I'd bandaged both of his hands. Given him ice.

My mind flashed to Amelia Trainor's testimony. Annie had skin beneath her nails. They couldn't make a DNA match, but she theorized Annie had clawed at her attacker. Likely, she had scratched his hands as he squeezed them around her throat.

I never thought twice about the injuries on Kent Tucker's hands that day. He'd given me an explanation. I knew in my heart now they'd been covered in scratch marks before he even walked in my office.

Tatiana's throat. Her gasps. Those same hands.

"Your hands," I whispered, unable to contain it. Then I snapped out of it. "Brian was blackmailing you, threatening to leak those videos of you with Tatiana. It would have ruined your career. The family wouldn't have endorsed that. Did they offer to make it right?"

"Top-notch girls," Tucker said. It was almost as if he forgot I was there. "That's what they promised me. I wasn't hurting them. They were into it. That's what I was paying for."

Kent shook his finger at me. "I blame myself for one thing. I shouldn't have trusted that piece of shit. I should have trusted my instincts and gone straight to Peter when Brian started asking for more money. I waited too long."

"You should have," I said. "Why didn't you?"

"I didn't trust him," Tucker said. "And when I *did* go to them, they blew me off."

"Surely the family didn't endorse Brian's little side business," I said. "You have to know that's not how these things are supposed to work. It's too messy, Judge. That's why I'm here. You're right. You paid for the girls. That should have been enough. This is helpful. It's exactly what the Thornes need to know. If the Liskis can't be trusted to solve these problems, I doubt my clients will want to continue with them."

I kept my tone neutral. I just prayed he couldn't read any fear in my eyes. I needed him to keep talking.

"I gave them a reason to make Brian disappear," he said. "I set it up for them. Gift-wrapped it."

"Because Brian beat her," I said. My mind was like a movie on jerky fast forward. Brian knew his way around the courthouse too well. He took Jack and me to the one room that made it hardest for courthouse security to find. He hadn't fumbled around. And he'd gotten in the building with a weapon. It meant he'd known how to get in another way besides through the main doors and the metal detectors. I should have connected it sooner.

Did he bring Tatiana there sometimes? Was that part of Kent's fetish too?

"He deserved to die," Tucker said. "The family knew it. They gave me carte blanche. As if that was helpful. Cowards."

"Then why didn't you just do it?" I asked. "Why didn't you take care of Brian? You're saying the Liski family wanted *you* to kill him?"

He had to say the words.

"Peter said he wouldn't stand in my way. Brian was *their* problem. He wasn't supposed to be mine. Promises were made. Tatiana was vetted."

Oh God. "You think she consented to having you beat her within an inch of her life?"

"She's a professional," he said. "You tell them. You tell Peter. This is his mess to clean up. Not mine."

"But you tried to clean it up anyway."

"It was never enough," Kent said, making a sharp gesture with his hand. "Brian wanted more and more."

My mind raced. Brian told Annie he had a plan to get out from under the family.

"Brian went rogue," I said. It was a statement and a question. If the Liski family were running a high-end human trafficking service, blackmailing a client on the side would have been bad for business. No wonder they were trying to cut Brian off. He was a problem. A liability.

Kent's words echoed through me.

"I was part of your plan?" I said. "Make Annie take him to court? Establish a record of what he did to her? Is that it? Were you going to kill him or were you expecting Annie to do it? Make it look like self-defense?"

"He deserved it," Kent said. "He was a monster."

"Right," I said.

"She was in on it with Brian the whole time," he said. "Tatiana. She made that tape without my consent. You make sure they know that. She isn't to be trusted. They need to take care of her. Annie never had to know. There was no reason for that. But even then, I took care of it. I protected the family. They owe *me* now."

Kent choked back a sob.

"How did you take care of it, Kent?" I asked. I started to sweat.

"Everything can go back to the way it was now," he said. "I did it. Okay? I've proven I can be trusted. You tell them that. It'll be better if the Thornes take control. If they protect me, I'll give them anything they want. I'll help them. Tell them."

He looked down at his hands.

"They'll need to know exactly what you did," I said.

"I killed her!" Kent shrieked. "Are you happy? She didn't understand. Tatiana got stupid. Brian got greedy. Annie didn't understand. She would have ruined everything. I couldn't make her understand. I know her. She wouldn't have kept quiet."

"What did she say, Kent?" I asked.

"Brian couldn't control Tatiana. That bitch went to my sister! I tried to explain. What I had with Tatiana wasn't like what Brian did to Annie. Tatiana knew what she was getting into. We were adults. She was getting paid. She was no victim. She went to the house! Tatiana didn't think I saw her. If I'd gotten there just a few minutes later, I wouldn't have seen her leave. But I did. She went in there and told Annie a bunch of lies."

"June tenth," I said. "Tell me what happened. Maybe I can make the family understand."

Kent let out a hard breath. He squeezed his glass in his hand. "She came over for dinner the night before and we talked. She wanted to get some things and she knew she wasn't supposed to go to her house alone. She said she had a meeting with you the next morning but could I meet her at the house on my lunch hour afterward. I did."

"What happened when you got to the house?"

"She didn't think I saw her," he said. "Tatiana. I saw her pulling out of the driveway when I turned down the street. If I'd have gotten there just a little bit sooner, Annie never would have had a chance to talk to Tatiana. She wouldn't have heard all of those lies about me. It was none of her business. I'm her brother. Her only family. I was there for her. The Liskis weren't. They thought she was trash. I warned her. But she was willing to turn me in because she didn't understand. And I couldn't trust Brian to handle it at that point. The family couldn't either. So I did."

"You tried to explain it to her," I said. "You tried to make Annie understand that this thing with Tatiana wasn't what she thought it was."

"Yes," he said. "But she didn't believe me. She said she had proof. She said she wasn't going to let anyone else get hurt like she was. Tatiana showed her one of the tapes. I said I'd turn myself in. I asked her if she'd go with me. She said she would."

If I closed my eyes, I could see it play out. Annie would have been horrified when she saw that tape. She confronted her brother. She tried to do what she thought was right, protect another woman from harm. He lured her away from the house to her death.

"But you killed her instead," I whispered.

"Yes!" he shouted. "I took care of it. And I told you. I practically gift-wrapped it all for the family. Brian was going to go down for it. He deserved it. He was the one who was supposed to die. Not Annie. If only she would have listened to me. It didn't matter. After that, she would have been dead anyway. As soon as the family knew her plans, they would have come after her. You know that. You know the Thornes would have done the same thing. I made it quick."

He buried his face in his hands. It was enough. It had to be enough.

Sweat poured down my back now. I felt the tape loosen from my skin. I got to my feet.

"It's time for me to go," I said.

"You'll tell them?" he asked. "You'll tell the Thornes I'm a team player. I'll do whatever they need me to do. Because I'm not gonna go down for this."

He looked up at me, pleading. Then a shot zinged through the fake palm trees lining the side of the pool. It took him in the shoulder.

Kent jerked backward. I froze for an instant then followed the orders shouted at me from all directions.

"Get down! Get down! Shots fired!"

Eric and at least a dozen members of the Delphi P.D. SWAT team poured through the gate, guns drawn.

Chapter 42

I sat in the back of the SWAT van sipping from a water bottle. It was eighty degrees out, but someone had put a blanket around my shoulders. It just didn't occur to me to shrug it off.

The ambulance had carted Judge Kent Tucker away over an hour ago. The crime scene unit had descended on his house. I watched as bagged items were carried out and placed inside another van parked in the street.

Eric barked orders to the various crews. In another life, he would have made an effective war general. Finally, after answering about the hundredth question from junior members of the Delphi P.D., he came to me.

"I'm fine," I smiled, answering the question on his mind.

"I'm sorry," he said. "That was never supposed to get that close." Carefully, he helped me lift my shirt and liberate me from the sticky tape and wires I'd been wearing. He deposited the microphone into a baggie and handed it off to another officer. Eric had been positioned in a surveillance van one block over listening to every word Kent Tucker and I uttered.

"You figure out who fired that shot?"

Eric raised a brow. "Not here," he said. Shrugging in the direction of his car, I got up and followed. He deposited me in the front seat and buckled me in. I let him. Then he began the slow drive back to my place on Finn Lake.

The lake was quiet. A purple-and-red sunset blazed across the horizon. I held my breath for a moment as Eric pulled up the winding drive. With the new house built upon a slight hill, it gave me far more privacy than the old place connected to the main road. Now, nobody had any business coming up that drive unless they were coming straight to my house.

"I can't stay long," he said. "Tucker's coming out of surgery already. I want to be there when he wakes up."

We walked into the kitchen. My two dogs, Marbury and Madison, jumped and yelped, more excited to see Eric than me for the moment. He was one of their favorites; mine too.

Eric leaned down to pet them.

"Hurry," I said. "Marby will pee."

I scooped him up and opened the sliding glass door to the deck. I set him down gently and Madison, his mother, ran out after him. We watched as the two dogs scampered down the steps and chased a squirrel out in the yard.

I turned to Eric. "What can you tell me?"

"The last call I took was from the Feds," he said. "They're going to meet me at the hospital. That's why I want to get there first. My guys grabbed a suspect coming out the other end of the neighborhood. We've got a positive ID. This isn't for public consumption yet, none of this is, but he's our shooter."

"The Feds know him," I said. My knees felt a little wobbly so I sat down at the kitchen table. Eric went to the fridge and poured me a glass of wine. I wanted him to join me, but he was still on duty.

"Yeah," he said. "They know him. A hitman connected to one of the Ukrainian mob syndicates working out of Detroit. He's on their wanted list."

"Their hitman was sitting on Tucker's place too?" I asked.

Eric shook his head. "That's about the size of it. Judge Tucker hadn't even made it on Feds radar yet."

"Well, that'll all change," I said. "You heard Tucker. The Liskis have been running a high-end prostitution ring. Tucker's a client. Brian brought him to them. But Brian started getting angry because he was never going to move up in the family. He was always going to be the least favorite cousin. That's mostly what he told me."

"Right," Eric said. "So Brian decides to work an angle for himself."

"He starts blackmailing Tucker and gets Tatiana in on it for a cut."

Eric went over to the slider and let the dogs back in.

"What Tucker said to me," I said. "He got sick of paying and tried to go over Brian's head back to the family."

"Bad for business," Eric agreed.

"He tried to use me," I said. "If he'll keep talking, I think you're going to find out that the family told Tucker to do whatever he had to to handle Brian. They weren't going to off a member of their own family, but they weren't going to stand in the way of someone else doing it. So, he was going to make it look like self-defense."

Eric reached down to pet Madison. "We'll have to wait and see what else he says. But that's what I think too. He kills Brian and makes it look like either Annie did it in self-defense or he did it in defense of her. Christ, after what happened at your office, I would have been a suspect too."

"Poor, poor Annie," I said. "Tatiana wanted out because it was getting too dangerous. I know it. I don't think she went to

Annie because she wanted more money. I think she was looking for help."

"I've busted guys like Tucker before," Eric said. "First it's the sex. But that's not enough. They want to inflict pain. They like the danger and coming so close to the edge. Tatiana is lucky. If it had gone on much longer, he would have killed her."

I swallowed hard. "Instead, he killed Annie to keep her from exposing him. She had no idea what she was walking into. She didn't know her own brother was an even worse monster than her husband. Both of them. God. Eric. She was brutalized by them both."

I covered my face with my hands. If only I'd pieced it all together sooner.

Eric came to me. "You were more than her lawyer, Cass. You were her friend. You listened to her. You believed her. And you tried to help. None of this is on you."

He drew me into his arms. I felt safe there but even that made me feel guilty. I knew in my heart that Annie Liski never had someone like Eric in her life. Every man she'd tried to trust, who should have protected her, had only hurt her until it finally cost her her life.

I cried. For the first time since Annie Liski died, I finally gave myself permission to cry.

Chapter 43

Two weeks later, Judge Kent Tucker went to prison. I got the news while sitting next to Eric in a conference room at the Delphi Public Safety Building. Across from him sat Special Agent Lee Cannon. Somebody higher up at the Bureau decided he was the perfect person to break the news to me.

"Manslaughter," Eric said. He'd gone completely purple. "He'll be out in ten years, Cannon. Less. He strangled the life out of that woman. Not to mention what he did to that call girl, Tatiana. You've seen the video?"

"Detective," Lee said. "You know there's a limit to what I can loop you in on. I'm only here as a courtesy to ... well, to Cass."

Fire shot from Eric's eyes. I put a hand on his leg under the table.

"What can you tell us?" I said.

Cannon had a folder in front of him. He slid it across the table. I opened it. It was sparse. Just the outlines of Judge Kent Tucker's plea deal. He'd pled guilty to voluntary manslaughter. He would serve his time in a maximum-security state prison. In exchange, he was spilling everything he knew about the Liski family.

"What's he giving you?" Eric asked.

"He's cooperated fully," Lee said.

"I'll bet he has," I muttered.

"Cass," he said. "This is bigger than Annie Liski. And I don't say that lightly. Tatiana Zavod was one of the lucky ones. We believe there have been at least a dozen women who weren't so lucky. Who ended up like Annie."

"At Kent Tucker's hands?" Eric said, rising from the table.

Lee grimaced. "No. But this ring the Liskis ran? These women were brought over from Ukraine and trafficked to very wealthy men with Kent Tucker's brand of proclivities. Some didn't survive. Tucker led us to Tatiana. In his own twisted way, he probably saved her life. You were right, she was trying to get out. She's in WITSEC now. We're going to take care of her. And that doesn't leave this room."

"Can you tell me what she said about Annie?" I asked.

Lee leaned back. "Your theory was correct. Brian Liski made her certain promises. He convinced her he had more power in the family organization than he did. But he was only using her to blackmail Tucker. What he planned to do from there is only a guess."

"Brian made promises to Tatiana too," I said. "I think she was foolish enough to believe he was her way out."

Lee nodded.

"And what about poor Dean Farnham?" I asked.

Lee squirmed in his chair. He was holding something back. Eric leaned forward. "Farnham reached out to someone," he said. "What do you know?"

"I'll tell you what I can," Lee said. "Don't feel too sorry for Dean Farnham. This also doesn't leave this room, but Farnham was also one of the Liskis' clients. Let's just say he had some similar tastes as Kent Tucker. We found more tapes. Tatiana provided them a few hours ago."

Eric sat slowly back down. "Christ. Farnham was trying to cut a deal for himself. He was talking to you guys."

Lee nodded. "I think Farnham knew how much trouble he was about to be in."

"Why the hell didn't you warn Cass?" Eric shouted. "If you knew how deep the Liskis were connected, you should have communicated with us. Jack LaForge is dead because of it. Cass could have ..."

"Eric," I said. "Please." But I leveled a hard stare at Lee Cannon. I had the exact same questions.

"I'm hearing all of this pretty much the same time you are," Lee said. "You honestly think I or anyone from the Bureau would have put you in unnecessary danger? Farnham went to another agent. He said he had information on the Liski family. But it didn't go far."

"So, who killed Farnham?" I asked.

Eric cleared his throat. "He was killed with a bullet from the same gun we lifted off the guy who shot at Tucker. The family took him out. They knew he had started talking to the Feds."

I shuddered thinking how close I'd come to being next.

"You should have communicated with us," Eric said. "The minute Cass asked you to look into the Liskis and told you why, I should have known about it. Farnham's been dead for weeks. If you had information that he was mixed up in all of this, your office should have coordinated with mine. You *knew* we had an open murder investigation."

"And what?" Lee said. "Last time I checked, you were the one who sent Cass into Tucker's house wired! And I don't answer to you. This was all in its early stages. We didn't know about the prostitution ring. We didn't know any of this was connected to Annie Liski's murder or your judge. It wasn't my case. It wasn't my field office. I swear to God I didn't know. *We* didn't know."

"That's a piss poor excuse."

The two men squared off across the table.

"Enough!" I shouted.

Eric's jaw jumped. He gave me a hard look but settled back into his seat.

"That's all I can tell you," Cannon said. "And if you think Kent Tucker's time is going to go easy ... the word is out. Things will be done to try and protect him, but ..."

"But he's a former judge," Eric said. "And it'll take all of three seconds for word to get out that he ratted on the Liski family."

"Exactly," Lee said. He rose and grabbed his briefcase. When he came around the table, Eric didn't extend his hand to shake Lee's. Eric's behavior wasn't warranted, and I think even Eric knew it.

I'd had enough of their posturing, so I was the one who opened the door and walked out with Lee. I stopped just short of the elevator.

"I appreciate you telling us what you could," I said.

Lee shook his head. "You just can't stay out of trouble, no matter what." His face softened and I knew he meant it as a joke. Partially, anyway.

"Neither can you," I said. "But I need you to level with me. Do I have anything to worry about?"

Lee's face hardened again. He was handsome in a blond surfer kind of way. "From the Liskis? No. They've got bigger issues right now and you're not the one giving evidence against them. Plus, it doesn't hurt that you know ... certain people."

He was referring to my past association with the Thorne

Law Group. As dangerous as the Liski family was, the Thornes were bigger. It's why I'd used it as leverage against Tucker. If it got back to the Thornes that I'd used them, even as a bluff, things could get complicated for me again.

"Can I at least count on the fact you'll give me a heads up if you hear ..."

"Cass," he said, putting a hand on my arm. "Yes. If the wind changes even slightly ... you're my first call. But it wouldn't hurt if you'd just do what you said you came here for. Stick to drunk driving cases. Parking tickets. I don't know ... maybe teach tort law at the community college."

I smiled. I felt Eric's presence behind me. Lee's eyes darted over my shoulder, then he looked back at me with new recognition.

Awkwardly clearing his throat, Lee pressed the down button on the elevator. "See you around," he said. "If there's anything else I can share, I'll be in touch."

Eric didn't answer, but I could feel his muscles relax behind me as Lee got in the elevator and the doors closed.

"I don't like him," Eric said.

"No kidding," I said. "Let it go. It's time to get back to work. I'll meet you later if you behave yourself."

"Six o'clock?" he asked.

"Make it seven," I said. "I've got one last appointment. Then head over to my place. I'll even cook."

I expected Eric to underscore his dislike of Lee Cannon. He didn't. Instead, he put his arm around me and kissed my cheek, making me blush.

We were in public. In the busy hallway of the Public Safety Building. And Eric Wray had left me speechless.

Chapter 44

I PLANNED FOR A QUIET DINNER, Just me, Eric, the dogs, and the lake. But it was Friday, in early August, and eighty-five degrees at sunset.

When I pulled up, I saw my brother Matty at the end of the dock with a pole in the water. Madison sat at his feet, her ears flopping down around her face as she stared in the water. She liked the silver flashes the minnows made as they swam in the shallower water.

Ten minutes later, my older brother Joe pulled in with my niece Emma in tow. She had the new boyfriend with her. He was nice. Tall and lanky, a high school basketball player. One of the stars of the team. His name was Cole and he was polite but called me ma'am. I tried to forgive him.

"You mind if we take the WaveRunners out, Aunt Cass?" Emma asked.

"Keys are on the hook," I said. "You know the rules."

Emma waved. "Gas tanks stay full," she answered.

Joe came up to me, brushing the hair out of his eyes. "You need a trim?" I said.

"Vangie's on her way," he said. "She can do it."

285

"Oh," I said. "You don't trust me?"

He smiled. "I wouldn't even let you trim the dogs, Cass. Stick with lawyering."

I sighed. Joe took the grocery bag out of my arms and peered inside of it. He wrinkled his nose.

"That's barely enough to feed Matty. Lucky for you I already ordered the pizza. It'll be here any minute."

Whistling, he let himself into the house and started putting my groceries away. It was only two steaks, some asparagus, a bottle of wine and enough vegetables to make a salad. You'd think that would have clued him in I'd made other plans. But boundaries weren't our strong suit in the Leary family.

Sure enough, my sister Vangie pulled in and parked behind my Jeep. My eight-year-old niece Jessa tumbled out and wrapped her arms around my legs.

"Hey, peanut," I said. "Emma's here. If you hurry and get your life jacket, she'll take you out on the WaveRunner!"

"Yay!" Jessa squealed and ran down the hill.

"Find Joe," I told my sister and made a scissor gesture with my fingers. "He's looking scruffy."

Vangie shook her head. "Would it kill him to pay for a proper barber?"

She headed for the house and yelled down to her daughter, reminding her about the life jackets. And just like that, my house became controlled, but very loud chaos.

I pulled out my phone to warn Eric before he got here. I didn't get a chance to punch in his number before my phone rang with a number I didn't recognize. It showed up as coming from Lansing.

I walked around to the back patio before I answered. From there, I watched Emma help Jessa with her life jacket and deposit her on the WaveRunner seat in front of her.

Cole had taken the second one just past the dock and waited.

"Hello?" I answered the phone.

"Ms. Leary?" a female voice asked.

"This is she."

"Oh good. I was hoping I could catch you. I called your office, but you'd already left. My name is Jane Witherspoon. I work in Governor Finch's office."

I sank slowly into one of the Adirondack chairs. "Okay?"

"Listen, I know this is out of the blue, but we'd like to arrange a meeting with you. Early next week? Can you clear your schedule and come to Lansing?"

"To meet with the governor?" I asked.

"Yes. And to meet with her staff," Ms. Witherspoon said.

"Can I ask what this is about?"

Silence. "My goodness. I'm so sorry. We sent an email this morning. I assumed you received it."

I pulled the phone away from my face and tapped my email app. Sure enough, there it was; I'd never opened it.

"It's been a busy day," I said. "I'm afraid I'm behind on a few things."

"Of course," Jane said. "I'll cut to it then. Ms. Leary, of course you're aware that there's a vacancy on the Woodbridge County District Court bench."

I shook my head to clear it. A vacancy?

"Yes," I said, trying to keep the sarcasm out of my voice. "I'm aware Judge Tucker is no longer serving."

"Of course. Well, your name came up. You're on a very short list of people the governor is considering for a special appointment to that seat."

"Excuse me?"

"Ms. Leary? Are you there?" she asked.

"I'm here."

Another car pulled into the driveway. I turned my head. Eric got out. His jaw dropped, then he smiled as he saw all the activity at the house. He caught my eye and shrugged. It warmed my heart. He was becoming one of us with all our glorious lack of boundaries.

"I'm sorry," I said. I put a finger up to Eric to temporarily silence him. "Can you say that again?"

"Well, we're hoping you'll consider submitting to the formal nomination process. I can't make you any promises of course, there is vetting protocol, but we think you'd make an excellent judge."

I shook my head. It felt like I had loose marbles rattling inside of it.

"Can I ask you who submitted my name?"

I could almost hear Jane Witherspoon's cagey smile through the phone. "We can discuss that in person. Are you interested?"

My brother Matty used a four-letter word that carried across the lake. Marbury had just pounced for minnows and scared the bigger fish away. I had no idea if Jane Witherspoon from the governor's office heard any of it.

"I think I can clear my schedule," I said. "It's certainly worth a meeting."

"Wonderful," Jane said. "Shall I communicate with your office manager then?"

"Yes," I said. Miranda was going to lose her damn mind. "That would be ideal."

"Fantastic. Enjoy your weekend. Governor Finch is looking forward to meeting you."

I swallowed past the lump in my throat and said goodbye. Eric made it to me as soon as I clicked off the call. He slid his arms around my waist and pulled me against him.

"You want to tell me who that was?" he asked. "Your face is all white."

I opened my mouth to answer. Cole and Emma made a circle near my shoreline and waved. Jessa's delighted squeal filled the air. Marbury ran up and down the beach barking. He was especially protective of Jessa.

"Full house, I see," he said.

"I'm sorry," I said. "I meant to warn you ..."

Eric kissed my cheek. "I don't think I mind. Though I was hoping to get you all to myself."

I blushed. There was an implication in Eric's words. A bridge we had yet to cross for so many reasons. But for now, I felt safe in his arms and with my family all around us.

Even so, I wasn't prepared for the next words he whispered against my ear. "I love you," he said. "Now, are you going to tell me about that phone call?"

Those three words thundered through me along with everything that went along with them. He loved me. He *loved* me. It was even odds whether my head or my heart would explode first.

"Cass?" he asked as he gave me that easy, charming smile. "Seriously, who was that?"

I touched his cheek and smiled back at him. "Later," I said as yet another car pulled up behind us and the dogs started their frenzied barking all over again. "Come on. The pizza's here."

Up Next for Cass Leary...

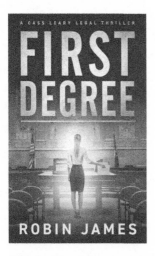

Cass's latest murder case hits far too close to home. Don't miss it! Click the book cover for more information or head to robinjamesbooks.com

Click for More Info

Newsletter Sign Up

Sign up to get notified about Robin James's latest book releases, discounts, and author news. You'll also get *Crown of Thorne* an exclusive FREE bonus prologue to the Cass Leary Legal Thriller Series just for joining. Find out what really happened on Cass Leary's last day in Chicago.

Click to Sign Up

http://www.robinjamesbooks.com/newsletter/

About the Author

Robin James is an attorney and former law professor. She's worked on a wide range of civil, criminal and family law cases in her twenty-year legal career. She also spent over a decade as supervising attorney for a Michigan legal clinic assisting thousands of people who could not otherwise afford access to justice.

Robin now lives on a lake in southern Michigan with her husband, two children, and one lazy dog. Her favorite, pure Michigan writing spot is stretched out on the back of a pontoon watching the faster boats go by.

Sign up for Robin James's Legal Thriller Newsletter to get all the latest updates on her new releases and get a free bonus scene from Burden of Truth featuring Cass Leary's last day in Chicago. http://www.robinjamesbooks.com/newsletter/

Also by Robin James

Cass Leary Legal Thriller Series

Burden of Truth

Silent Witness

Devil's Bargain

Stolen Justice

Blood Evidence

Imminent Harm

First Degree

Mercy Kill

With more to come...

Mara Brent Legal Thriller Series

Time of Justice

Price of Justice

Hand of Justice

With more to come...

Made in United States
North Haven, CT
22 May 2024

52840183R00182